A CLOSE REACH

A NOVEL

STEVE MYRVANG
JOANNE JURGICH

Volume 2 of The Reach Series

Also written by the authors:
Volume 1 of The Reach Series,
A Broad Reach

Cover Layout and Design by Crave Design Studio

Acknowledgements

Thanks to Don Redding for sharing his inspirational journey down the road less traveled. Thanks also to our team: Dr. Robert "Rob-dog" Roth, Luther Hintz, and Rod and Jody Mager, for their support and suggestions. To our learned editor, Bill Buck, your tireless forbearance and effort can never be adequately acknowledged by mere vodka alone. Last but not least, a very special shout-out to Cher, Beyoncé and Danna.

Prologue

The William Thornton Floating Bar and Restaurant, or *Willy T* as it is known locally by boaters familiar with the colorful establishment, was packed. Stepping onto the dining deck, Paul and Sienna gave the hostess their name and were told that their table would be ready shortly.

While waiting, they ordered rum punches from the harried bartender. The uproar from the bar patrons made communication difficult, if not impossible. Once their table was available, they were ushered into the dining area of the old schooner. Away from the roar of the bar, they were now able to converse. Their conversation, however, was abruptly cut off as Paul stood suddenly, his face blanched. Holding tight to the rail of the ship, he watched, stunned, as the couple made their way toward him. She was young, shapely and blonde. The man helping her laughed when she stumbled into his arms. His nose had been altered and the hair color was different, but the voice was the same. Turning toward Paul, Andrew Sherman's smile froze.

For Renée and Jack

1

Sal was late two martinis ago. Daylight briefly flooded the dimly lit room as two men entered from the street. At six-ten and just south of four-hundred pounds, Tiny was Sal's bodyguard. Sal, barely five-six, exercised regularly and watched what he ate. He'd kept trim for the ladies when he was younger. Now with seventy in his rear view mirror, it was his fear of death that kept him on the treadmill.

Tiny scowled at the row of olive skewers, the empty cocktail glass and the overflowing ashtray. "You better not be fuckin' drunk."

Sal held his hand up. "Hey, Tiny, ease up. We're late and what's the fella supposed to do in this hole, throw darts? Although, I tell you Stinger, those cigarettes are like nails in your coffin."

"Been trying to quit, Boss, but it's hard with not working and all. Also, I just found out I have SAD which means I'm—"

"I know what the fuck it means." Sal glanced over at Tiny, smirking. "Hard to feel sorry for a guy whose only responsibility, other than lying low for a few years, is to work on his tan." Tiny's high-pitched laugh reminded Stinger of his six year old niece when he tickled her.

"How was Florida?"

"Come on Boss, you know I'd rather be working. Don't get me wrong, I appreciate the way you've taken care of me. I'm just going stir crazy." The bartender delivered Stinger another martini. Ignoring Tiny's glare, he pulled two olives off between his teeth, placed the olive skewer on the table alongside the others and took a long sip. Tiny wasn't the problem, it was Sal he had to be careful of. "Florida was OK. I got my license like you told me."

"That's good. So now you're a private investigator."

"In Florida anyway."

"Doesn't matter, it makes you look legitimate no matter where you do it. So look, I went to see my dumbass nephew in the joint."

"How's Buddy doing?"

"Still pissed off as hell and swears he didn't kill Sherman. Wants me to put a tail on Sherman's former business partner, an architect named Paul Armstrong. Thinks Armstrong was in on the deal and can lead us to Sherman. Buddy's been a pain in the ass for as long as I can remember, but he's my dead sister's son, and I promised to look after him." Sensing the end of his forced retirement, Stinger straightened out of his slouch as Sal continued. "We kept tabs on Armstrong for a while. Last I heard, there's not much left of the guy after his company went tits-up and his wife left him. He moved in for a while with some farmer who grows weed and helped out with the farm chores. Frankly, I don't see a connection with Sherman, but I promised Buddy I'd put someone on it."

"I'm your man, Sal. So I'm headed out to Seattle?"

"Slow down. You'll like this, being all sun-deprived and everything. You're headed to the Caribbean. The guy lives in the Virgin Islands now. One of our associates took a vacation

2

on St. Croix and recognized him from Buddy's trial. He's playing a fuckin' guitar at some restaurant down there."

"St Croix, Paul Armstrong, got it. I'll be all over this guy before he has a clue."

"That's good to hear, Stinger. It's still too early for you to be representing our interests in this part of Jersey, but you'll be my go-to-guy in the Caribbean. Can't imagine you'll turn up anything, but keep me posted anyway." Sal placed a hundred dollar bill on the table. "Don't fucking spend it on cigarettes."

Tiny helped Sal on with his overcoat then held the door open as the boss passed easily under his huge arm. He threw one final scowl at Stinger before the door closed behind them.

Stinger finished his martini. Images of white sandy beaches and topless bathers fueled his gin-soaked stupor. He asked the waiter to call him a cab, left the hundred on the table and after a couple of misdirected efforts, teetered outside, talking to himself. "You want to know who I am, Sugar? I'm Clark 'Stinger' Gifford, Private Investigator." He repeated the line until he was satisfied. "Now, for sure that's gonna get me some pussy."

2

Paul Armstrong leaned forward, prepared to leap onto the dock and run him down if Sherman made any effort to escape. Andrew Sherman appeared in good shape, but Paul was 20 years younger and had 30 pounds on him. Andrew turned his head and looked back at his Zodiac. Realizing any effort to escape would be pointless, he resumed leading the girl, stepping from craft to craft, toward *The Willie T.* After a brief, heated discussion, Andrew dumped his companion off at the bar and approached Paul and Sienna's table.

"Well, this is awkward."

"But better than being dead, I'd imagine. Nice nose, Andrew."

Andrew acknowledged Paul's comment with a weak smile then turned toward Sienna, "I don't believe we've met."

"Sienna Meyers," she replied, with a brief nod.

Andrew appraised Sienna then took a seat. "Well, Paul, you're looking fit."

"What the fuck, Andrew?"

Andrew glanced around nervously as nearby diners looked over. "What the fuck indeed. Look, I'm willing to talk, but you need to keep your voice down. There are people, as you might guess, who—"

"Oh, I'm sorry. Is this better? Now, what the fuck, Asshole?"

Andrew winced, then glanced at Sienna, "Perhaps you'd like to join my friend at the bar while we boys talk some things out."

"No thanks. I wouldn't miss this for the world. Besides, it looks like your friend might not appreciate the company."

Andrew looked back at the bar. His companion laughed coyly, then playfully punched the shoulder of a young, muscular man who had taken the barstool next to her.

"Sienna's my fiancée," Paul said, bringing Andrew's attention back to their conversation. "She knows as much about you as I thought I did."

Staring down at his hands, Andrew began slowly. "I had no choice, Paul. It was either fake my death and live, or stay in town and be murdered. Maybe not immediately, but once Buddy realized that I had run out of repayment options, he would have used me as an example of what happens when you stiff Buddy Falco."

"Bullshit! I can't believe that there weren't other options. Oh, I don't know . . . say . . . something that didn't include destroying our company and framing an innocent man."

"Innocent? Oh no, this is a bad man, Paul. Maybe if I hadn't been so panicked, I might have figured out another way to disappear. I feel terrible about what I did to you and T-Squared, but I have absolutely no remorse about Buddy Falco."

A long silence followed. "You mentioned the *why*, what about the *how*?" Sienna asked. "How'd you do it?"

Andrew was momentarily lost in thought. When he spoke, his voice seemed thick with genuine regret. "I can just imagine what you two must think of me. I left you holding all the bags, Paul. Believe it or not, I'm truly ashamed and really sorry."

"You had to know what this would cost me and the rest of the company. Sorry's not enough, Andrew. You've skated through this whole mess apparently untouched. Everyone suffered except you."

Andrew's head dropped, his eyes averting Paul's as he spoke. "I don't blame you for hating me, but I haven't skated through anything."

"What? Is your yacht too tiny? Do you miss your 50-yard line Seahawk tickets? Gosh, I hope I haven't hurt your feelings."

Andrew looked up, "No, Paul. It's that I can't forgive myself for what I did."

Paul snorted derisively.

"Look, I don't expect you to care one way or the other, but I feel hollowed out and empty, like I'm just waiting to die. I know who the bad guy is in all of this. I've never felt so much loathing for anyone as I do myself."

"So why go on then?" Paul asked, ignoring Sienna's reaction to his question.

Andrew smiled cynically. "That question is currently under review. I'd hoped that I'd be able to let go of my past and start fresh, but I've realized over the last few months that I can't. You're right, I caused the problem. I should have been the one who paid for it."

Sienna, quietly watching the exchange, could practically hear the explosions as the two men sorted through their minefield-laden past. The sudden roar of a cigarette boat's powerful engine igniting pulled their attention toward the rumbling vessel. Smiling back at them, his youthful date gave Andrew the finger and took her seat next to the man from the bar. The large powerboat was packed with a young crowd of partiers. Its sound system blared as the missile-shaped craft roared into the night.

Andrew sighed, "I spent six months in a Costa Rican addiction treatment center kicking the coke. My one remaining vice, my penchant for companions young enough to be my daughter, now seems nothing more than an embarrassing charade."

"More like grand-daughter."

"Too true, I'm afraid. Look, you guys came here for a meal, let me buy you dinner."

Paul appeared to have not heard the offer as he silently stared back at Andrew. "Actually, I'd like to hear how you pulled it off, and I'm hungry," Sienna said, glancing at Paul who indifferently nodded his agreement.

After the waiter took their orders, Andrew turned to Sienna, "When I first met Paul three years ago, I was already in deep with Buddy Falco. It started pretty small at first. Nothing I couldn't cover, but Buddy ran with a fast crowd. Women, booze and coke were everywhere. He was always eager to cover me when I was short. I felt like I was just one big score away from pulling even, getting well. I started going after larger stakes, but a horse would pull up lame, twenty-five yards from the finish, or I'd hit a full house and lose to four of a kind. The final blow came when the Packers took out the Steelers in the Super Bowl. My credit dried up with Buddy at close to four-million. I started T-Squared with Paul hoping that the money would come in fast enough for me to keep Buddy and his friends happy. But as successful as we were, starting a business is capital-intensive. So, I kept asking Buddy for more time. The last time I saw him, we were playing the ponies from his box at Emerald Downs. He told me that his 'friends' were concerned that I wasn't trying hard enough. They wanted his boys to rough me up and he couldn't hold them off much longer. Then he stood up and began screaming at me. He kept hitting me with his rolled up program. Told me that I had thirty days and the clock was ticking."

"What a psycho. So how did you pull-off the fake murder?"

"Oh, it wasn't fake.

Sienna looked at Buddy, confused.

"I was pretty shook up at that point. Buddy said he wanted me to be crystal clear on what things could look like in thirty days. He told me that his boys were dropping another deadbeat off The Tacoma Narrows Bridge the next morning."

Paul rejoined the conversation. "So that was Buddy's Escalade filmed by the bridge video cameras. How did your blood, skin and hair turn up in the trunk of his car?"

"I'd actually thought of disappearing for some time. Buddy's behavior was all the push I needed. After he calmed down, he told me to meet him back at the car. Gave me the keys to let myself in. Planting the evidence and reporting his car stopped on the Narrows Bridge were all really pretty simple."

After the waiter served their entrees, Andrew pushed the food around on his plate and continued, "I had anticipated the situation with Buddy becoming ugly and set aside a small nest egg that would provide me sufficient funds if I needed to leave in a hurry. Some of the funds were in cash and some in an off-shore account I had set up years ago. Nothing close to what I owed Buddy and his partners, but sufficient to provide me with a quick exit and some walk-around money. I'd also purchased fake ID which included a California driver's license and a U.S. passport."

"Why rob T-Squared for more money, if you already had money set aside?" Paul asked.

"I had enough money to survive for a period of time, but I needed enough to disappear, which, as it turns out, is very expensive. I hadn't put away enough and I knew Buddy's crew would turn over every rock looking for me."

"So, you headed to California?"

Andrew looked at Paul and let out a long breath, "Look, Paul, before we go on, I'd like to know what you two are going to do about all this. Misappropriating investor funds from T-Squared to pay down my gambling debt was certainly illegal. I don't know how much I should tell you. As I said, Buddy has very long arms and I can think of better ways to orchestrate my demise than being murdered in prison."

Sienna deferred to Paul, who thought for a minute before replying, "As far as T-Squared goes, I can't see anything good coming out of reopening that can of worms. The investors received dollar for dollar on their investment from the sale of our projects. The lawyers picked everything else clean and I ended up walking away without owing anything. Since you're dead, there isn't a warrant for your arrest. So, I guess as far as I'm concerned, Sienna and I are having dinner with . . ."

"Alan Sloan, it's a pleasure meeting you," Andrew extended his hand toward Paul then dropped it back in his lap when the gesture wasn't returned.

Sienna asked Andrew what his future plans entailed. Admitting to the fear of staying in one place too long and an all-pervasive loneliness, Andrew was hopeful that his next surgery would bring about an unrecognizable transformation into his new persona and provide him with the opportunity to settle into a less transient lifestyle.

"I'm having the work done in Canada. I'm a bit apprehensive about the next surgery, but when it's done I don't expect that anyone, even you two, will be able to recognize me. After that, I'm not sure where I'll live. Maybe I'll start a small business down-island. Who knows, maybe I'll end up on St. Croix."

The end of their evening together came a little after 11:30. Andrew's eyes filled with tears. "I know I can never make it up to you for what I did. Take care of each other and I'll see to it that our paths cross again one day."

Andrew made his way out to his Zodiac. Paul and Sienna watched as he started his engine, untied the line and waving back at them, slowly motored away until swallowed by the darkness.

"Not the evening we signed up for, but a good one none-the-less." Sienna leaned into Paul as he put his arm around her shoulders.

"Do you think I let him off too easy?"

"Not at all. He knows the pain and trouble he caused. Nothing can change the past."

Brilliant stars blanketed the clear night sky as they motored toward Sienna's yacht, *Star Gazer*, a forty-six foot, three berth, 2000 Beneteau. Paul and Sienna, accompanied by Paul's Aunt Charlotte and Sienna's five year old son, AJ, had sailed from their island home on St. Croix and were enjoying a leisurely ten day vacation in the British Virgin Islands. The unimaginable encounter with Paul's former business partner released in Paul an avalanche of memories and emotions. Distracted, he responded to Sienna during their run back to Star Gazer in clipped utterances.

Once they were aboard, Sienna checked on AJ while Paul brought a bottle of brandy and two glasses top-side. Joining him, she asked, "OK, what's up?"

"Not sure. It might be that I've never had a dead business partner come back to life and I'm a little thrown by it all."

"That's understandable. Are we going to tell Char?"

"I think the fewer people that know, the better. Buddy Falco knows that he didn't kill Andrew and will never stop looking for him. It wouldn't be good if he found out that we ran into Andrew. Not that I don't trust Aunt Charlotte, but something as strange as this could just pop out in a conversation on its own, before she even realized it."

"OK, so it's just between you and me."

"And Alan Sloan."

***

The next morning came earlier than Paul and Sienna had hoped. It was just past 6:00 when the door into their forward berth was thrown open by AJ. "OK you two lovebirds, time to rise and shine," the precocious youth announced.

Aunt Charlotte had mango pancakes already on the grill when Paul and Sienna joined her and AJ in the salon. "Well, Paul, it looks like you two made good use of your night out. I was awake reading until 11:00. What time did you get back?"

"It must have been a little before midnight."

"So what kept you out so late? Did you meet somebody interesting?"

"Not really. Just your typical world explorers, pirates and expatriates."

"Oh? Anyone I might have heard of?"

Realizing that Aunt Charlotte's antennae were fully extended, he filled his plate with pancakes, muttered an incoherent reply and took a quick exit.

Undeterred, Char followed him topside. "Look Paul, something happened last night. I can see it on your face."

Paul let out a long sigh. "It's Andrew. He's alive."

"And your reason for trying to keep this from me was?"

"Buddy Falco is a bad man. Our encounter with Andrew might not seem coincidental to him if he ever hears about it. He might think I was in on Andrew's disappearance from the start and send his goons to get me to talk."

"And you're concerned that I can't keep such an important secret?"

Paul felt fifteen as he shook his head no.

"Don't make the mistake of thinking you need to shield me from your problems, Paul. I'm sharper than you might think and I'd never say or do anything that would harm you, Sienna, or AJ."

3

A high-pressure area had been building over the Leeward Islands. Wanting to make sure they arrived early enough to secure a mooring for the evening; immediately following breakfast Paul unhooked *Star Gazer* from its buoy. Early morning sunlight stretched deep into the turquoise water as Sienna carefully guided the sailboat through the maze of quietly rocking vessels. Sir Francis Drake Channel was glass-smooth as they motored northeast to Manchineel Bay off Cooper Island. Sienna thought that with the calm seas, they would have a comfortable night's stay in the crescent shaped bay's exposed location. Paul took the helm, while Sienna leaned against him and hummed softly over the muted rumble of the ship's diesel engine. AJ entertained himself at the base of the galley stairs with a video game. Paul could hear bits and pieces of Aunt Charlotte's animated conversation with Andy via a strong signal off the St. John cell tower as the ship's hull cut smoothly through the placid water. He felt Sienna's warmth as she snuggled against him. It was a perfect morning and it made Paul's discomfort all the more unsettling.

Two cheek-filled exhales alerted Sienna to his unrest. "Still thinking about last night?"

"I guess. He always was a great salesman. In spite of all his apologies and regrets, I feel like I just bought another load of his bullshit."

"I don't know. It seemed sincere to me."

"That's how good he is. He once told me that to sell you have to believe. I'm sure he believed what he was selling last night, but it just doesn't add up. For instance, what's with this getaway fund he had squirreled away? If he already had enough money to disappear, why take so much from the company just before staging his murder? The auditors estimated that he stole over a million from the company within two weeks of his disappearance. I'm sure Buddy Falco never saw a penny of it."

Sienna took his hand, "I'd still let it go. We have a great life ahead of us. If it weren't for Andrew, you'd probably still be in Washington and we never would have met."

"I know that," Paul replied sharply. Sienna withdrew her hand. He took a deep breath. "I know that Honey, but it still doesn't make it right. Too many people were hurt while he got off scot-free, *banished* to paradise with a new identity and a bottomless bank account."

Startled by an air-horn blast close off-port, they watched as a large powerboat quickly over-took them. Standing on the foredeck, a tall, red headed boy waved exuberantly. Paul and Sienna returned the wave and follow-up salute from the boat's operator; a large shaggy gray-haired man in shorts and an unbuttoned purple and green flowered shirt, parted wide by a generous brown belly.

Curious over the air-horn blast, Aunt Charlotte and AJ appeared from below and braced themselves as Star Gazer dipped and rolled through the powerboat's wake. "*Caribe*

Daze," Paul read off the boat's transom as the distance between the two boats rapidly increased. "Sounds like a cocktail."

******

Caribe Daze rested calmly on a nearby mooring as Paul and Sienna hooked onto the last available buoy at the south end of Manchineel Bay and tied off. Paul noticed the absence of the Zodiac that had previously hung from the vessel's back rigging. Shielding his eyes from the sun's glare, he spied the red headed boy and flower-shirted boat captain standing at the end of a long wooden dock just south of the recently remodeled and upscaled Cooper Island Beach Club. Ball-capped now, the large man offered his hand to the red headed woman. She stood out in a bright yellow bikini top and a colorful flowered sarong as she stepped off the Zodiac onto the dock.

"Come on, Paul, let's go explore."

Paul turned to see AJ, already suited up in fins, mask and snorkel. The two were soon face-down in the 85 degree water, silently finning over the nearby reef off Cistern Point. Sienna and Char lounged under *Star Gazer's* Bimini enjoying the occasional bursts of incomprehensible *snorkeleze* as Paul and AJ reacted excitedly to the multicolored assortment of tropical fish and coral formations.

The drone of a small engine brought Paul's head out of the water. "Ahoy, *Star Gazer*," the floral shirted man shouted to Sienna and Aunt Charlotte as he brought the Zodiac alongside the stern boarding platform.

"Permission to come aboard?" The red headed female crew member asked as Sienna took her hand and helped her step on deck. Paul and AJ swam back to join them a few minutes later.

"Hank and Roxanne Johnson," the man said offering a beefy hand to Paul. "Son's name is Dusty, but he likes to be called Red."

"It's because my hair is red. Can I snorkel with him, Hank?" Red asked, pointing at the much younger AJ.

"You don't have your suit on, Honey," Roxanne observed.

"Hank doesn't wear his suit a lot of times."

"I was telling your lady, Sienna, here," Hank explained after shaking hands with Paul, "we saw you two at *The Willie T* last night. I was concerned there might be a problem. Thought you might be having a heart attack when that fella and his girl came aboard. Then, I thought you were going to punch him out when he sat down at your table."

"You'll have to excuse the big guy. Hank is always sticking his nose into other people's business," Roxanne explained. "Once a cop, always a cop."

"Who was the man? Why did you want to punch him?" AJ asked Paul.

"I, ah, well . . ." Paul stumbled momentarily, but was saved by Aunt Charlotte.

"AJ, let's take Red down below and make some lemonade. Maybe you would like to show him your iPad."

Once the two boys had left, Paul shrugged off Hank's observations, "It was an ex business partner who I hadn't seen since our company went under and we lost contact."

"Well it seemed like you all patched things up. Guess you couldn't say as much for him and his girlfriend though."

"Oh for Christ's sake Hank, will you let it go? We've just barely met these nice folks and you're already giving them the third degree."

"I'm sorry, it's just that I'm kind of used to picking up on people's problems. It's what I do. Try and help."

"Actually, he's really quite harmless, my big Hanky-Bear." Roxanne stood on tiptoes and kissed him on the cheek.

Smiling warmly, Sienna said, "I don't know about you two, but I'm sure it's five o'clock somewhere and I'm thinking that something a little stronger than lemonade might be in order. Would anyone care to join me?"

"Why Sienna darling," Roxanne replied, "you just read my mind. It's like I always say—"

"Everything goes better with Grand Marnier," Hank finished for her.

The Cadillac Margaritas and conversation continued topside with Aunt Charlotte joining them for the second round after it became obvious that Red and AJ were getting along quite well.

"Red is my angel. When I met Hank, I was concerned that he might find my son, you know . . . challenging. Developmentally he is probably pretty close to AJ's age. But I'll tell you, the way he lights up over the little things . . ."

Hank picked up the thread, "Marrying Roxanne and adopting Red were the two best moments of my life. My first wife, not to speak ill of her, liked music but didn't like to dance. She liked kids but not as much as cats. After ten years of trying, we filed for an amicable divorce." He reached over and took his wife's hand. "Roxanne was in real estate and helped me find a condo. I liked the first place she showed me, but kept asking her to show me more. Don't really remember any of those other places."

"He was a smitten kitten."

"Then later, after our second date, she introduced me to Red and right off the bat I got it . . . I'd always known they

17

were out there somewhere. You see, I'd finally found my family."

Roxanne reached over and gently brushed the tear trailing down Hanks cheek. "Oh Honey, you've really got to hold back a little. You're scaring our new friends."

"No he isn't," Sienna and Charlotte said in unison.

"That was one of the sweetest things I've witnessed in a long time," Charlotte continued. "Every day, say how much you love each other, then you'll never be sorry when . . ."

Charlotte's eyes filled as she thought of her husband, Ernie, who had died less than a year earlier of a heart attack. Paul and Sienna each took her hand, unable to hold back their tears as well.

"Why is everybody so sad?" Red's voice rang out as the boys clambered topside.

"We're not sad, Honey," Roxanne answered. "We're just happy to have so much love in our lives."

"Then why are you crying?"

"That's just what adults do sometimes," AJ explained. "They cry when they're happy *and* they cry when they're sad."

"Go figure," Red replied with a shrug.

"Amen," AJ seconded, following his new friend back down the stairs.

4

As it was now approaching dinner time, Hank suggested they reserve a table for the two families at the Beach Club. Charlotte, however, offered to stay on board and make macaroni and cheese for the boys, which was met with shouts of approval from AJ and Red. Roxanne nodded her consent to Hank and the plan was set in motion. Sienna made reservations on the ship-to-shore radio and Hank and Roxanne returned to *Caribe Daze* to shower and change.

An hour later, the two couples were led to their table at the waterside rail of the open-aired restaurant. The sky was darkening into a brilliant crimson as the sun dropped slowly into the Caribbean.

Their drink orders taken, Paul noticed that Hank had become quiet and seemed distracted since their arrival at the restaurant. Roxanne, however, was in full stride relaying a recent conversation with a friend whose marriage was on the rocks.

"Excuse me, there's someone at the bar that I recognize," Hank said, during a break in her story. Hank approached the man at the bar and tapped him on the shoulder.

The man's dark hair and tanned face were in sharp contrast to his ultra-white teeth as he turned and faced Hank with a broad smile. "Well, well, if it isn't my favorite ex-law enforcement hero. How's it hangin' Chief?"

Hank ignored the offered hand. "I'm kind of curious. What brings you down this way, Stinger? Not any subways that I know of in the Caribbean."

The man's face darkened. He started to stand, but sat down quickly when Hank's large hand clamped on his shoulder. Leaning forward, Hank quietly repeated his question.

The man shrugged off Hank's hand. Then nodding back toward the dining area, replied, "It's about your friend. Seems like somebody's looking for him."

The surprise in Hank's face emboldened the man. "Careful now, Chief. You wouldn't want to step into something that doesn't concern you, what with you and your pretty wife now being retired and all."

Hank's eyes blazed. For an instant, the man feared he may have guessed wrong about Hank's unwillingness to cause a public scene as he nervously watched the pulse beat on the side of the big man's forehead. Leaning forward ominously, Hank whispered in Stinger's ear, "Listen carefully, Barf Bag. I'm going to assume that you didn't just threaten my wife and me."

"No way, man. I didn't mean nothing."

"That's good then," Hank replied, straightening up and brushing off the man's shoulder. "You know, Stinger, you really shouldn't wear black shirts with all this fucking dandruff. Stick around, I'll be back."

Returning to the table, Hank picked up the tail end of Roxanne's story. "I think her first big mistake was marrying him after he told her that his mother would be singing *Born Free* at their wedding."

"Born free?" Sienna said, laughing. "Seems like maybe there were some issues right out of the gate."

"Not to mention that the mother ending up living with them."

After dinner, Hank asked Paul if he'd like to hang around for some guy talk. Sienna was anxious to return to the boat to relieve Aunt Charlotte and Roxanne was happy to join her to check on Red.

Following Hank into the bar, Paul was surprised to see him stop beside a dark-complected man who stood and smiled broadly as the two were introduced by Hank. "Paul, this is an acquaintance of mine from New York. His real name is Clarabelle, but he goes by Stinger."

Irritated, Stinger corrected Hank, "Actually, Mr. Armstrong, the name is Clarence and my associates call me Clark."

Paul was momentarily stunned. "How do you know my last name?"

"That's what we're going to find out. Isn't that right, Clarabelle, I mean Stinger, Clarence, Clark."

Paul and Stinger followed Hank and seated themselves at a low table in a remote section of the restaurant's outside deck. "Before we start, I think a little explanation is in order. Stinger and I once represented different opinions regarding a New York subway station fatality. As the chief of police for the Port Authority, I was of the opinion that the victim had been purposely pushed in front of the oncoming train. The video of the incident, although inconclusive, did show Mr. Stinger standing behind the man moments before the incident. Mr. Stinger's attorney, however, argued convincingly that the evidence was circumstantial. He also claimed that Mr. Stinger's known associations with members of a New Jersey crime syndicate were immaterial. The fact that the victim had recently been subpoenaed to provide testimony regarding money

21

laundering against the president of one of the syndicate's waste disposal companies was also determined immaterial."

Clearing his throat and holding his hands out, palms up, Stinger replied, "Justice was served. I was innocent and fortunately the terrible accident wasn't made worse by sending an innocent man to prison."

Paul had the sinking feeling that justice hadn't been served and his life was about to become much more complicated. "So how do you know my last name?"

"Well, it's what I do. I find people. I'm licensed as a private investigator in Florida." He shot a look at Hank. "I'm no murderer or scumbag, or whatever Henry wants you to think."

When Paul and Hank didn't respond, Stinger cleared his throat and continued. "So this client of mine . . . I hope you can understand that I am bound professionally to keep his name confidential."

Hank snorted.

"Actually, finding you was pretty easy."

"It should have been. I've never tried to hide from anyone or anything. So, now what? You found me. What happens next?"

"I was supposed to send a picture of you along with how my employer can get in touch with you. After that, I'm not sure."

"Have you sent anything yet, *Mr. Detective*?" Hank asked.

Ignoring the sarcasm, Stinger replied, "I sent him an email earlier today when I found your girlfriend's boat anchored off-shore. Also, I sent a photo that I took of you two having dinner with your ladies."

Paul's mind was whirling. *What if they already know that I had dinner with Andrew last night?*

Stinger stood up and stretched. "There is one other thing. I was supposed to ask if you'd seen your old friend Sherman lately?"

Paul quickly tumbled through his options and found nothing better than the truth. *Sorry Andrew, but this was your doing. I can't put Sienna and AJ at risk.* "Actually, we had dinner with him last night."

Stinger appeared surprised by the admission. "OK, where was this?"

Before Paul could answer, Hank interjected, "Stinger, excuse yourself for ten minutes. Paul and I need to have a brief discussion."

When Stinger didn't get up, Hank stood, pulled him up by the collar of his shirt and propelled him toward the bar. Scowling murderously back at them, Stinger took a seat and immediately pulled out his cell phone.

Hank sat across from Paul. "Here's the thing. You don't know me very well and I only have an inkling of what might be going on here. So you can keep me in the dark and deal with this scumbag as you think best, or you can give me a brief description of what this is about."

Paul chose the second option, after which Hank advised, "Don't say anything more to Stinger. We go to the police tomorrow morning and you tell them what you know. You're a concerned citizen who is reporting that your former partner pulled a hoax to avoid criminal charges, which sent an innocent man to prison. This will put you right with the law. As far as Stinger's bosses go, when they contact you, you tell them that you already notified the authorities and that you had nothing to do with Sherman's actions."

Hank walked over to the bar and after a heated discussion, Stinger followed Hank back to Paul.

"Well, it's been a pleasure meeting you Mr. Armstrong. I hear you're quite the musician over there on St. Croix. Also, congratulations on your upcoming marriage. From what I could see, you've got yourself one tasty lady." Looking at Hank he added, "We kinda' miss having you around the playground, Chief. Don't be a stranger." His white-toothed smile practically luminescent, Stinger winked and returned to the bar, paid his tab and left.

"Classy guy," Paul said, sarcastically.

"Oh yeah, he' a real gem."

Sienna appeared in the doorway. Spotting the two men, she walked across the deck and joined them. "Hey guys, I just dropped Roxanne and Red off on *Caribe Daze*. Aunt Charlotte was reading to AJ so I thought I'd see if there's still a party going on here." Her smile disappeared as Paul's worried eyes met hers. "Something I should know about?"

5

    Arriving home to St. Croix's Salt River Marina two days later, Sienna and Paul washed down *Stargazer*, stowed gear and pulled bed sheets and luggage onto the dock while AJ and Aunt Charlotte searched for iguanas and cane toads along the edge of the lagoon. Carmen and Kate, close friends of Paul and Sienna's visiting from Winthrop, Washington, arrived in Paul's double-cab truck.

    "Andy's cooking up a big feast for your homecoming," Kate said as Paul drove to their west-end home they were sharing with their guests.

    "He thought you'd be tired of 'boat food,'" Carmen explained, laughing.

    Andy had been Kate's trail-cook on horse camping trips she led through Washington State's Pasayten Wilderness. Carmen, her partner, operated an accounting practice from their home, The Wilderness Ranch; a one-hundred-and-sixty acre spread at the north end of Washington State's pristine Methow Valley.

    "I never met a man who likes to cook so much," Aunt Charlotte said. "Believe me, I'm not complaining."

    "So, what do you think of our island?" Sienna asked.

"Paradise," Carmen replied. "I've never seen my Kate so relaxed. The weather is to-die-for and the white sandy beaches . . . there just aren't enough superlatives to describe them."

"We met another couple who introduced us to a bunch of their friends," Kate added. "Back at the ranch, I'm usually in bed by nine, but down here, seems like we're always heading off to a dinner party at someone's home or restaurant. Andy's tagged along a few times when he wasn't too pooped from all the gardening he's been doing."

"Gardening?" Paul asked.

"You know Andy. He's always looking for something to do," Kate explained. "I used your truck to bring in a few loads of good topsoil from one of our new friends who owns a nursery. Andy's been building raised beds with the ATV and cart he bought off the classifieds; collecting large rocks for the walls from all over the property. You should see him, sitting on that little buggy just like he used to on his tractor back home. He's pretty worked up about the cost of food here and says we should be growing our own vegetables."

"Sounds great to me," Sienna said. "Maybe we should look at growing enough for the restaurant as well."

Slight of build, clad in overalls, white T-shirt, cowboy boots and hat, Andy waved to them from the covered terrace as they drove up. Located at the northern edge of St. Croix's Rainforest, the expanded and remodeled original residence on the twelve-acre parcel provided more than ample temporary accommodations for Paul, Sienna and AJ as well as their Washingtonian guests. Prior to leaving on their sailing trip, Paul had turned in a permit application for a six unit, off-the-grid development he had designed for the property. The financial backing and idea for the project had come from Andy, who was also the father of Sienna's deceased husband Aaron, and grandfather to AJ. Andy had envisioned the project as providing a home away from home for the very close-knit yet wildly diverse cast of characters he called family.

"Well if it isn't my favorite denizens of the sea," Andy greeted them as he approached the truck.

"Still playing Scrabble it would seem," Sienna commented to Carmen.

"Oh yeah," Carmen replied, laughing. "He adores his Z words."

******

While the sailors unpacked and cleaned up, Kate set the large table on the covered terrace for dinner. Carmen decanted two bottles of Washington State's Chateau Ste. Michelle Merlot. Andy brought out steaming platters filled with slices of smoked pork shoulder, potatoes, mixed vegetables and homemade bread. Ringing the same dinner triangle he used on horse camping rides, he called the group to the table. "Come and get it! Chow time!"

Sitting next to Andy and patting his leg, Aunt Charlotte commented, "Doesn't our Andy just thrive on his cowboy theatrics? My ears are still ringing."

"Plenty of time after we're gone to be quiet," Andy replied.

"I think that should suffice as Grace," Carmen said, helping herself to the potatoes.

"So tell us about life on the high seas," Andy asked AJ.

"I saw a loud boat with mostly ladies who weren't even wearing their bathing suit tops. Also, Paul and I saw a big sting-ray, three turtles and two squid when we were snorkeling."

"Back to that loud boat, AJ," Andy interjected while Charlotte pinched his leg. "What do you think was going on there?"

"They were dancing like this." AJ stood up and thrust his hips back and forth. "Then I saw two of them jump into the water without any clothes."

"Maybe they were looking for their swimsuits," Carmen suggested.

"Or their brains," Aunt Charlotte added, joining in the laughter.

After Carmen's apple pie dessert, Charlotte and Sienna cleaned up while Kate played catch with AJ. Carmen and Paul followed Andy for a tour of the 'work-in-progress' vegetable garden.

After Andy described his vision of living off the land, Paul surprised himself by blurting out, "We ran into Andrew Sherman at a floating restaurant off Norman Island."

Carmen and Andy stopped in their tracks and stared at Paul. Understanding he was serious, Carmen spoke first. "So he faked the whole thing. What a monster. What'd you do?"

Before Paul could reply, Andy burst out with a string of curses ending with, "That rotten bastard.

Before I was through with him, he'd have wished Buddy Falco had killed him."

"I had the same reaction at first. Let's wait until AJ goes to bed, then Kate can join us and we'll give you the whole story."

Keyed up by the house guests and overtired, AJ reappeared from his bedroom three times before finally falling asleep wearing his baseball glove, on the floor next to his bed. Once they were convinced he was down for the count, Paul and Sienna filled the others in on the details of their encounter with Andrew Sherman and their new friendship with Hank and Roxanne. When Paul described the meeting with Stinger, Andy couldn't remain quiet. "I don't like the way this is goin'. Seems to me that this Stinger fellow is tied in with some pretty bad company. What if they think you were in cahoots with Sherman and come after you?"

"Hank's contacting Stinger's employer. He'll let us know if we have anything to worry about," Sienna answered.

"Won't you be in trouble if the police find out you met with Sherman and didn't report it?" Carmen asked.

"The morning after meeting Stinger, Hank and I motored *Caribe Daze* over to Road Town and filed a report with the Tortola police."

"What was their reaction?" Kate asked.

"The detective that Hank and I spoke with thanked me and asked for my contact information in case he had any follow up questions."

"It's not the authorities that concern me," Kate replied. "Seems likely that you'll hear from this Stinger-fellow's employer, even with Hank interceding. I just hope he believes that you were also a victim in Sherman's faked death." Refilling her wine glass she added, "That man Sherman has sure been a burr under your saddle blanket."

"Ain't that the truth," Andy added. "Still seems to me, you might have been too easy on him with all he's put you through."

"You're probably right, but Sienna and I have too many positive things in front of us to waste anymore energy on Andrew Sherman. We start clearing for the foundations next week. Then there's this little shindig we're planning for November where Sienna'll make an honest man out of me."

"I'm buying the cow, even though he's been giving the milk away for free," Sienna said, smiling.

"Never heard that expression used by a woman," Andy mused. "Ok, so enough Shermanizing. Now, what are we going to call this little village we're building?"

"AJ likes *The Funny Farm*," Sienna replied, straight faced.

"That kid's a hoot," Andy laughed.

"How about something a bit less descriptive," Carmen joked. "Kate and I were thinking *Latitude 17*."

"I like it," Aunt Charlotte replied. "But doesn't it sound like a tropical bar?"

"*Windsol?*" Paul offered. "We're off the grid and proud of it."

"Hey, that one should stick," Andy replied. "What do you all think?"

Aunt Charlotte and Sienna gave thumbs up.

"Until we retire, Carmen and I'll just be part-time occupants." Kate replied. "If you like the name, I'm all for it."

"Tell you what, let's call up to Quilcene," Paul suggested, referring to the absent members of the *family* still up in Washington State. "See if they go for it."

"No, Son," Andy replied. "I'm all for democracy, but we've got a quorum here. My times a-tickin' and the fact that I'm paying the bills should count for something."

"To *Windsol*," Carmen toasted, raising her wine glass, "and many years of love and friendship in our island home."

"To many years," Andy repeated, looking wistfully at Aunt Charlotte.

6

"We'll see you in six months," Carmen said as she hugged Paul and Sienna goodbye in front of the American Airlines ticket counter.

"Wish we could stay longer and help with the project," Kate added, "but there's already too much for us to do in a short period of time, with the first ride coming up in two weeks."

"We're just glad you could stay until we got back from our sail," Sienna replied.

"OK, Pardners," Andy said to Paul and Sienna with tears hidden behind his dark glasses. "You take care of yourselves."

"Andy, we'll be back in a few months. Get a grip on yourself," Aunt Charlotte chided, dabbing her eyes with a handkerchief.

After waving one final time, they watched as the four passed through the *Passengers Only* door.

"Well, back to our real life," Sienna announced on their way home. "Can you pick up AJ from my folks at 4:30? I won't be home 'til 9:00. Maybe you can stop at the Chicken Shack on your way and pick up dinner."

"Sounds good. I've got to stop at the phone store to straighten out a bill. Then I thought I'd check with DPNR and see where we stand with the building permit. Should have had it by now. I called Ms. Hodges yesterday and got a 'Soon come, Sweetie.'"

******

Having lived on St. Croix for less than a year, Paul was still adapting to island time changes in attitude. "There is no Crucian word for *expedite*," he was told by a bar patron early one evening at The Inn On The Cay in Christiansted. It was this insight, coupled with Dorothy's understated observation; *We're not in Kansas anymore* that provided him with the necessary perspective to ease through the inevitable Crucian encounters that had sent many fellow continentals rushing back to the states.

As the lone customer in the phone store, Paul waited thirty minutes for his ticket number to be called while employees plaited each other's hair. Later, at the building department, he was at first elated when Ms. Hodges announced the building permit was ready for pick-up. But then she went on to explain, "The cashier, she went home early so you can come back Tuesday to pick it up."

"Why not Monday?"

"Monday the staff'll be at an *Improving Customer Service* seminar on St. Thomas," she replied, without a trace of irony.

At his final stop, The La Reine Chicken Shack, Paul stepped back and smiled in disbelief as a fireman cut in front of him to pick up his take-out order, then saunter back to the blaring siren and flashing lights of the double-parked fire engine.

"Reminds me of my last heart attack," an elderly man standing in line with Paul volunteered. "My wife called 911 and

33

the ambulance was there in ten minutes, which is fast for this island. But on the way to the hospital, the driver swung by a barber shop to pick up a fellow'd gotten nicked with a straight edge. I'm still here, obviously, so I can't really complain, but if we'd known I wouldn't reach the ER for thirty-five minutes, my wife could have driven me there in twenty."

It was after 9:30 and AJ had already been down for half-an-hour when Paul heard Sienna's Jeep Liberty pull up. Paul greeted her on the terrace with two glasses and a bottle of Courvoisier.

"So, did they miss you?" he asked, referring to her first day back at The Green Flash, a beachside restaurant Sienna owned and operated on the north shore of St. Croix.

"I have to give Bob and Gigi credit. The place looked spotless and even without Paul Armstrong's Friday and Saturday night performances, business was good for this time of year."

"Always feels great to be missed," Paul kidded. "By the way, I talked with Barney and he told me that Claire called him. She loves South America, but there may be some problems with Paulo."

"I hope she's OK. What kind of problems?"

"It seems that her Latin lover has come up a little short on the dinero. Claire sent Barney a $5,000 check drawn on her account at a Port Townsend bank and asked him to wire her the funds."

"Poor Claire, I can't imagine how terrifying this bipolar business must be."

"She feels invincible when she's in the manic phase, but coming down's gotta be like waking up in a nightmare."

"When you were married to her, did you ever notice anything like this?"

34

"No, nothing like this. I worry about Barney too. You know, he says that he's not in love with her anymore, but I don't believe it. I think it really tears him up when she writes about what a great guy Paulo is."

"It must be hard on you too," Sienna replied leaning over and kissing him on the cheek. "You were with her for fifteen years and Barney's your best friend."

"Well, there's not much Barney or I can do about it until she asks for help, if she ever does."

"Did Barney say when he's coming down?"

"Now that we have the permit, he plans on arriving late next week. He wants to be here for the foundation work and said he'll stay as long as we need him."

"You guys haven't seen much of each other over the last year. How do you think Hank and Barney will get along?"

Paul chuckled, "I'm looking forward to finding out."

******

Following the island-wide decimation in '89 by Hurricane Hugo, Don McGowan arrived on St. Croix with his twelve year old son, Adam. A competent handyman, Don found work immediately and was in constant demand rebuilding and repairing homes. Through careful management, hard work and a reputation for dependability, he slowly built his business into the most respected construction company on island. Paul was referred to Don by the manager of St. Croix Lumber and the two struck an agreement in which Don would work on the house remodel as a first phase. The second phase, the construction of a six-unit off-the-grid village would follow if their relationship stood up to the initial test.

The two worked well together. Paul appreciated Don's pragmatic and knowledgeable approach to construction, as well as the careful planning he put into lining up the subcontractors and materials for each week's work. For Don, any associations he might have had with architects and prima donnas were quickly dispatched by Paul's genuine interest in incorporating Don's ideas. Paul was a good designer, but he relied on Don's experience for building on St. Croix.

On Tuesday, after picking up the permit, Paul parked his truck in Seaborne Airline's downtown Christiansted parking lot and walked the waterfront boardwalk to Angry Nate's, a favorite of Paul's for its fresh mahi sandwich and great coffee. Don was sipping an iced tea and enjoying the harbor view at an outside table shaded by a palm frond umbrella when Paul arrived.

"Don't tell me you got it?" Don asked, as Paul sat down and dropped the permit on the table.

"Looks like we're in business. How soon can you get Cheech and his brush cutter on the site?"

"We should be clearing the site by Wednesday."

"Barney will be here the end of the week to help with the foundation work on Monday."

"Not sure what we'll need him for. My men can handle things just fine."

"I realize that Don, but I don't want any power equipment in the area around the cabins. It's steeply sloped and the helical piles can be installed with a two-man power auger."

"That sounds like a tough job for two men. Power augers are hard enough to work on level ground."

"Barney's six-eight and weighs close to 300 pounds. He works on his farm seven days a week and I guarantee that if you give him a good helper, he's the right man for the job."

"I'm sure you're right. It's just that I like to know the people I have working under me. What if he and I have a difference of opinion on how deep he needs to go with the piles?"

"You already said it. He's working under you. Let's start him out and if you don't like the way it's going, you can fire him. No problem."

"Six-eight, close to 300 pounds, how 'bout you fire him?"

"Deal," Paul replied, opening the lunch menu.

7

Joseph Barnswollow (a.k.a. Barney) and Paul were sixteen when they first met their junior year at varsity football tryouts for Seattle's Franklin High School in the fall of 1984. Riding on the back of a summer growth-spurt, gaining twenty pounds and two inches to his six foot height, Paul decided to expand his athletic endeavors beyond golf and wrestling. Barney, at six-seven and two-hundred-forty pounds had already lettered as a sophomore and was on track to make All-Metro his junior year.

Lacking experience, Paul was overlooked by the coaches. A week before their first game, a scout squad was put together to run the expected offense of their perennial rivals, the Garfield Bulldogs. Not wanting to risk injuring a valuable player, Paul was selected to play quarterback for the scout squad. At first, there was little opportunity for Paul to even run a play as Barney and company pushed easily through the scout squad's offensive line. Paul was repeatedly pancaked under Barney and one or two linemen even before he had a chance to hand the ball off, let alone throw a pass. Fifteen minutes into the onslaught, Paul was hit exceptionally hard by Barney. Landing on his back, he absorbed the additional force of four other linemen piling on top.

"That all you got?" Paul said to Barney, as the pile was clearing.

"You're a tough little shit," Barney replied, his large, grinning face stuffed tightly inside the football helmet.

Although Paul hadn't played organized football, he had plenty of experience playing neighborhood pickup games. Tired of the ass- kicking, he put this experience to use in the huddle by calling a roll-out with a pump fake. "If I can get outside, I think the defensive halfback will buy the fake."

The improvised play went off perfectly, while teammates and coaches alike watched open-mouthed as Paul connected with a pass that traveled over 50 yards in the air. The ensuing silence was broken by Barney's loud, baritoned announcement, "Fuck' n egg, we got ourselves a quarterback." Their friendship was forged at that moment and remained intact ever since.

While Paul accepted a football scholarship to Washington State University in Eastern Washington, Barney confounded major college recruiters by turning-down a dozen full-ride offers to work out of Dutch Harbor in the Bering Sea with his father on the family's crab boat, *Kodiak Kate*.

Paul found little joy in the regimented approach to football at Washington State and quit his sophomore year. Six years after high-school graduation, he received his Bachelor of Architecture degree and Barney, after his father's retirement, took over the helm as one of the youngest ship captains in Alaska's crabbing industry. The two lost contact during a two-year dark period that followed the accidental drowning of Barney's younger brother while working on *Kodiak Kate*. Barney blamed himself for the accident, sold the boat and disappeared. He wandered aimlessly throughout the bars and back roads of the Pacific Northwest and British Columbia until an attempted suicide landed him in a Port Townsend, Washington hospital, finally having hit rock-bottom.

Aunt Charlotte was a volunteer at the hospital and alerted her husband of Barney's condition. Uncle Ernie sat with the depressed patient each day of the month-long hospital stay. Years later, after Ernie's sudden, fatal heart attack, Barney spoke at his funeral. He recounted Ernie asking him in the hospital when he'd be done feeling sorry for himself. "I told him to leave and not come back. But he showed up the next day like nothing had happened. Finally I told him about my brother's death and how I blamed myself for it. He told me that we all make mistakes and that I'd suffered enough. He said I should come back and make a life for myself. Something clicked inside me and I've never been the same since."

Barney purchased a 120-acre farm in Quilcene, located in the eastern foothills of Washington's Olympic Mountains. He bred a Wagyu bull into his herd of Hereford cattle. Organic and delicious, the meat was packed and sold as fast as it was produced. Same too, with the high-grade marijuana he produced in the eight-hundred square foot greenhouse he had added to the farm's outbuildings.

Paul, meanwhile, had married Claire and was up to his eyeballs in work after opening Armstrong Architects, A.I.A. For the fifteen years of their marriage, Claire had little use for Barney, whose booming voice usually contained some derivative of the word fuck in every third or fourth sentence. Also on her *why I hate Barney list* was his bushy red beard, soiled coveralls, a 1966 rusted red pickup with a rag hanging out of the gas tank, and his penchant for ganja. "Definitely not the kind of person you want to be associated with," she would repeatedly advise. Paul, generally ignored her advice, but other commitments kept him from spending much quality time with his friend. Barney was bitter for the wedge she had driven between them and referred to her privately as "Paul's Psycho Bitch-Snob Wife."

That all changed, however, quite suddenly. With his sudden divorce and the simultaneous destruction of the newly-formed company he had started with Andrew Sherman, Paul accepted Barney's offer to live with him on the farm while he figured out his next move. Soon after, Claire returned to Paul's life by way of a completely unexpected occurrence . . . Barney and Claire fell in love.

Now, driving to the airport to pick Barney up, Paul's mind skimmed over events of the last year. He recalled his surprise when first hearing that Barney and Claire had become a couple. The understandable awkwardness between the three of them hadn't lasted long as Paul and Claire were now able to continue their friendship without the burden of a passionless marriage they had endured for too long. The friendship and good times were short lived however, as Claire soon fell into an inexplicable depression. The psychiatrist's diagnosis of bipolar disorder or manic depression couldn't prepare Barney and Paul for what would come next. Her mania became delusional as she hacked into Paul's email and sent copies of his tax returns to former clients, caustic emails to his friends, and a threatening email to Sienna. All of these actions were minor compared to the heartbreak Barney suffered when Claire ran off to Columbia with Paulo, a South American juggler, to "find her bliss."

******

Barney's white, tree-trunk legs stretched down from his plaid bermuda shorts to the size 15 Jesus sandals as Paul watched him wedge through the arrival doorway. A Seahawks jersey stretched over his massive chest. Mirrored sunglasses and a cloth Stetson completed the ensemble. Paul prepared himself just in time for Barney's crushing bear-hug. "I've missed you, Ace," Barney announced loudly, as they waited for his bags at the luggage carrousel. "Looks like you're being well-fed though. Is it always this fuckin' hot? I hear all the beaches are nude. So this is what paradise smells like. Must be a landfill nearby."

Barney's bags finally arrived and Paul carried them out to his truck while Barney took advantage of the free rum drinks at the hospitality kiosk. "Here, I got one for you too." Barney folded himself into the truck and handed the drink to Paul for the drive home. "Can't believe they serve you free rum for the road and call it a traveler . . . Beats the shit out of the flowered leis they give you when you land in Honolulu. What's the plan for tonight?"

"Sienna made reservations for us at 7:00 at The Green Flash. I play a set at 9 and 10, then we might head down to the boardwalk to see what's happening in Christiansted. Speaking of getting laid."

"I've got nothing to report from that neck of the woods. Since Claire, I've got no interest. Hey, Dear Abby, can you maybe find me a little ganja to smooth out the jet lag?"

"Already taken care of by the best roofers on the island. They did a great job on the remodel. I paid them a bonus and they gave me a baggie that has your name on it."

"Excellent, Amigo. I thought of shoving a zip lock up my ass for the flight, but didn't think I'd have the stomach to smoke it."

"Just as well. A handsome cowboy like you is just beggin' for a cavity search."

"What? You don't like the duds? I was going for Kenny Chesney. You know, still western, but with a tropical edginess."

"Didn't say I didn't like it. Just meant that you're flying way above the radar."

"Always have. Always will."

"Well, there is that. Why throw in a winning hand?"

"My point exactly, Ace. How much longer before we arrive at the homestead? I've got to piss like a race-horse."

"Ten more minutes. Want me to stop when we hit the rainforest? Everyone pisses on the side of the road in the rainforest."

"No need to stop." Barney set his drink in the cup holder and unbuckled his seat-belt. Unzipping his pants, he rolled down his window, lifted off the seat and turned. "I'll just let it loose in the wind."

Paul's chuckle turned into a full belly-laugh as, swearing loudly, Barney cut off the stream that had curled behind the cab onto his luggage.

When Paul was finally able to talk, he said, "Doesn't seem like we're much different than we were at Franklin High, does it?"

"My point exactly, Amigo." Barney stuffed his race-horse back in the stable and zipped up. "Why throw in a winning hand?"

Sienna and AJ were standing on the terrace waving when Paul and Barney drove up.

"That's one beautiful little family you have there, Partner. You're a lucky man."

Uncle Barney threw AJ ten feet skyward when he reached the truck. Holding him upside down with one arm, he embraced Sienna with the other. "Damn, but it's good to see you two again." Paul uncoiled the garden hose and sprayed-down the side of his truck and Barney's bags.

Once AJ was deposited back on the ground, he jumped up on the back bumper of the truck. "Why are you spraying Uncle Barney's bags?"

"Oh God," Sienna moaned, guessing correctly. "You idiots are fourteen. Come on AJ; let's show Uncle Barney his room."

******

AJ had Uncle Barney shagging grounders while Paul threw him underhand pitches. Play was interrupted when Barney's wolf-whistle acknowledged Sienna's appearance on the terrace wearing a short denim dress with a gold chain belt and high heeled sandals. Smiling, she announced, "AJ, I'm heading to work. Remind your friends that they need to have you at my sister's by 6:30 if they want to make their 7:00 reservations. Also, it might be a good idea if you remind Uncle Barney to use the bathroom before you boys head out."

Paul followed Sienna to her car. She kissed him briefly before getting in. "I want you and Barney to have a great time," she said, after rolling down the window. "I'll pick AJ up after work. Just promise me that if you guys stay out real late, you'll call me so I don't worry."

"Promise, and thanks for understanding. He can be a little much sometimes."

"Yes, but fortunately his heart is the biggest part of him." She waved goodbye to Uncle Barney, who returned the wave while galloping in circles with AJ on his shoulders. "I love you, Paul," she said as she backed the car up.

"Love you more."

44

"Probably." She drove off with a grin.

Barney set AJ down and walked over to Paul. "Everything OK there Amigo? Did I cause a squabble? You know, I can get a room in town. Might be easier on you guys."

"What are you talking about? Have you already gotten into the baggie?"

"What's a baggie?" AJ asked from a distance that Paul and Barney had assumed incorrectly was out of ear-shot.

"A powerful elixir for the young at heart," Barney ad-libbed. "Now let's go inside and clean up. Come on, I'll race you."

AJ took off squealing with Uncle Barney close on his heels. Paul picked up the baseball equipment and followed them inside.

******

"OK if I roll a joint?" Barney asked, as they pulled away from Charleese's, the youngest of Sienna's four sisters.

"Sure, it's no more illegal here than anyplace else."

"Doesn't that fuckin' fry you? People are still being sent to prison for getting high. They ought to legalize pot down here. That'd fill the hotels."

"You're preaching to the choir, but there's a strong fundamentalist sector on St. Croix. They probably think it would turn the place into a tropical Gomorrah."

"Yeah, well some people just can't be reached. Probably the same folks that raised the big stink when the gay cruise ship docked here a few years ago. Heard about it on NPR. Don't think that did much for the island's image." Barney took a deep drag and offered it to Paul.

45

"Maybe later, I need to be clear-headed for my two sets."

Barney shrugged his shoulders and took another toke. "Thought you artiste-types drew inspiration from weed. Say, not to change the subject, but heard anything more from the mob since your dinner with Sherman?"

"I got a text from Hank. He spoke to Buddy Falco's Uncle Sal, who told him they're working on having Buddy's sentence overturned. His only interest in me is as a witness to Andrew being alive."

"Seems pretty cut and dried to me. He's alive, so Buddy didn't murder him."

"Hank thinks there are a lot of folks in criminal justice that are blocking the process. I'd imagine there's plenty of good reasons for Buddy's incarceration and the DA is hoping that another one turns up in time to keep him locked up."

"Well, just as long as it doesn't come back and bite you in the ass. Good thing you ran into this Hank fella. At least you got somebody looking after you down here. God knows, I can't be everywhere."

"He actually reminds us of you."

"Shit, most days I can barely even stand myself. I'll probably hate him."

"Well, we'll find out soon. He's on island for business and flying back home to St. Thomas tomorrow morning. I asked him to join us for dinner."

"And I was looking forward to some quality one-on-one time with my Amigo."

Surprised, Paul looked over at Barney, who suddenly burst out laughing. "Relax Ace, the more the merrier."

8

Hank was sitting at the bar when Paul and Barney arrived. He stood and greeted Paul with a hug and Barney with a firm handshake.

"You guys could probably have turned a lump of coal into a diamond with that hand shake," Paul observed as Hank shook his hand in the air grimacing.

"Remind me to get on a hugging basis with Barney real fast. I heard you were strong, but Jesus . . ."

"Shit, I'm sorry Hank. It's probably the weed that Ace laid on me. Usually I'm more careful. Plus, you remind me of a sheriff-friend I have back home. Tex and I always try to get the better grip on each other."

"You'll meet Tex and Sally next month," Paul added. "They're coming down to help on the project for a few weeks. By the way, Barney's hugs are harder on you than his handshakes."

"Hey, I'm right here you know," Barney complained, while signaling the bartender over. "Now, how about I order us up some fancy-assed, umbrella, sissy-drinks."

"I'm in," Hank said. "But first, did I hear something about weed?"

"You guys enjoy." Paul handed Barney the truck keys. "I'm going in the back to see Sienna."

"Did you see Don?" Sienna asked when Paul entered her office. "He's here with his son and daughter-in-law. They're down from the States for a couple of weeks."

"That's great. What's the daughter-in-law's name? Annie, isn't it?"

"Good memory. She seems really sweet. So how are Hank and Barney getting along?"

"Too early to say. Barney kind of crushed Hank's hand when they shook. He apologized and blamed it on the weed I gave him."

"I hope Hank's OK with that. I'd imagine he's a bit uncomfortable with pot, given his years in law enforcement."

"Well, they're out in my truck getting high, so he must not be too uncomfortable."

Sienna rolled her eyes. "Looks like you boys are headed for quite an evening. Just remember—"

"I'll call you if we stay out late." He leaned down and kissed her.

Heading into the dining room, Paul spotted Don with his son and daughter-in-law. Barney and Hank hadn't returned so he walked over to their table.

"Paul, I'd like you to meet my son, Adam and his wife, Annie."

"It's a pleasure to meet you," Adam said. "Dad says that you're his all-time favorite client."

"Wow, that's an honor. Did he say why?"

"I'll tell you why," Don said. "Because you're so involved, I don't waste time waiting on decisions. Also, since you don't micro-manage me, I never have to explain what I'm doing."

"Sounds like a great client to me," Annie agreed.

"Yeah, I guess. Although, I would like to have heard something about what a brilliant designer I am," Paul kidded.

"I'd say that's Sienna's job," Don replied.

"What's my job?" Sienna asked as she approached the table.

"Don's suggesting that my fragile ego often requires buoying-up by you."

"It's true. It's constant and I don't get paid nearly enough for it either."

"No you don't," Barney's loud voice boomed as he and Hank arrived from the parking lot. "Excuse me for eavesdropping, but I can tell you all first-hand the amount of work it takes to keep our boy's head above water." Gently hugging Sienna he added, "You *are* a Saint."

"It takes a village," Hank added, then joined Barney in a *high-five*.

Paul introduced the new arrivals to Don and his family.

"So you're the great contractor Paul's been telling me about," Barney said as he carefully shook Don's hand. "Looks like I'll be helping out for a little while. Don't you worry now about hurtin' my feelings if I'm not doin' something the way you'd like."

"I appreciate that, Barney. We'll be out there on Monday morning bright and early."

Sienna led Hank and Barney to their table while Paul went up to the stage to do a quick sound check. "You boys enjoy your meal," Sienna said as the two lumbering hulks sat down. "Can I start you out with drinks?"

"Hank here would like something fruity with rum and an umbrella. I'll have the same please."

"Paul needs to focus so he's abstaining," Hank volunteered.

"Oh my god," Sienna muttered as she turned for the bar.

Barney looked over the menu. "Think I'll start with a hamburger as an appetizer. I see here where they have those sweet-potato fries. First cabin, just like up in the States."

"Shit!" Hank said, looking down at the beach. "That skinny fuck just threw his puppy into the surf like a football. Training it for fighting. Let's go pay him a visit." But Barney was already half-way down the outside stairs when Hank jumped up from the table in pursuit.

Arriving alone and with a full head of steam, Barney plucked the shivering pup out of the owner's raised hand just before another cruel launching.

"What the fuck?" The man's eyes blazed from the intrusion, but cooled quickly when he turned to face the red bearded giant glaring angrily down at him, cradling the dog in his massive arms. His demeanor softened even more with Hank's arrival. "You could get arrested for the way you're treating your dog."

"What? You mean throwing her in the water? That ain't nothin'. Just trainin' the lil' bitch. Been doin' it with all my dogs. Don't hurt 'em, just makes 'em tough. Shit, you don't know about trainin' dogs."

"Last I heard, fighting dogs was illegal," Hank said, taking out his cell phone. "What's your name?"

"I don't know where you're from, asshole. People 'round here knows I'm Carlos, and they know not to fuck with me or my dogs. Now, have your big friend give me back my property, 'fore I be takin' your names down for the police."

"What's the pup's name?" Barney asked.

"Fuck you."

"I think we can do better, my friend. She's kind of reddish. I think Rose is a good name for her. Here, hold her for a second Hank."

"What are you fixin' to do?" Carlos asked as Barney turned toward him.

"Thought I might see how you like it." Barney clamped his big hand onto the back of Carlos's shirt and grabbed the seat of his pants with the other. Easily lifting the struggling man above his head, Barney bent his legs and tossed a screaming Carlos ten feet into the shallow surf. Hearing the commotion, Paul joined a growing number of onlookers at the rail of the restaurant and watched as Barney waded into the water and pulled the gasping man out of the surf.

"What's going on?" Sienna asked.

"It appears our friend, Barney, had a disagreement with a jerk-off regarding his method of dog training," Don explained, standing at the rail on the other side of Paul.

"So how was it?" Barney asked, dragging Carlos back to shore. "You feel tougher?"

Still coughing up salt-water from his open-mouthed landing, Carlos choked, "Get the fuck away from me. I've got friends who are going to sorry your big ass when they hear 'bout this."

"Tell you what." Barney took his wallet out after pulling Carlos to his feet, "Let's you and I make a deal."

******

Sienna set Rose on a towel in the cardboard box Paul had cut in half as a temporary puppy bed. Paul placed a bowl of water and a plate of meat scraps in the box as the ravenous little fur-ball gobbled down the meal.

Barney and Hank were already into their third round of drinks bought by Don and other appreciative patrons for their heroic deed when Sienna and Paul rejoined them at the bar.

"Hope I didn't cause a problem for you two. Just couldn't watch that asshole torture Rose like that."

"We call the police several times a month for that kind of thing," Sienna replied. "Never seems to do much good though. Dog fighting's illegal, of course, but most people just look the other way when they see the abuse."

"That's not what our boy here just did," a well-lubricated Don boasted, raising his drink. "Yes sir, he turned the tables on that creep . . . World would have been a better place, though, if you'd let him drown."

"Don't know what I was thinking," Barney roared laughing, having mistaken Don's statement as hyperbole.

The rum-fueled love fest for Barney broke up with the arrival of hamburgers and sweet-potato fries. "I've got to tell you Barney," Hank said, his mouth half full of food, "that punk won't change his ways, but there were a lot of island kids down there who saw him fly through the air and you pulling him out of the surf. Kinda destroyed his tough guy image. Give those kids something to think about."

"Yeah, well at least we rescued Rose." Barney signaled the waiter for another round.

Paul finished his meal while his two friends continued to drink. He opened his first set with Bob Marley's *Buffalo Soldier* followed by a Taj Mahal's, The *Callypsonians*. During Buffet's *Margaritaville*, Barney was pulled to his feet and kept on the dance floor by "several very friendly island ladies," he later described after shoehorning himself into the back seat of Paul's truck. "So let's get this show on the road. I'd imagine there's no shortage of beach bars on this rock." Hank slumped against the passenger door while Barney continued his nonstop chatter. "I hope old Barn doesn't spoil it for the rest of you guys down here. Kinda hard to enjoy a Slurpee after you've tasted Champagne."

"No problem, Barney. Paul and I already got the picks of the litter. You're welcome to the rest."

"Picks of the litter. Hah!" Barney shouted, pounding him on the shoulder. "Hank, you're my kind of asshole."

"I thought you just wanted to be friends," Hank replied, which brought another roar from the backseat giant.

There's not enough booze on the island for me to get through tonight, Paul thought as he considered their next landing site. "So where do you wild and crazy party-dudes want to go next?"

Barney's answer surprised Paul, who had visions of being dragged through several beach bars with another righteous confrontation thrown in just for fun.

"Somewhere we can talk. Music would be OK, but not too loud. I could go for some dessert."

"Sounds good to me," Hank chimed in.

"Well, there's a fire pit with chaises at the west end of the property. I've got a cooler and cd player I can bring down from the house."

"S'mores!" Barney shouted and high-fived Hank who had faded back against the door. "Damn fine idea, Ace. Hey Hank, what time do you fly back to St. Thomas in the morning?"

"I'm taking the float plane out of Christiansted at 8:00. Thought I'd get a room in town tonight."

"Shit, I don't see you needing a place tonight. This shindig's not slowing down before breakfast tomorrow. We've got a lot of figuring and coordinating to do if we're going to keep our boy here out of trouble."

9

Barney and Hank had the bonfire roaring by the time Paul arrived on the ATV with Rose in his lap. He pulled a cooler full of Jamaican beer and a wicker picnic basket out of the cart.

He didn't mention how relieved Sienna was that they had moved the party into the back yard. "I'm just glad the *Justice League* is kicking it back for the rest of the night," she said, handing Rose to Paul.

Paul had also packed some pillows, blankets, AJ's boom box and a small collection of CD's. "Marshmallows, graham crackers and Hershey bars," Barney reported, looking into the picnic basket. "Gentlemen, we have a green light for s'mores!"

Barney and Hank sat hunched forward, carefully holding skewered Marshmallows over fading red embers. Paul was stretched out on a chaise with Rose sleeping in his lap. "So you gonna keep the dog?" Barney asked.

"What's your guess now that AJ's played with her.?"

"Well, I think that's all right. I have a sixth sense about animals and there's no doubt she's a good one." He flashed an irritated look at Hank who was pulling a blazing Marshmallow out of the fire. "Jeez, I've told you Hank, they taste better browned than charred."

"Who the fuck made you Betty Crocker?"

"Sorry, it's just hard for me to see good Marshmallows going to waste."

Paul was glad to see the two getting along, but was hoping they'd wind down soon. Sienna was in bed, naked, less than 100 yards away.

"So tell me Hank, do you think Ace has anything to worry about with Falco and his friends?"

"Honestly, I can't say for sure." Hank blew the flame out on another Marshmallow. "There's no reason to think he would, but we're not dealing with reasonable people here. I've spoken with Falco's Uncle Sal, who's the head honcho of the Jersey syndicate. He and I have had a few frank, off-the-record conversations in the past. I always found him to be pretty straight with me. He said that their lawyers are trying to get his nephew's sentence vacated based on the report Paul filed with the Tortola police."

"Seems pretty fuckin' clear to me. Paul had dinner with the asshole, so he's obviously not dead. How can they keep Falco in prison for his murder?"

"The majority of people in law enforcement familiar with Buddy Falco consider him guilty on many counts. Sherman told Paul that Falco admitted he was disposing some deadbeat's body off the Narrows Bridge. That's how Sherman got the idea to fake his demise."

"Yeah, but that's just hearsay. He might have just been trying to scare Sherman."

"Don't forget Falco's car was videotaped crossing the bridge. That's what drew the police to him in the first place," Paul reminded Barney.

"Look, I'm sure they think he's thrown several people off the bridge, but they can't prove it," Hank said, blowing out another flaming Marshmellow. "So they go with what they have. Without Andrew Sherman's appearance in the flesh, the authorities can delay or even deny the vacation by claiming that the mob got to our boy scout over there."

"Can't they investigate? You know, interview the bartender, waiter and other employees at the Willie T? And why *boy scout?*"

"I think I've got the last part of that," Barney said. "With most people, there's a good side and bad side, a light and a dark. One morning we wake up singing with the birds, another morning, we're throwing our shoe at the fuckin' robin for waking us up. With Ace, here, there's no dark side." Paul started to object, but was waved off by Barney who was on a roll. "Now I'm not saying that he's never down. You should have seen him draggin' his mopey ass all over my farm after his business and marriage went TU. But the thing about my Amigo here is that his basic reasonableness keeps him from staying pissed-off. If a robin woke him up, he'd blame himself for not wearing ear plugs. Shit, he forgave Sherman for chrissake."

"That's bullshit. I get mad. I almost punched Andrew when he came up to our table."

"Why are you so touchy about being described as a nice guy? Look, I didn't say you don't get angry. You just don't have a dark side to turn it into anything. By the time you ordered your dinner, fairness, forgiveness and understanding had, once again, completely taken over."

"Pretty tough talk coming from a lard-assed pussyboy."

Barney roared as he lunged toward Paul, who quickly set Rose down on the chaise. He easily side-stepped the drunken charge and jumped on the big man's back. Hank watched in amazement as Barney unsuccessfully struggled to shake and twist Paul off. Finally collapsing on the ground,

Barney groaned, "Not fair, jumping a man who's inebriated. Plus you know all those fuckin' wrestling holds."

Paul brushed off his knees while Barney climbed back into his chaise. "Good thing I can't stay angry, Doctor Freud. I might not have let you up."

"Well, that was unexpected," Hank admitted, after the dust settled. "You two have done this before?"

"Used to do it all the time," Barney replied, leaning toward the open cooler. "I'd needle him about something. Try to make him mad. Then we'd go at it. He wrestled in high school, but it'd usually end up with me getting him in a bear-hug. Might've lost a step or two since then," he added, popping the cap off the last bottle.

"Well, all right then," Hank said, shaking his head. "Back to your question, Paul, yes, they could investigate and maybe come up with a corroborating witness, but what's their motivation, if they still want Buddy behind bars?"

"I'm not anxious to testify or even give a deposition. In fact, I'd just as soon never hear anything more about Andrew or Buddy, but isn't it the job of the authorities to find out whether or not Buddy had been framed?" Paul asked, then glared at Barney who mouthed, *Boy Scout.*

"Well, you'd like to think so. Anyway, Buddy's Uncle Sal doesn't see much help coming from the Justice Department. Says that they're focusing on finding Sherman themselves. Either way, it looks like they don't have a beef with Paul."

Half an hour later, the night sounds of the rainforest were joined by Barney and Hank's resonant snores as Paul headed back to the house to join Sienna in their comfortable bed.

******

Sienna kissed Paul awake. "I'm headed for yoga. AJ's with Barney and Hank. They're out on the porch drinking coffee."

"What time is it?"

"Six-fifteen. Hank's flight's been delayed 'til nine. So you've got plenty of time for the *Real Man Breakfast* that Barney says he's making."

Sitting up, Paul rubbed his eyes. "Hank needs to catch his plane, but I figured Barney would sleep 'til noon after all the liquor and pot."

"Barney said he didn't sleep very well. I can't believe they slept on that old lawn furniture. Why didn't you have them come into the house?"

"They had blankets and seemed comfortable."

"Well, he said he was sore from you jumping on him and got all kinked up sleeping on the chaise. You jumped on him?"

Paul explained their tussle to Sienna's amazed reaction, "I think I overshot it by a couple years when I said you two act like fourteen-year-olds."

Paul laughed and stepped into the shower.

"So I'm headed to work after yoga. I was going to swing by and pick up AJ, but Barney said he wants some quality time with his nephew. Calls him 'Little Ace.'"

"That's great. Maybe I'll play golf after I drop Hank off."

She blew him a kiss from the bathroom doorway. Pots clanging and Barney's loud laugh could be heard from the kitchen as Paul quickly shaved and dressed. He found Barney standing at the stove with AJ perched on a stool beside him. A low cloud of smoke partially hid the iron skillets filled with charred bacon, scrambled eggs and thin-sliced russet potatoes. Hank was buttering toast and Rose was devouring a bowl of kibble.

"Good Morning, Sleepyhead. Make yourself useful, I thought we'd eat out on the porch."

Paul grabbed placemats, glasses and utensils and soon the four were quietly wolfing down Barney's *Real Man Breakfast.*

"Very good, Cheffy," Hank commented, as he served himself seconds.

"I used the bacon grease in the potatoes and scrambled eggs. It makes everything taste better."

"I'll say." AJ seconded, proud to be included as a *Real Man.*

Paul dished-up seconds for himself and AJ. "I heard you and Uncle Barney are hanging out together today."

"Yeah, we're going to look at a boat to buy."

Paul looked at Barney.

"Well, if I'm going to be spending much time down here, I need something to keep me busy. I used to be a pretty good boat captain. Haven't done much . . . actually any boating since the accident. Think maybe I could take people sport fishin'. Saw a five year old Cabo 35 for sale in that little island paper over there," he said, pointing to yesterday's copy of *The Avis.* "I called the owner and think AJ, Rose and I'll ride down to Christiansted when you take Hank. Go check it out."

"If the price is right and the boat's been taken care of, that's a good vessel to get into," Hank said. "I have a friend who has one. Says they're built like a brick shit-house. Twin-diesels. Nice interior trim-out. Stable, but they really fly. Says she cruises at thirty-knots with a low swell."

******

Standing at the west end of the harbor side boardwalk, Paul, AJ and Barney watched the De Havilland Twin Otter's pontoons lift off the calm water just outside Christiansted harbor. Holding Rose, AJ waved and shouted to the climbing aircraft, "Bye, Hank. Say Hi to Red for us!"

The plane made a wide turn to the north and soon became a small speck in the clear, morning sky as it covered the forty miles between St. Croix and St. Thomas.

"So you're sure you don't want me to go with you?" Paul asked Barney.

Rubbing AJ's curly black hair with his huge hand, Barney replied, "I know you want to go chase that little white ball around. Little Ace, Rose and I are gonna check some things out. Probably give you a call just before dinner for a ride home."

10

Carrying his clubs up to the practice area at the Buccaneer Golf Course, Paul spotted Doc James hitting balls into the driving net while Arthur Green and Luke Bradshaw practiced their putting.

"Hey, Paul," Billy Rawlins, a retired sixty-five year old counselor called out as he appeared from the clubhouse. "I heard you were tied up and that's why they called me."

"No problem, Billy. I got a last minute hall pass. My friend, Barney, wanted some one-on-one time with AJ. I thought you were off-island for the summer."

"I'm just here for a couple weeks while Sandy and her gal pals enjoy a week at some overpriced spa on Dominica."

Overhearing their conversation, Arthur asked, "Is Barney that big guy that frisbee'd Carlos Desmond into Cane Bay?"

"You heard about that already?"

"Word travels fast on this little rock," Luke said, bending at the waist and stretching his hamstrings. "Billy and I were talking to a couple of women at The Galleon last night and they told us all about it. One of the women—"

"Paula," Billy interjected.

"Right, Paula. After dinner, her friend left and she joined us at the bar. A couple drinks later she left saying that she was going to look this giant up and check out his beanstalk."

"Doc James is on the phone with his exchange," Arthur said, interrupting the laughter. "We might have an opening."

Minutes later, the doctor left the course explaining that he was meeting a patient at the hospital. "Shit. It's probably Braxton Hicks contractions, but it could be early labor. What lousy timing. I really had a good feeling about my swing today."

Billy commented after they watched the doctor throw his clubs into the trunk of his car and drive off. "Let's see . . . bring a new life into the world or play golf? Doesn't seem like that difficult of a decision to me, but what do I know?"

"Reminds me of the story about the golfer who straightened-up over a putt and took his hat off as a funeral procession drove by," Arthur recalled. "His caddy complemented him on his display of respect. 'It's the least I can do,' the golfer replied. 'She was a good and faithful wife for thirty years.'"

******

Paul pull-hooked his tee-shot on the scenic par-three third hole and watched as it sailed into the ocean. Having hit two balls into the pond on the second, he now resigned himself to forgetting about his score and merely enjoying the companionship and exercise. His pitch from the drop area stopped six-feet short of the hole, but two putts later, he shouldered his bag and headed for the fourth tee after recording a double-bogey five.

"It's a beautiful day for golf, isn't it, Paul?" Luke needled from the golf cart.

"Ka-ching," Arthur happily added, having birdied the last two holes.

"I'm just glad my shitty play is making somebody happy, even if it's you two," Paul replied sourly, after he hooked his drive into the bushes on the par-5 fourth.

"C'mon, Partner. Don't let those assholes get inside your head," Billy said, as they walked down the fairway.

"Not much in my head related to golf these days. We break ground on Monday and I picked up a job designing a home for an off-island couple. Add Barney to the mix and there isn't much time left for golf right now."

"I'm retired, but I remember what being swamped feels like. Still, I'd appreciate it if you'd turn it up a notch. Luke is Mr. Smack-Talk and I really hate losing to these guys."

Paul did manage to improve and by the end of the front nine, he and Billy had drawn even.

"Get you guys a drink?" Arthur offered as Paul and Billy walked to the next tee.

"No, but you guys go ahead," Billy replied, chuckling. "In fact, have three or four."

"You know, for a counselor, you're pretty competitive."

"Yeah, so? I'm no Mr. Rogers, Paul. Call me competitive, but I've always liked winning more than losing."

Paul's cell chirped from inside his bag. Sienna and Barney had each called within two minutes of the other. "I'll see you on the tee, Billy." Paul set his bag on its stand and called Sienna.

"Have you talked with Barney?"

"Not yet. He called right before you. Everything OK?"

"No one's hurt, but Captain Barney ran his craft onto the reef in Christiansted Harbor and is waiting for the Coast Guard to pull him off. He wasn't going fast, but the hull is pretty scraped-up."

Paul took off his hat and wiped the sweat from his forehead. "Well, he's not the first to do that. I'd imagine he'll be fined by the Coast Guard."

"I'm surprised the owner let him take it out by himself. Those channel markers are confusing."

"Well, we know how persuasive Barney can be. I'll give him a call."

"How are you playing?"

"I'm four over, but Billy and I are all even with Luke and Arthur."

"Well, have fun. Let me know what you hear."

Paul called Barney, whose voice boomed over the cell, "Cover your ears Little Ace, Uncle Barney is probably going to say some bad words."

"How's your day been so far?"

"Fantastic until somebody put this fuckin' reef in front of us."

"What a bummer." Paul signaled Billy that he'd be another minute.

"The good news is that my mate here and I love this little skiff. You can unplug your ears now, AJ . . . She's fast and sturdy. Once I get the hull back in shape, *The Last Hurrah* will be good as new."

"So I guess running her up on the reef secured the sale, huh?"

"Woulda' bought her anyway. Even Rose likes her. Hasn't yakked once. Captain Marvin has priced her to sell and

I'm buyin'. Look Ace, I'd like to chat some more, but Coast Guard's here so I gotta run."

Paul described his call with Barney when he rejoined the group.

"We'll be able to watch from the next tee," Arthur said.

After all four players parred the tenth, they let the group behind play through and watched from the elevated eleventh tee while Barney and AJ were pulled off the reef.

"OK, you still with me?" Billy asked, as Paul pulled his four-iron from the bag for the downhill 215-yard par-three.

"What? You think a little thing like watching Barney and AJ being pulled off a reef is going to mess with my concentration?" His hooked tee shot onto the roof of the water treatment building suggested that it may have.

Billy held their loss to one point with a 30-foot par putt and they remained just one-down through the next six holes. On the final hole, a four-hundred and thirty-six yard par 4, all players were in the fairway off the tee. Billy hit his second shot safely right of the pond guarding the front of the green. His ball came to rest pin-high on top of a short mound.

Arthur's ball came off the shank of his club and careened out of bounds. Dejected, he shouted over to Luke, "Looks like it's on you now."

Paul made good contact with his shot but his ball bounced hard on the green and rolled just off the back.

Luke hoisted a sand wedge high into the air which landed softly ten-feet past the pin. He pumped his fist in the air. "That's what I'm talking about."

Billy was determined to fight to the finish. His pitch-shot struck the pin dead-center and disappeared in the hole. Paul cheered as Billy jumped excitedly and threw his club high into the air. Landing off-balance on the back slope of the mound, he rolled painfully over his ankle and landed hard in a nest of fire-ants. His putter landed solidly on the back of his head. Dazed and screaming, he scrambled to his feet and frantically brushed the voracious creatures from his legs, while Paul, Arthur and Luke ran to his aid.

"They're inside my jockeys!" Billy shouted, pulling his clothes off. He ran naked into the pond hoping to drown the remaining ants in the dank, murky water.

Exiting the pond proved more difficult. He struggled unsuccessfully to pull a foot loose from the pond's muddy bottom. "Fuck me, I'm stuck."

It was all too much. Luke started to laugh.

"What the fuck's so goddamn funny?"

Luke stared vacantly back at him through watery eyes and managed momentarily to stifle his laughter. Billy looked down at his mud-covered, bruised and bitten, naked body. Arthur and Paul's faces were screwed tight, fighting valiantly to keep from joining Luke. Billy started to chuckle. Soon, all four were laughing hysterically.

After regaining control of themselves, Paul and Luke took their shoes off and waded into the water, forming a chain with Arthur anchoring the rescue from shore. Their progress was slowed by repeated bursts of laughter, but was sped up with the arrival of a foursome of women on the nearby seventeenth tee. The ladies stared open-mouthed at the spectacle, but broke into cheers as Billy's naked torso finally reached shore. Turning briefly, he bowed, bringing another wave of cheers.

Wiping off as best he could with golf towels, Billy quickly threw his clothes back on. There was a knot on his head from the putter, but no blood. His legs and torso burned from the ant bites, but his swollen ankle seemed the most serious injury. Paul volunteered to take him to the hospital for x-rays, but Billy wouldn't hear of it. "I've rolled my ankle enough times to know it's not broken. I'll ice and elevate it when I get home. I've got some clothes in the car and once I get cleaned up I'm thinking there may be some money and drinks coming our way. I'm in with a three. Play on boys."

Paul's chip stopped four-feet short of the hole. Arthur sank a thirty footer for a six after taking a two stroke penalty. Luke's birdie putt lipped-out. He back-handed the remaining short putt in for a par. Paul now stood over his four-footer for the match. He knew immediately he'd pushed it to the right. Catching the edge of the hole, the ball swung three-sixty, coming to rest at the cup's edge.

"Nice try, Paul," Billy said.

"Fuck me." Luke groaned.

Paul looked back at the hole. The ball was gone.

******

"I can't believe it dropped," Arthur said, as the four enjoyed drinks on the clubhouse veranda.

"Never a doubt," Billy replied, gingerly touching the back of his head.

"I was more surprised when you showed that little pecker of yours to those ladies on 17," Luke said.

"So might we infer that there's more than one reason people refer to you as a big dick?"

"I think they were so distracted by the body hair, they didn't even notice his dick," Arthur speculated.

Billy sighed. "Look boys, I'm fifteen years older than any of you. Been married to the same woman almost as long as

Luke-here has been alive. May I offer some advice to my younger compatriots?"

"Please O'Ancient Holy One. Grace us with your wisdom," Luke begged sarcastically.

"Patience my son. First, in golf, as with women, remember that being long off the tee, has less impact on scoring than a properly timed delivery."

The sound of footsteps climbing the stairs up to the veranda interrupted the soliloquy. Three of the four women that had watched Billy's adventure headed for a corner table while the fourth ordered gin and tonics from the bar.

"I'm surprised they didn't head directly for their cars, with you showing them the Full Monty and all," Luke needled.

"You just don't get it, my lad."

"Get what?"

Standing up, Billy announced, "Ladies, I'd like to buy your drinks. Thanks to our trouncing of these two humbled associates," nodding at Arthur and Luke, "my partner and I are flush with cash."

Delivering the drinks to their table, Billy was rewarded with hugs by each of the appreciative women. One of them took his hand and asked shyly if he was married.

"Yes, very," he replied, leaning down and kissing her hand. "But thank you so much for asking."

Billy returned smugly to the table. After taking a sip of his drink, he quietly said to Luke, "Watch and learn, Luke, watch and learn."

11

Paul walked to the parking lot with Billy. Luke and Arthur stayed for another round of drinks with the ladies.

"Hope you're not too sore tomorrow. Let me know if you need anything."

"I should be fine. If I don't see you before I leave, we'll be back after Thanksgiving. Then you and I can give those two losers a shot at redemption."

They hugged goodbye. Paul climbed into his truck and called Barney as Billy pulled away.

"So how'd you play?"

"Do you really care?"

"No, not really. Little Ace and I are at the Brew Pub working out details with Captain Marvin. Should be done in a half-hour or so."

Paul called Andy, who he knew would be preparing to leave on Monday's trail ride with Kate in Washington's Pasayten Wilderness.

"That Barney sure is a mess of trouble," Andy laughed after Paul brought him up to date. "You make sure he's got a life jacket on my grandson when he takes him out in that damn boat."

"Will do. Although, I know Barney wouldn't let AJ into a boat without a life jacket."

"Just the same, better safe than sorry. Say, I talked to Sally yesterday. She and Tex are heading down there the third week of June. I think Char and I will fly down with them. Think you can put up with a crowd while construction's going on?"

"Absolutely. I know that Tex and Sally want to help with the construction, but I'm not sure what they'll really be able to do. Don has a pretty tight grip on things and doesn't really appreciate volunteer labor."

"Can't blame him for that. My experience is that you usually get what you pay for. Still, with all that remodeling Tex and Sally did on their home, seems like they could be useful for something."

"We'll work it out. Might smooth things over if Barney proves helpful. Don was concerned, but agreed to Barney's help with the helical piles installation."

"Well, keep me posted Son. Give my love to Sienna and AJ. We'll miss you up in them mountains."

Paul recalled the horse camping trip where he met Andy. Driving to the waterfront brewery, he reflected on how much his life had changed. Sienna, AJ, and St. Croix were not even a glimmer on the horizon when he had joined Kate's ride early last fall. Now, his plate was full as he spent his days with friends and family on a beautiful tropical island. He'd never known a love like he had with Sienna. Soon after their wedding, he would adopt AJ. He couldn't imagine a better life. A wave of concern came over him as he replayed his meeting with Stinger. With so much love in his life, he couldn't help but feel vulnerable, now having so much to lose.

******

Monday morning Paul and Don watched as Barney and his assigned down-island helper, Cleo, wrestled the two-man power auger over to the next drill spot. Don was happy with their progress. "Starting tomorrow, we'll come in behind them and form the pile caps. After they're poured, we'll set the Sonatubes and place the rebar for the piers. We should be ready to pour all six cabins' foundations within two weeks, as long as Barney doesn't burn himself out."

"That's great. How soon before we pour the floors?"

"We'll set the insulated slab forms and rebar right after pouring the piers. The piers should be cured enough within a few days to start the slab pours. We'll be erecting the wall panels within a month."

Don yelled over to Barney and Cleo to knock off for lunch. Sienna had made sack lunches for Paul and Barney which they took over to the lawn chairs on the bluff overlooking the ocean. Don and Cleo joined them. A cooling breeze rose up from the sea.

"What island are you from?" Paul asked Cleo.

"Saint Lucia. I came here two years ago with my wife and kids. I've been working for Mr. Don ever since I got here."

"You're a good man," Barney said, carefully patting Cleo on the shoulders. "It's a pleasure working with you."

Cleo's leathered face cracked open into a wide smile. "You're a good man too, but you must move slower. The weather's too hot. It'll boil your blood if you don't rest sometimes."

Don raised his hand, stopping Barney's inevitable rebuttal. "Cleo's right Barney. The heat and humidity sneak up on you here. I don't have a man who works harder than Cleo, so if you move like he moves and rest when he rests you'll get more done in the long run."

Barney surprised Paul by deferring to Don, "OK, if you say so. You're the boss."

The afternoon's heat set in and made clear the wisdom of Don and Cleo's advice. By four o'clock, Barney had completely sweated through his clothes. Overheated and overtired, he didn't need to be asked twice if he'd like to join Sienna, AJ, Rose and Paul in a ride out to Cane Bay. Once they arrived, Paul and Barney immediately waded out into the ocean while Sienna and AJ played with Rose on the beach.

"You know, Ace," Barney said as the two friends floated in the glass-smooth 85 degree water, "I don't seem to have much desire anymore to . . . you know."

"Maybe you should have it checked out. Could be low T."

"Nah, I'll tell you what it is, but you have to promise not to freak out when I do."

"OK," Paul agreed with some hesitation, having no clue what would come next out of Barney's mouth.

"I know I brag about what a stud I am and all, but honestly I can't get Claire out of my head. I really don't want to be with anybody else."

Paul was relieved by the innocent admission, but was sad for his friend as well. "I know, Barney, but that ship has sailed. You've got to move on. She's with Paulo or Pablo or whatever his name is."

"Yeah, I suppose, but you know how fast things can change with her."

"That's just my point. How can you have a relationship with a person who changes so much? It truly sucks how her bipolar condition has affected her life. I'd just hate to see it dragging you down as well."

"Yeah, I hear you."

"Look, Sienna has a single friend she thinks you might really like. How about we ask her to join us for lunch on Saturday? It might just be the jump start you need."

"Yeah? I don't know. What's her name?"

"Colleen. She's Sienna's yoga instructor."

"Bendy, I bet." Barney said feigning interest.

"Probably real bendy."

"Well . . . suppose it wouldn't hurt to meet her. I'm not really into it, but OK."

"I'll make sure Sienna tells Colleen how thrilled you were with the idea."

******

"Remember, Uncle Barney, have fun and stay possessive," AJ advised.

"Ah, I think that would be *positive*, Little Ace." Barney pulled AJ out of the truck and set him on the ground. "But message received loud and clear, Mate."

"Roger that," AJ said, grabbing his back-pack from the cab. "Gi' me five." Barney squatted down and completed the high-five, then engulfed AJ in a hug.

I got to get me one of those, Barney thought as he watched AJ run up the walk toward his aunt's front porch.

Sand Castles, just south of Dorsch Beach on the island's west end, was a low-key, favorite restaurant of Paul and Sienna's. *Maybe this will be fun. Might as well stay possessive.* Barney followed Paul and Sienna's wave over to their table. Even sitting, the sandy-haired woman appeared tall. Standing, she rose to his shoulders, *just over six feet,* he guessed.

Paul introduced them. "Barney, Colleen. Colleen, Barney."

73

"Hello, Barney."

He smiled into soft green eyes and leaned forward as she greeted him with a kiss on the cheek.

Barney liked her natural looks and easy smile. Her voice was pleasant. *Not like Claire's, but still nice.* He played back the last few words of the conversation and realized that Paul had asked him if he wanted a drink.

"Yeah, I'll have a painkiller."

"Are you in pain?" Colleen asked, sitting down.

Barney looked at Paul, who shrugged his shoulders while Sienna asked, "Well, are you?"

"I wouldn't say in pain, maybe uncomfortable and out of my element. You seem like a nice person, Colleen. I'm just not sure I'm ready to . . ."

"To what?"

"Be charming I guess. I get all tongue tied and I miss my old girlfriend."

"Thanks for being so honest, Barney. Let's just see if we might like being friends and not worry about all the rest."

Barney smiled, sat down and joined them.

"Thanks for dropping AJ off at Lenay's," Sienna said.

"Don't need to thank me for that. I've really taken to that little guy. On the drive over, he told me not to feel nervous because a lot of women think big guys are sexy."

"Where does he get this stuff?" Paul asked, laughing.

"I might have said something similar to that when we were in the boat the other day. Actually it was right before I ran us up on the reef. He told me that he was worried that I'm not married. I told him not to worry because—"

"A lot of women think big guys are sexy," they all repeated.

After lunch, Colleen suggested they take a walk on the beach.

"I should be heading back to work," Sienna said. "But you two go ahead."

Barney carried her oversized purse as they strolled barefoot along the beach. Colleen stopped and plucked small pink shells from the coarse sand just north of Sandy Point.

"Sienna told me you're buying a fishing boat."

"I am. I need to tie up a few things in the States first, but hope to be available for charter by early winter."

"That's great. I'd love to see the boat sometime."

"Sure, anytime." *She knows what she wants, just like Claire. Shit, I did it again.*

Colleen noticed Barney's look of discomfort. "Hey Barney, let's take a swim." She stepped out of her skirt and began unbuttoning her blouse.

Barney wasn't sure what to make of this sudden departure from decorum. "The thing is, Colleen, I don't wear underwear."

"I'm not looking." She unhooked her bra and peeled off her panties. "C'mon, nobody's around and it'll feel great."

Barney noticed she had no tan line before her brown bottom disappeared into the water. He also realized a stirring that would make his naked run into the surf a bit conspicuous. However, true to her promise, she treaded water, facing out to sea as Barney quickly stripped and lumbered in after her.

"Are you still standing?" Colleen asked when he reached her side.

"Still standing. You?"

"See for yourself," she said mischievously.

She has a beautiful body and obviously not shy about showing it, he thought as he dropped underwater for the viewing. *Is this what friends do on this island? Skinny dipping? Probably. She's just uninhibited. But what a body. Down boy. This isn't about sex. It's about feeling*—Colleen took hold of the heel of her left foot and raised it up above her head, her legs now spread wide apart as she sunk slowly until standing one legged on the sandy bottom.

—*horny. I'm so fucking horny. Shit, Down Boy. She's into Yoga. Just being natural and . . . so fuckin' bendy.*

In spite of his attempt to remain calm, Barney's penis had its own hopes about what the lady's intentions might be. Surfacing, he turned away from her and feigned interest in a pelican that was dive-bombing for Ballyhoo, hoping to buy enough time for his protuberance to settle.

The tactic failed as Colleen's arms circled his neck from behind. He felt her soft breasts flatten against his back. "Look, don't worry about all this. I know you haven't dated lately and you miss your old girlfriend, but it's so beautiful here." She slid around to his front and wrapped her long legs around his waist. He lifted her onto him as she added, "And doesn't this seem like a good idea?"

12

"Uncle Barney's making pancakes!"

AJ's excited announcement pulled Paul from a vivid flying dream, but not quickly enough, as Rose slathered his face before he could pull the sheet over his head.

"Off the bed, Rose." Sienna ordered from the doorway. "I stalled them as long as I could, but it's almost seven."

"Seriously?" Barney yelled from the kitchen. "If anybody deserves to be left in the sack, it's me. Let's see how Mr. Sunshine feels after a day in the hot sun working for *do-it-my-way Don*."

Paul stumbled into the bathroom before appearing, still half asleep, in his boxers. "May I have some coffee, please?"

"Nice that you got dressed up for our guest." Barney handed him a steaming mug.

"Don't give him a hard time," Colleen admonished.

"At least his fly is buttoned," Sienna sighed.

"Oh, hi Colleen," Paul said turning sideways just in case. "Didn't know you were here."

"Enough chit chat," Barney said. "Let's down these vittles and get on with our day. Right, Little Ace?"

"Yeah, come on Paul, time's a-wasting," AJ replied, imitating Barney.

Sienna followed Paul into the bedroom and sat on the bed.

"Barney and Colleen?" she said, smiling.

"She spent the night?" He stepped into shorts and pulled on a T-shirt.

"I don't think so. I was up at three-o'clock and Barney wasn't home yet. They probably slept at Colleen's, if they slept at all."

"So it looks like they're hitting it off. Guess she's coming with us?"

"Oh, Ace?" Barney's voice rumbled from the kitchen. "You gonna eat these pancakes or do I feed 'em to Rose?"

An hour later, they motored out of the Salt River Marina and were soon under sail heading east on a close reach for Buck Island.

Barney and Colleen were on the foredeck with AJ. Sienna was at the wheel. Paul sat next to her relaying portions of his ongoing cell phone conversation with Hank. "They left St. Thomas harbor an hour-and-a-half ago. Sounds like we'll make Buck Island at about the same time as they do."

Barney overheard Paul on his way to the cooler. "Is that my favorite asshole? Tell him that I warned Colleen about him so he'd better behave."

"That was Barney. I have no idea what he was babbling about. You can ask him when you get here."

Barney, now gripping the necks of a couple Red Stripes and a root beer in between the four fingers of his right hand stopped momentarily before heading back to the bow. "AJ already spotted a school of dolphin and the biggest fuckin' turtle I've ever seen. Colleen's having the time of her life."

Sienna snuggled against Paul as Barney made his way forward. "They seem to be hitting it off, don't you think?"

78

"I never can tell with Barney. I think that he's trying to fit into this romance, but it's an effort for him."

"With some reward, it seems. He often looks sad, but I don't see it today."

"It's Claire that he's missing. I agree with you, though. He seems happier today."

One of the few protected marine areas in the National Park System, the 176-acre Buck Island Reef National Monument was established in 1961. On its east side, snorkelers and scuba divers can enjoy the clear warm water and the magnificent array of multicolored sea life, fields of coral and an occasional encounter with a curious barracuda. The leeward side of the island offers a protected sandy mooring ideal for daily and overnight anchorage. Located a little over a mile off-shore but at the eastern end of St. Croix, Paul, Sienna and AJ made the three-hour sail as often as they could, which had only occurred once since their return from the BVI's.

"We need to do this more often," Paul said, taking in a deep breath of ocean air.

"I agree. But do you really see it happening before we finish Windsol's construction?"

"There's always something that takes priority over relaxing together. Life's too short. Windsol may take a year to complete."

"What? I thought you said six months?"

"It's possible, but everything would have to go off like clock-work, and on this island—"

"But what about our November wedding?" Sienna asked, growing more upset. "Welcome everybody, and please grab a shovel?"

Paul realized his mistake, "I should have updated you on the construction schedule after we got the permit."

"And?"

Clueless, Paul could only shrug.

"No idea? Really? How about, 'I should have told you before we planned the wedding that we might still be under construction?' Where are we going to put everybody up if the cottages aren't done? Oh, that's right, we'll just buy some more cheap-ass lawn chairs. They can eat s'mores and sleep around a bonfire with Barney." Sienna continued after a few calming breaths, "It's just that I wanted the wedding to be perfect." Then, hearing herself, "I sound like one of those self-absorbed brides I've had to deal with catering their wedding receptions." She turned to Paul, "Perfect? We're perfect and all this other stuff is just garnish."

"I like the food metaphor, but really, I'm sorry about this. I'll figure something out."

"We'll figure it out."

"Hey you two lovebirds!" Barney shouted from the foredeck. "I'm just a lowly powerboat captain, but unless you want to sail right up on the beach, you might want to turn the engine over and drop the sails?"

"Excellent suggestion," Sienna replied, as Paul hurriedly furled the jib and dropped the main-sail.

Already a dozen boats bobbed on their anchors off the pristine white sand beach. Picking a spot at the north end of the designated anchoring area, they motored through a tight 180-degree turn and then reversed slowly until they were about ten- yards offshore. Paul jumped into the water while Barney heaved an aluminum anchor onto the beach. Paul buried the anchor in the sand. Sienna slowly motored away from shore about twenty feet where Barney dropped the bow anchor and secured *Stargazer* by tightening the two anchor lines.

AJ was next in the water, quickly followed by Colleen and Sienna. AJ scampered up on the beach excitedly announcing the arrival of *Caribe Daze*. Roxanne and Red waved from the powerboat's foredeck while Hank carefully brought the vessel alongside and rafted-up the cabin cruiser to *Stargazer*.

******

Paul, Barney and Hank stretched out under *Caribe Daze's* rear deck Bimini top, drinking beer and watching AJ and Red run tirelessly onshore. The ladies had set out on a walk to see the lemon sharks skirting through the shallow reef waters on the northwestern section of the island's shoreline.

"So how long have you known Barney?" Roxanne asked Colleen as the three bikini-clad and barefoot women made their way along the beach, their progress occasionally slowed by downed trees and sharp boulders protruding from the sand.

"Not quite twenty-four hours," Colleen replied, straight-faced. "But, and I know what a cliché this is, I feel like we've known each other much longer."

"I know what you mean. I felt exactly the same way when I met Hank," Roxanne replied. "What about you and Paul?" she asked Sienna.

Cautious after her conversation with Paul and not wanting to jump on the Barney/Colleen bandwagon too early she replied carefully, "I've felt that before with several people."

Seeing through Sienna's response, Colleen said, "Don't worry Sienna. I have my big-girl panties on . . . actually my big-girl bikini bottoms," she corrected herself, laughing. "I know Barney's still in love with Claire. That's mostly all he talked about after we had sex in the ocean."

Roxanne and Sienna stopped in their tracks. Sienna knew Colleen had an off-beat sense of humor and asked, "No kidding? On the beach walk?"

Although Roxanne and Colleen had just met, Colleen showed no hesitancy as she described the experience, ending with "I thought he might be too big, but he actually fit quite nicely."

"Well that's a huge relief," Roxanne replied, tongue in cheek.

After they helped each other through a maze of trees that had sloughed onto the beach, Sienna asked Colleen, "Did it bother you . . . him telling you his feelings about Claire?"

"A little, but not because of jealousy. I was bothered that he needed to say anything more about her."

"Maybe he was worried about hurting you and didn't want to give you the wrong impression," Roxanne offered.

"Holy Jesus, Sweet Mary and Joseph, I've crossed over!"

The startled women quickly spotted the source of the proclamation. Pulling his snorkel and mask off and carrying fins, a long knife in a scabbard hanging from a canvas belt around his small waist, he emerged from the surf. If there was a patch of skin covering the wrinkled and sinewy old body that wasn't tattooed, it would have to have been under his Band-Aid-sized red Speedo.

Surprised, Sienna called to him. "Hey, Edgar."

"Sienna? Lord, I didn't think my day could be any better and now this."

"Ladies, this is my friend Edgar. I've known him since I was a kid. We used to dive together off of Green Cay."

Turning his light blue eyes on her companions, he gave each the once-over. "When I saw you three, I thought I'd died and gone to heaven. Are there, by any chance, any men accompanying you on today's outing?"

"There are," Roxanne, the shortest and most well-endowed of the three replied, now standing a little straighter.

"Well, my loss and their gain then." Edgar said, feigning disappointment. "But, seriously, three lovely women like you shouldn't be prancing about so far from civilization without a bodyguard. May I accompany you?"

"He's harmless," Sienna whispered to Roxanne and Colleen as Edgar stowed his gear behind a bush just back from the beach.

Sienna and Edgar chatted as they continued down the beach while Colleen and Roxanne eavesdropped, following close behind.

"I guess you heard that Dharma passed-over 'bout ten-years ago?"

"Of course. I was with you when you scattered her ashes. Remember?"

"That's right. Of course I do, but to tell you the truth, I don't remember much after she died. I was so upset, I had to leave the island and, well, I just poked around Florida for a bunch of years. But everybody acts so goddamn old up there. I got fed up and came back to St. Croix. The little house I had up above Coakley Bay was all grown over, a real mess. I spent a couple years fixing it back up. Thought maybe when I finished, I'd sell it, but by the time it was done, I guess I couldn't think of a place I'd rather live."

"Was Dharma your wife?" Roxanne asked.

"No, Dharma was my dog. Had her for fifteen years. Pretty much broke my heart losing her." He appeared ready to burst into tears, but shook his head and said, "But that's more than enough sadness for today. How long you girls got before you need to get back to your balls and chains?"

"We were just taking a walk before lunch to see the lemon sharks," Sienna explained.

"You're a tall one aren't you?" Edgar eyeballed Colleen. "How do you ladies know each other?"

"Well, Sienna met Roxanne when they were in the BVI's and Sienna is in my yoga class."

The lemon sharks must have been napping or, as Edgar conjectured, found a better hunting ground. After several disappointing minutes with not a dorsal fin in sight, they started back.

"Well, you ladies should be OK from here." Edgar said, a few minutes later, as he recovered his gear. "I don't want to be a nuisance to anybody, so I'll just say goodbye and thanks for brightening up an old man's day."

"That's ridiculous, Edgar," Sienna protested. "Stop by and have a drink with us later this afternoon."

"Well, if you're sure. Wouldn't mind meeting your lucky stiffs." He attached his belt and steadying himself against Sienna's offered shoulder, pulled on his fins. Backing into the water, he signaled a *thumbs-up,* flashed them a big smile before pulling his mask down and disappeared back into the sea.

"Wasn't he something?" Roxanne commented. "I'll bet that guy doesn't need Viagra. I've never been so openly undressed by a man's eyes in my life."

"I kind of enjoyed it," Colleen said.

"No kidding. Poor Barney, already just a vague memory."

Sienna laughed. "Go easy on her, Roxanne. Let the girl enjoy her Robinson Crusoe fantasy."

"Very funny. Look, I'm not kidding myself with Barney. He's a gentle giant, who's still in love with his old girlfriend. We're having a good time together. It's nothing more serious than that."

13

After lunch, Paul and Hank challenged Sienna and Roxanne in a game of cribbage, while Barney and Colleen took Rose and the boys on a trail hike across the island. Before they left, Sienna reminded them to stay away from the poisonous Manchineel trees, which can cause severe skin and eye irritation just by taking cover under their branches during a rainstorm.

"I know all about that, Mom," AJ replied, impatient to be underway.

They had been hiking for less than five minutes when Red tapped Barney on his back. "Hey Mr. Barney, did you know that the Carib Indians used the sap from the Manchineel trees to poison the tips of their arrows?"

"No Red, I didn't. Think we'll see any of them up here?"

"There's one right over there," Red pointed, correctly identifying a lone Manchineel tree.

"No, I mean Carib Indians."

"Of course not, they're all dead."

"Just the same, I'd keep on the look-out for some very old Carib Indians." Barney winked at Colleen.

Red appeared concerned as he stared at Barney.

"Don't worry, Red," AJ shouted back from the front of the line. "He's trying to be funny."

Barney winced and looked at Colleen for support.

"Hate to say this Big Guy, but trying was probably an apt description."

"I thought he had what Grandpa Lou had before he died," Red said, circling his index finger around his ear.

"Uncle Barney isn't crazy. He just likes to make people laugh."

"Also true." Colleen pulled down on Barney's shoulder until she could kiss him on the cheek.

They climbed out of the low-lying beach forest onto gentle hillsides. Reaching the crest of their climb, some three-hundred feet above sea level, they took a side trail to an observation point and were treated to dramatic views of the multicolored ocean below as lighter colored sand and coral reef waters gave way to the darker, deeper waters just outside the islands underwater shelf. Rested, they rejoined the main trail and continued down along switchbacks through colorful frangipani trees, organ pipe cactus and bromeliads.

"Check out the size of these caterpillars," Barney said pointing at the white ringed, orange headed, velvety black creatures moving slowly along a barren branch.

"Those are frangipani caterpillars," AJ announced knowledgeably. "They eat the leaves and flowers of the frangipani and their poop fertilizes the tree to help it grow."

"You should see how big they are when they turn into moths," Red added, holding his hand up with spread fingers. "The first time we saw one, Hank thought it was a bird."

Arriving at the trail's end on Dietrich's Point, it was a short walk along the beach back to the designated anchorage area. As they approached the two vessels, Barney spotted Sienna helping an old tattooed man in a red Speedo onto *Stargazer*.

As AJ, Red and Rose ran ahead, Colleen hung back with Barney and described their earlier encounter with the man.

Barney enjoyed Edgar's *balls and chains* and *lucky stiffs* metaphors. "You've got to give the horny old goat credit."

"Speaking of being horny, after dark how about you and I find a little privacy down the beach?"

Barney was so distracted by Colleen's suggestion that he continued walking right past *Stargazer*, until he noticed that Colleen had stopped some thirty yards back. The last to board, he was approached immediately by their guest.

"Edgar Bourbon, at your service," Edgar announced, proffering his large hand.

Being careful not to squeeze too hard, Barney was ill-prepared for the knuckle popping vice-grip Edgar put on him.

Seeing the big man flinch, Edgar apologized. "Oh, sorry 'bout that. I'm an old aerialist, used to fly trapeze for Ringling Brother's. Did a stint as a strong man as well. Anyway, always had a pretty strong grip," he said, releasing Barney's hand.

"Hey, I like this guy already," Hank said, bumping fists with Edgar. "Gave the big guy a taste of his own medicine."

"All right," Roxanne interjected, "if you boys are done peeing on the ground and marking your territory, Paul's down in the galley asking for drink orders."

Noticing that Edgar had taken his drink up to the foredeck, Barney joined the solitary figure who happily greeted him.

"Colleen was telling me that you might be interested in some yoga classes," Barney said, sitting next to Edgar on the cabin roof.

"Might as well," Edgar replied. "I've abused this old body pretty bad over the years. Been curious about yoga, but never got into it. Might help me get out of bed easier in the morning. Plus, and I don't mean anything by this, but your girlfriend gets a man's blood pumping, which is a good thing at my age."

"Yeah, only she's not really my girlfriend. We just met yesterday."

"Oh, OK then, I still have a chance," Edgar said, straight-faced.

"Well, I suppose that's true," Barney agreed hesitantly.

Edgar burst out laughing. "What's she gonna do with an old fart like me? Probably kill me, that's what. No sir, I missed my chance. Back in the circus, there was this older woman named Edna Rush that I was seein'. She rode around on our show elephant, Jumbo, and did tricks; you know handstands, flips and such. Anyway, she was trampled by that elephant during a big tent fire we had. I've never been under a circus tent since."

"Haven't there been other women since then?" Barney asked, wondering why he cared enough to ask.

"Oh, I've had my share. Almost married a couple times. See, I was in the Merchant Marines for a while. I tell you when we made port; I was drawn to women like a moth to a flame. But nobody stuck. Only one I ever loved was the one that got trampled by the elephant."

"Shit, that's too bad."

"I'm not complaining mind you. I've had a great life, but if I could do one thing over again, I'd-a run-off with Edna before the fire and started a family. We'd still be together. Probably have a mess of great-grandchildren by now. You can't always count on a second chance."

"What story is this crazy Crucian telling you, Barney?" Sienna asked, making her way up to the foredeck with Paul.

"Was telling him about Edna Rush and the Hartford fire."

"The elephant woman who was the love of your life," Sienna recalled, freshening up their drinks from a pitcher full of rum punch. "I remember every story you told me when we used to dive together."

"You were a curious kid," Edgar recalled. "Always asking questions. I think I talked to you more than anybody else on the island, other than Dharma, that is."

"Who's Dharma?" Paul asked.

******

AJ had run out of steam an hour earlier and was asleep on the floor next to Red who lay still and coverless on the bed above him.

Shutting the door quietly behind her, Roxanne whispered as she followed Hank, Paul and Sienna out to *Caribe Daze's* rear deck, "I think those two Ever-Ready bunnies finally ran out of juice."

"I think I'm ready to join them," Hank said, yawning. "It's been a long day."

"It's not over yet," Roxanne said, taking his hand as the two couples said good-night.

Back on *Stargazer*, Paul and Sienna snuggled and quietly watched the eastern sky slowly brightening as the full moon neared the crest of the island's hills.

Paul broke the comfortable silence, "Barney was sure disappointed when I told him the park service prohibited night time beach access."

"Oh yeah. I think they had more than walkin' in mind or his 'Fucking turtles' was quite an overreaction."

90

"Good thing we stopped them. Might have given those volunteer marine biology students a view of nature they hadn't expected."

"Well, they didn't retire to AJ's berth early to play his Nintendo."

Paul went below and came back with a bottle of Black Sambuca. "Maybe you were right about them." Paul filled their two shot glasses. "Barney seems pretty swept up with Colleen."

"Actually, we talked about that on our walk this morning. She knows that Barney's still in love with Claire. If you believe what she says, and I'm not sure I do, she doesn't expect things to become more than *friends with benefits.*"

"And Colleen's OK with that?"

"Like I said, if you believe what she says." Sienna sipped the licorice-flavored digestif.

"Well, good for them then. So, changing the subject, you knew Edgar when you were a kid?"

"Yeah, Mom used to clean hotel rooms at Green Cay. She'd bring me along and I'd hunt for lobster and reef fish while she worked. One day Edgar showed up on the beach with Dharma. I was coming in with a full sack of speared fish. He started asking me questions about my pole-spear and how to use it. The next day he joined me and we started hunting together. Mom knew of Edgar. He had a reputation for being a recluse, 'maybe a little nuts' is how she put it."

"And she felt OK with you diving with him? How old were you?"

"I was probably 12 when we started diving together. At first she was uncomfortable with it. She'd come out and check on me every chance she had to make sure I was OK, but she knew I was strong and like a fish in the water. Also, I did have my pole spear . . . Anyway, she did feel better that I was hunting with a partner. Dharma swam with us sometimes. She'd put her face under the water, find lobsters then hang back while we used the snare. Really was an amazing animal. Almost seemed human at times."

"When was the last time you saw him?"

"I didn't dive much once I started high-school and we sort of lost touch. Before I left the island for college, I ran into him at Schooner Bay Market. Dharma had just died and he looked terrible. He asked me to join him at the Green Cay Beach and say a few words while he scattered her ashes in the sea. After it was over, we hugged goodbye and he moved off-island for a few years."

Paul put his arm around her and she leaned her head against his shoulder. "I think we should have him over for dinner soon. I really liked him," Paul said.

"Maybe when Andy's here. They'd get a kick out of each other."

"I would have hated to have gone up against either one of them in their day."

Suddenly bathed in moonlight, they watched silently as the full moon rose above the island's ridgeline.

"Speaking of gratification," Sienna said, leaning back against him and sliding her hand between his thighs. "Will you ignore me when I'm old and wrinkled?"

"I should be the one asking that. I'm nine years older than you and my Nordic shell wrinkles easier than your African skin," He kissed her while cupping her breast.

"That's true," she said, taking his hand and guiding it under her skirt. "So, are you going to ask me?"

"Ask you what?"

"I forgot."

14

"I think the island agrees with you," Paul said, passing the joint to Barney who was flying back to Washington State the next morning.

"Yeah, I haven't felt so relaxed . . . maybe ever."

"Do you think it's the yoga, or the yoga instructor?"

Barney took a deep drag on the reefer. "You know, while I really enjoy being able to touch my toes again, it's the woman who's changed me."

After returning from their weekend at Buck Island, Barney had fallen into a three-day-a-week routine, joining Colleen's early-evening yoga class at the studio in her west end home. His instruction most often continued long after his classmates rolled up their mats and headed home. "Stay for dinner?" was Barney's invitation for aromatic and succulent vegetarian meals followed by night-long sessions of tantric sex.

In spite of little sleep, his energy level had never been higher as he and Cleo completed the last drillings almost a full week ahead of schedule.

"So, will there be the patter of larger than normal children's feet scurrying around the ashram one day?"

"Don't think so, Ace. Don't get me wrong. I love the woman and I'm grateful for the time with her. The sex is out of this world, but she's not the one. She sees it too. We're a rest

93

stop for each other, a place to recharge our batteries. We're not like you and Sienna. We're not *home* for each other."

"Will you see her when you come back?"

"Of course, if she's here. Last night she said that she was going back to India to study and work with some master. Not sure when or if she'll be back."

Paul's eyes softened. "It's still Claire, isn't it?"

Barney leaned back in the chair and pulled his cowboy hat over his eyes. Paul looked out over the ocean while his friend attempted to compose himself. The sun had become a burnt orange ball as it dropped close to the horizon. Barney wiped the tears from his face and stood facing the water. "I know in her right mind she feels the same. That's why I keep waiting and hoping."

"I wish there was something we could do."

"My thought exactly. I feel so goddamn helpless and time just keeps ticking away. Do you realize it's been four months since she left with that Latin Loser?"

"Yeah, I know, but at least you haven't been lying around doing nothing. I think Colleen and you have been good for each other."

"Colleen has been great for me. I'm not sure that I've been much help for her."

"She wouldn't have spent so much time with you if she hadn't enjoyed herself."

"I think there was a part of her that thought I might come around and let go of my feelings for Claire. Maybe I'm a dumbass, probably am, but I just can't, not yet anyway. This is all so fucked up."

******

A week after Barney's departure, Colleen notified her classes that she would soon be leaving for India. Two weeks later, Sienna drove Colleen to the airport.

"How long do you think you'll be gone?"

"I'm not sure. I'll be teaching classes at an Ashram in Simlah that caters to westerners. If it's a good fit, I may stay for a while."

"How are you doing without Barney?"

"It was inevitable, wasn't it?"

Sienna was about to change the subject when Colleen added, "You knew all along I was crazy about him."

"Yeah, I thought that may be the case."

"I'm so full of shit. 'Not serious, no expectations,' blah, blah, blah. I almost convinced myself."

"He told Paul that he loved you."

"But not like he loves Claire. The hold that woman has over him is unbreakable. Believe me, I tried." Tears filled her eyes. Sienna reached over and took her hand.

Riding the rest of the way in silence, they arrived at the airport. After hugs and kisses goodbye, Sienna pulled away from the curb and watched in her rear view mirror as Colleen totted her bags through the queue while engaged in a conversation with a tall, handsome middle-aged man in line with her. *She'll be fine*, Sienna thought to herself, smiling.

******

"Mr. Armstrong, my name is Curtis Blossom. My wife, Deidra and I are coming down your way next week. We own a four-acre piece of waterfront land on the east end we want to build on. We'd like to meet and talk about hiring you as our architect. You come highly recommended."

Paul did a quick mental inventory of his commitments before answering. "I'd be glad to meet with you and your wife, but I couldn't commit many hours on the project for a month or so."

"That suits us just fine. We don't want to rush. This is something I've been planning to do for a long time and I want to do it right: I want to be completely off-the-grid using wind and solar power. Deidre wants marble floors, fountain courtyards, a lap pool, a *Top-Chef-kitchen*, the works. Of course I can't wait too long if I want to take advantage of the lower construction costs down there. What with Hovensa leaving, and the economy tanking. I'd imagine people in the construction trades are pretty desperate to find work."

The eagerness in Curtis Blossom's voice while describing the very sad, but true plight of his fellow islanders had Paul's asshole-meter climbing to yellow. Nevertheless, he agreed to meet the following week and would firm up a time after talking with Sienna. Mr. Blossom was very insistent they meet over drinks and dinner at The Buccaneer. "I like to get to know somebody before talking business. Monday, we'll be arriving at the Buccaneer, he explained, before disconnecting. "Give me a call and we'll set up a time."

After a long day of work, Sienna was less than enthused when he told her about the phone conversation. "We have so few evenings alone with me working 'til nine most nights. Blossom sounds like an asshole. Why don't we find something fun to do instead?"

But by the next morning, after doing a Google search, she modified her position. "He may be an asshole, but he's a rich asshole. We could use some extra money with our wedding coming up. I'll ask Mom to watch AJ."

******

Don and Paul watched as the wall panels were lifted into place by the truck-mounted crane. The final cabin's floor slab was scheduled to be poured that afternoon.

"If these panels go together as fast as the distributor promised, we could be setting roof joists next week," Don said.

"Any word on the containers?"

"Last I heard, they were en route from Louisville. Should ship out of Jacksonville first part of next week."

"Well, keep on top of it. I need to be able to house guests by our wedding in November, or—"

"Should be OK," Don interrupted, "assuming there's no screw ups."

"Screw ups never happen down here."

"Don't worry, Paul. Sienna's lived here most of her life. She's used to screw-ups, present company excluded, of course."

"Funny. Maybe so, but it's never the same when women wear the bridal veil."

"No shit? She's gonna wear a veil?"

"No, I was just being . . ." Paul sighed. "Actually, Sienna will be cool if we're not ready. I'd just really like to make it happen for her if we can."

"I'll do everything I can. Just don't have a stroke over it."

The following Tuesday, after dropping AJ off at his Nana's, Paul picked Sienna up at The Green Flash. Driving to The Buccaneer, Sienna filled Paul in on her day at the restaurant. "I fired Jimmy this afternoon. He was having Samuel deliver complimentary drinks again to hot girls down on the beach, even after I talked to him about it last week. I was pretty calm until he tried to convince me that it was good for business."

"Yeah, *monkey-business*. What a dog."

"Anyway, could you tend bar this weekend? I'll be short-handed."

"Of course. I'd enjoy it. Take my mind off the project."

"I appreciate how hard you and Don are pushing to finish before the wedding. How's it looking?"

"The windows, cabinets and finish materials are scheduled to arrive any day. Barring any major inventory screw-ups, we're looking pretty good."

"That's great, Paul. So, did you find out anything about Mr. Blossom's property?"

"Yeah, it's out on the south shore near the old Grapetree Resort. We'd need to apply for a minor development permit with Coastal Zone Management which will add a few months to the process. I'll find out what kind of schedule they're on. I know he's anxious to take advantage of anyone who's desperate for work."

"Maybe we should give him a pass on that. Might have just been a bad choice of words."

"Yeah, maybe, but I know what Don would tell him if Blossom tried to bend him over."

Climbing the outside stairs from the western parking lot, they were greeted by the long-time Buccaneer bartender and PGA golf instructor, Darrell Love. "Hey you two. I haven't seen you since forever. Understand you're dining with Mr. Blossom and his wife tonight." He nodded toward the back of the stocky, pink polo-shirted man talking on his cell-phone. "I think he's talking to his wife. Sounds like she was late getting back from her afternoon at the spa."

"All right, Honey, we'll see you shortly," Blossom said, finishing his call. Turning on his bar-chair, he smiled at Paul. "Darrell here was telling me that you were the architect for the terrace remodel. I remember the old roof's low arches. They had character but nothing as nice as this. Had dinner here last night, the lighting is spectacular. Nice to finally meet you Paul, I'm Curtis Blossom," he said, extending his hand.

"Thanks for the compliment, Curtis. My fiancée, Sienna Meyers."

Sienna later described to Roxanne that Curtis's hand felt like an eel. "It was the first of several creepy feelings . . . "

"So, Deidra's down at our room waiting for a ride up in the hotel's courtesy cart. Say, I've got an idea. Paul, would you mind driving down there and picking her up? I'm anxious to get this evening started. I'll keep your beautiful fiancée company."

"See you in a few minutes," Sienna said brightly. Paul heard the effort behind her smile.

******

The door to their second level room was already open as Paul knocked and called out, "Hello, Deidra. It's Paul Armstrong. Curtis sent me to bring you back to the terrace."

"Oh, come on in Paul. I'll be just a minute." Paul stood admiring the ocean view with his back facing the entry into the bathroom and dressing area.

"Oh, rats."

Framed in the doorway, her long blonde hair cascaded over large, bare breasts. Her brow was furrowed as she bent down and picked up the white knit dress she had dropped in front of her. Wearing only a white thong, she looked up at Paul.

Smiling, she slowly turned on red high-heeled sandals and disappeared from view.

"Sorry about that," Paul said after a few beats. "I'll just wait outside on the porch."

But before he reached the open door she reappeared, this time wearing the dress. "No need for that, Silly. You didn't see anything different from what I wear when Curtis and I go to the Riviera." Walking over to him she turned away, and pulling her hair off her neck she asked, "Would you do me, please?"

His fumbling fingers joined the dress clasp. Turning quickly to walk outside, he stopped when she asked, "Paul, can you help me find my purse?"

"Is this it?" he said, finding a small jeweled bag on the entry table.

"Oh, yes." Taking it from him, she walked outside. "Please close the door behind you, Paul."

Arriving at the terrace parking lot, Paul had already started up the stairs, when he noticed that Deidra remained inside the truck. Returning to the vehicle, he opened the passenger door and took her offered hand. Once on the ground, she tugged down the hem of her short dress and proceeded up the stairs with Paul in tow.

"What took you two?" Curtis greeted them, as they approached the bar. "Honey, meet Sienna."

"How do you do? Excuse me for a minute; I need to use the little girl's room. Sienna, how about joining me? We can girl-talk."

Sienna followed her after exchanging quick *what the fuck* looks with Paul.

"Yessir, Paul, I'd say we're two lucky hombres," Curtis said, as his eyes followed Sienna and Deidra's exit.

Speechless and confused, Paul ordered a dry Tito's vodka martini from Darrell, who delivered the drink with a knowing wink. "You know, Paul, I have to be honest about something." Curtis drained his Manhattan. "The last time we were on-island, Deidra and I went to The Green Flash for dinner. Sienna was our hostess and I was knocked over by her exotic beauty."

The confusion was starting to clear. Paul listened, looking straight ahead and sipped his martini.

"You performed later that evening and for some unknown reason, Deidra found you sexy. You're not buffed up, but you look like you can handle yourself."

Darrell appeared busy wiping dust out of cocktail glasses, but Paul caught the smile and knew he was enjoying Curtis's confession and Paul's dilemma.

"I don't know if you're aware of it or not, but there is a very active swingers club on St. Croix. Deidra, as you might imagine, has been quite a hit at the few local mixers we've attended and, well, that's one of the reasons we picked St. Croix. Am I starting to make myself clear?"

"Clear about what?" Deidra asked, as she returned with Sienna.

Playfully pulling his wife against him, he explained, "I put the cards out on the table, about how beautiful I think Sienna is."

Paul decided it was time to enter the discussion. "Curtis was also saying that there's an active swinger's club on St. Croix. How cool is that?" He imagined Sienna's expression as he looked down at his drink.

"So you two might be into it?" Curtis asked, hopefully.

"Us?" Paul looked over at Sienna. "God no."

"Oh," Curtis replied weakly.

"I could have told you that, Dumbass," Deidra said to her husband. "He would have sprinted out of our room if I hadn't asked him to find my purse."

"Here's a question for you Curtis," Paul asked. "Are you really looking for an architect?"

"Of course. I just wanted to understand the . . . landscape of possibilities before we talked business. I think its best that we understand each other. I've asked around and seen your work. I want you to be our architect and this won't come up again. Right, Deidra?"

"Whatever. The whole swinging thing's your idea anyway."

"Paul, I'd like to talk with you," Sienna said, standing up.

They walked out through the lobby and found a bench near the hotel's entry court fountain.

"When did you figure it out?" Paul asked.

"He was pretty obvious while you were gone. Said I had pretty feet . . . So what happened in the hotel room?"

"She flashed me in a thong."

"Bet that was painful for you."

"I may need therapy."

"Seriously, Paul, is this the kind of client you want?"

"Tell you the truth, I haven't decided yet. We can see how the conversation goes at dinner. I think he put her up to it. Let's see if he can let it go."

"Actually, I kind of like her," Sienna confessed. "Doesn't seem afraid to speak her mind. When we went to the restroom, she said that Curtis has some goofy ideas, but is kind and good natured once you get to know him."

"He told me that Deidra thinks I'm sexy," Paul boasted.

"But did she say anything about your feet?"

Dinner with the Blossoms was a pleasant surprise. Curtis had a ready reserve of entertaining stories he enjoyed telling about his business and travel adventures. After giving their order to the waitress, he also received points for being able to laugh when Paul kidded him, "If you had ordered raw oysters we would have left."

"So I take it, you won't let me off the hook easily," Curtis replied chuckling.

Deidra, as it turned out, was a voracious reader with a very quick-wit and a dry sense of humor. "This wasn't the first time his *damn the torpedoes, full speed ahead* approach has almost landed us on the rocks," she commented to Sienna, as Curtis signaled for the check.

"No, I insist," Curtis said, holding his hand up as Paul offered to foot the bill. "God knows I owe you and Sienna something for your kind-heartedness. In retrospect, I'm surprised you stayed for dinner."

Outside by Sienna's car, Paul and Curtis shook hands while Deidra and Sienna hugged good-bye. "I'll email the contract for your review tomorrow," Paul said.

"Great, I'll have the retainer when we meet at the property on Thursday."

"Ever had an interview like that before?" Sienna asked, as Paul drove them home.

"Not even close. It sure ended differently than I'd expected after the way it started."

"So I bet she looked good in that thong."

"No. Terrible. It was disgusting."

"Poor guy," she said, leaning over and nibbling his ear. "I'll see if I can come up with something tonight that will take your mind off it."

15

Andy's arm was tight around Aunt Charlotte's waist when they appeared. Sheriff Tex and Sally Reed, waving happily, followed close behind. Paul and AJ had been waiting over an hour at St. Croix's Henry Rohlsen Airport for the delayed flight's arrival from Puerto Rico and were relieved that the small twin engine Cessna had arrived safely.

"Well, that was an experience," Aunt Charlotte said, after hugging and kissing Paul and AJ.

"That was the longest sixty-mile flight I've ever taken," Tex noted, picking AJ up and setting him on his shoulders.

"At one point, I thought we were headed back to Miami," Sally said. "I sat in the co-pilot's seat and could see the thick clouds he avoided. I'm glad he took his time."

As they waited for their bags, Paul said, "Sienna's at the restaurant. We'll drop your bags off at the house and you can freshen up. We have a table reserved at The Green Flash for dinner."

"Is Paul Armstrong performing?" Aunt Charlotte asked.

"Performing and bartending. Sienna's short-staffed and I'm filling-in until she finds a replacement."

"Well, dinner at The Green Flash sounds perfect," Andy said. "I used to cook there, you know. Wouldn't mind helping out in the kitchen again."

"Thanks, but everything's under control, Andy."

Once underway, Andy asked AJ, sitting next to him in the back seat, "What are you going to have for dinner?"

"A hot dog," AJ replied without hesitation. "And a salad," he added, catching Paul's look in the rear view mirror.

As they drove through the gate into Windsol, Paul announced, "We're running late for our dinner reservation, so how about we hold-off on seeing the project until tomorrow morning?"

Tex hoisted AJ back up on his back, grabbed a suitcase and headed for the house. Sally and Aunt Charlotte followed, while Andy hung back with Paul, helping him finish unloading the bags. "Might as well get this off my chest. Char and I have kicked it up a notch. We're co-habitating these days, or shacking-up, as I think you young people call it."

Paul wasn't surprised. "So we'll have one extra cabin available then."

"Looks that way. You got someone in mind?"

"Hank, Roxanne and Red. I've gotten the feeling they're getting tired of living on their boat in St. Thomas. I think we'd be lucky to have them."

"It's your call, Son. By the way, thanks for understanding about me and your aunt. I know it doesn't seem very long since your Uncle Ernie passed on, but I ain't getting any younger. You know, I need to strike while my iron still gets hot, if you understand my drift."

"Andy, I think it's great."

"Well, that's a load off, especially for Char. She was afraid you might've felt uncomfortable."

Thirty-minutes later, showered, shaved and shined, they all piled back into Paul's double-cab truck, and headed out for dinner. There was a strong early-evening breeze bending the coconut palms across the street from the restaurant when they arrived. Even still, at 85 degrees, Aunt Charlotte could leave her sweater in the truck as they climbed the wooden steps into Sienna's Cane Bay restaurant, The Green Flash.

Sienna greeted them warmly and led them to a long table near the outside guard-rail. After the drink orders had been taken, Don, who had been cooling down at the bar, came over to say hello. "Well, I see that the fresh troops have arrived. I'm Don McGowan, the contractor Paul's probably been complaining to you about."

"I haven't heard anybody complaining." Andy stood and shook his hand. "Andy Meyers, and this is my girlfriend, Char. From what I hear you're doing one hell of a job."

"It's a pleasure to meet you, Don," Aunt Charlotte added. "Paul speaks very highly of you and I love the work you've already done on the main house."

"Well, that's nice of you to say." He looked over at the 6'-6" 245-pound Jefferson County Sheriff. "So you're Barney's replacement. They sure grow 'em big up in Washington."

"Actually, I grew up in Amarillo," Tex said, shaking Don's hand.

"A fact my big Texas cowboy never tires of telling people," Sally added, laughing.

Tex looked contritely at Paul. "Afraid I won't be able to be much help with the project on this trip. I'm short-staffed with the budget cuts and could only wrangle ten days away."

"Tex has been working 60 hours a week," Sally interjected. "I made him promise he'd use his time down here for a vacation. I could stay longer, but since we'll be back in November for the wedding—"

"Honestly, it's no problem. You guys need a vacation and Don has everything under control."

Relieved by the announcement, Don added, "With things moving so fast while we're setting panels, it would be hard to find something that you could help with."

"See, I told you it would all work out," Andy said. "Remember, if you two get bored lying on the beach and drinking rum, I can put you both to work in the garden. Hasn't gotten much attention since I was here last," he added, throwing a look at Paul.

"Now Andy," Charlotte said, patting her soon-to-be 80-year-old boyfriend on the back of his hand. "You know that Paul already has more than enough on his plate. We'll work in the garden together when we're here and when we're not, we'll hire a gardener."

"Guess this is what I get for falling for the boy's aunt," Andy joked, looking helplessly at Don.

"Seems to me, you came out all right on the deal."

"Better than I could have dreamed," he replied happily.

After dinner, Tex and Sally were Texas-two-stepping over most of The Green Flash's small dance floor, while Paul played and sang their request for "Boot Scootin' Boogie". Andy and Sienna watched from the table and laughed as Aunt Charlotte and AJ bravely tried to follow them step for two-step.

"I'm so happy that you and Char are shacking up," Sienna said, almost causing Andy to spit out his last swallow of beer. "Is there a wedding in the near future?"

"If it were up to me, we'd-a tied the knot some time ago. But I have to respect Char's one-step-at-a-time approach. Ernie hasn't even been gone a year."

"Of course, Andy. I understand completely."

"Where are you two having your wedding ceremony?"

"We're booked at the Carambola Resort. We're having both the ceremony and celebration on the beach."

"Sounds perfect. Hard to believe you two didn't even know each other a year ago."

"Andy," Sienna said emotionally, taking his hand. "I thought after Aaron was killed, that I'd never love anybody so much again."

Andy had to compose himself before replying, "You know, losing Aaron was devastating for both of us. Paul didn't come into our lives as his replacement, but he is like a son to me and I see the way you two are together."

When the song was finished, Andy smiled and squeezed Sienna's hand as they watched Sally, Tex, AJ and Char take a bow to the loud applause when Paul announced, "Let's give it up for our Texas-two-steppers."

"It wasn't that long ago, I was a bitter, lonely, old man just waiting to die. Probably would've been dead by now, the amount of booze I was drinkin'. But now, I've got a beautiful girlfriend, an incredible grandson, you and Paul; a loving family. It's the whole kit and caboodle."

"I worry sometimes," Sienna said wistfully. "Paul, AJ and I, it's all so perfect. You and I both know how fast things can change."

16

Stargazer gently rocked on her mooring in White Bay, as Paul and Sienna Armstrong enjoyed an afternoon beer.

Thirteen days earlier, following the busiest five months either could remember, their beach wedding had been an intimate ceremony witnessed by just their closest friends and family. The reception, however, included a wide circle of island friends. Nearly 400 feasted on a smorgasbord of island cuisine and danced to Jonjon Marley's reggae band until the pink hued eastern sky hinted at morning. Even at 4:30, most of the revelers were still there to throw bird-seed as Barney rowed the bride and groom out to *Stargazer*, anchored just off the beach. Now, anchored just a stone's throw off the island of Jost Van Dyke, their aimless and deliriously happy honeymoon voyage through the British Virgin Islands was down to its final evening.

"Wanna take the Zodiac over to Foxy's for dinner?" Sienna asked, with Paul's head resting in her lap.

"Sounds like too much work. How 'bout after a nap, we just swim to shore and grab a burger and a drink or two at The Soggy Dollar?"

"You know, we're going to have a tough time getting back into the pace of our lives."

"I agree, so let's not rush it." Paul gently pulled her face down for a kiss.

The nap was relaxing, if not restful. Paul stuffed his wallet, T-shirt and Sienna's sarong into a water-proof belt pouch. After locking the cabin door, they climbed over the side into the warm, crystal clear water. Careful not to dislodge their sunglasses, they swam ashore. Arriving at the venerable outdoor bar and restaurant, Sienna asked, "Remember how good AJ was at that?" She pointed to the small, steel ring suspended from a tree branch by a long rope. The idea was to catch the ring on a hook embedded in the tree with a pendulum swing, while standing about 12 feet from its trunk.

"Maybe we should order a couple drinks and practice. We could surprise him next time we're here."

"You're such a show-off. It's like when you pretended that you didn't know how to juggle and had me thinking you learned after two tries."

"I'm just trying to create a reputation for the amazing."

"You're plenty of that already. Don't worry, I'll still find you amazing even after I've kicked your ass in the swingy ring game."

"That sounds like smack talk. Well, you're on, Woman."

After an hour of playing and four shots each of iced Patron Silver, Sienna was up, nineteen to five. "OK, I surrender," Paul announced reluctantly, "on account of, I'm really hungry."

"I'll bet. That ass-whoopin' must have really built up your appetite."

"Yeah, that and if I don't eat something soon, those shots of Patron will have me swimming off to Puerto Rico instead of back to our boat."

"Oh, my sweet little light-weight. I hope I haven't bruised your ego with all my smack talkin'."

"Nothing that a juicy hamburger won't cure."

At dinner, Paul asked, "Weren't you surprised that the Blossoms flew down for the reception?"

"Curtis told Barney that since his job was paying for this soirée, they might as well come and enjoy it."

"Never seen a guy that likes to flaunt his money more than Curtis."

"Maybe so, but their job was a godsend and at least he's not an asshole."

"That's true. Also, he's been true to his word about keeping the swinging thing out of the conversation."

"I noticed him talking with Carmen. I hope he didn't suggest that she and Kate join them in a four-way."

"I bet that's one on his swinger's bucket list."

"So tell me, Mr. Armstrong. Any fantasies you'd like to share with the class?"

"Honestly, Mrs. Armstrong," Paul replied, signaling for the check. "You're my favorite one."

After leaving the restaurant, they stripped down to their swimsuits and took a slow, moon-light swim back to *Stargazer*. Climbing on board first, Sienna immediately noticed a sealed envelope partially shoved under the cabin door. "Paul, somebody was on our boat." She picked up the envelope which was marked "Newlyweds."

Paul sat next to her as she opened the envelope and unfolded the sheet of paper.

By the time AJ applies for college, tuition will be through the roof. A trust account has been set up to help. Contact Attorney Pascall in St. Thomas for details.

Congratulations and wishing you both the very best,
A S

After several moments of stunned silence, Sienna asked Paul the obvious, "A S is Andrew Sherman, right?"

"Or Alan Sloan. I wonder how he found us."

"He's obviously been keeping track of us. He's never met AJ. Why the trust account in his name?"

"He knew that I wouldn't accept any money from him. But a trust account . . . set up for AJ by an anonymous benefactor; I'm not sure we could refuse it even if we wanted to."

By sunrise the next morning, they were already under sail. Four hours later, they arrived in St. Thomas harbor and the bustling city of Charlotte Amalie. After clearing customs, they were met by Hank, whom Paul had contacted by cell on the way in.

"I don't know much about this Pascall fellow," Hank reported, "except that he's young and just recently started his own practice."

"We appreciate the help, Hank," Paul replied. "I'm glad he could see us on such short notice."

"AJ's mysterious benefactor might be his only client," Hank joked. "You know, Paul, as generous as this might seem, I'm not too thrilled about his contacting you again. If Uncle Sal or Buddy hear about it, they might think there's more to this than Sherman working down a karmic debt. By the way, how was the honeymoon?"

112

"It was wonderful," Sienna said, looking worried as she took Paul's hand and stared out the window.

Sparsely furnished, Herbert Pascall's one-room office seemed to reflect his understated, island-boy appearance. Sandals, cream khakis, yellow shirt, messy straw-colored hair above intelligent, bright green eyes, the attorney looked as if he might have just returned from a sail himself.

Smiling warmly after introductions, he motioned Paul, Sienna and Hank over to an old conference table where they sat in mismatched wooden chairs. "Mrs. Armstrong, I've received the fax of AJ's birth certificate from your mother. Now, if you and Mr. Armstrong will show me your passports, as we discussed on the phone this morning, I'll fill you in on the details of the trust left to your son."

"All right if I stay for the show?" Hank asked Paul and Sienna.

"Of course," Sienna said. "Paul and I consider you our most trusted advisor."

"First let me say," Herbert began, "that the donor wishes to remain anonymous. As administrator for the trust, I am bound to honor this condition. There is also a stipulation regarding the use for which the trust's funds may be applied; namely for costs associated with AJ's pursuit of a degree from an institution of higher education. Should AJ elect not to attend college by his twenty-third birthday, the funds shall be transferred with the same stipulated condition of use to your next child, should the two of you have another. If no children follow AJ, the money is to be given to a non-profit charity of your choice."

"That seems pretty clear," Paul said. "How much money is in the trust?"

"One hundred and fifty thousand dollars. There will be interest earned between now and when AJ's ready for college. My instructions were to place the funds in Certificates of Deposit."

Stunned by the amount, they could come up with few follow-up questions before thanking Attorney Pascall for his time.

On the ride back to the boat, Hank said, "Well, I feel better about the way this is all being handled, the anonymity part especially. It's unlikely that any of this could get back to certain people who may have an axe to grind." When there was no response from Sienna and Paul, Hank continued. "Wow, $150,000. That's one hell of a start. Of course, my nephew enrolled in Swarthmore last year and one year set my sister and her husband back over $60,000."

"I remember when I went to Washington State; tuition, room and board was around $15,000 a year," Paul replied, not wanting to appear as conflicted as he felt over Andrew's benevolence.

Standing outside the car, they thanked Hank for his help. "No problem. Say, listen, Roxanne and I talked and we're going to take you up on your offer. The name sounds a little hippy/dippy, but Windsol seems like the right place for us to put down some roots. The only problem I have is the price."

"Oh, don't worry, Hank, it's negotiable."

"Jeez Paul, $750. a month is giving the place away. Does Andy realize he could get four times that?"

"Probably, but he doesn't need the money."

"And you guys come highly recommended," Sienna added. "Say Hi to Roxanne and Red and let us know when you're ready to make the move."

"Will do. Love you guys," Hank said, as he drove off.

Trying to lighten the mood, Paul laughed. "That's my second surprise of the day. A big tough cop saying he loves me."

Returning to the Zodiac, Paul started the engine while Sienna released the lines. "Paul, I'm worried. Up until last night, I thought we'd seen the last of Andrew and the creeps he was associated with. Now, it seems like we'll be looking over our shoulder for years."

"Yeah, I know. But like Hank said, there isn't much chance of any of those guys finding out about the trust. I just don't like the idea of where the money came from."

"That part doesn't bother me at all. Consider it a portion of the money he screwed you out of. I'm sure that's the way Andrew looks at it."

"Maybe we're both being a little nuts here. I bet there aren't too many parents who would complain if $150,000 fell out of the sky for their child's education."

"Speaking of whom, the "child" asked me before we left, how much longer before you're going to adopt him."

If Paul felt any residue of remorse over the money, it was instantly overshadowed by the love and responsibility he felt for AJ. "Right away, of course." Leaning forward, he kissed his wife softly on the crown of her forehead. "If this is a dream, I never want to wake up."

17

Nearly eight months had passed since their dinner with Andrew at *Willie T's*. Accustomed to blatant typos in the island's newspaper, Paul smiled when he read the morning headline, *Murdered Businessman Turns Himself In*. His mirth disappeared immediately, however, as he continued reading.

Alan Sloan, aka Andrew Sherman, is in the protective custody of British authorities on Tortola after requesting asylum. No charges have been brought against Mr. Sherman. Mr. Sherman was believed to have been murdered in 2011, leading to the well-publicized trial and eventual manslaughter conviction of Frank "Buddy" Falco. Mr. Falco is currently serving a 20 year sentence in The Leavenworth Penitentiary. Mr. Falco's attorneys expect a prompt release of their client, once Mr. Sherman's identity is confirmed.

At Sienna's insistence, Paul hired an attorney in Seattle who reassured him that they would be shielded from most of the fray for the time being. Paul and Sienna followed Andrew's plight on the internet over the next several months. Finally, embezzlement charges were filed by the state attorney general and Andrew was poised for extradition to Washington State.

Now a free man, Buddy brought additional civil charges against Andrew for the pain, financial and personal losses he suffered as a result of the two-year false imprisonment. Tied up in a clogged court system, a trial wasn't expected for 24 months. In the meantime, Andrew, now considered a flight risk, would travel in the custody of federal marshals, ultimately arriving in Seattle for transport to a small holding cell in the King County Jail.

Just prior to stepping aboard the short island-hop from Beef Island's Terrance B. Lettsome International Airport to St. Thomas, the first leg of his journey back to Washington State, Andrew stopped on the tarmac and read a prepared statement to the small gathering of press. "My present situation is the sole result of my own improprieties. I apologize to the many people hurt by my actions. I can only offer, in my defense, that it was the legitimate fear of being murdered that prompted those actions."

The hole could be covered by a dime. Andrew simply dropped like a sack of salt. The bullet hole appeared in the center of his forehead while the plume of blood and tissue that had once been the back of his head dripped slowly off the plane's fuselage. The report from the fifteen hundred-yard shot followed the bullet one and three-quarters of a second later. Island investigators determined that the shooter had to have factored in a stiff cross-wind after they located the sniper's perch on Little Mountain, a small hill across Long Bay from the airport. "The shooter was quite skilled to have pulled this off. Must have had sniper training, maybe in the Marines or somewhere," one inspector speculated. The rifle used in the killing was thought to be a 338 Lapua Magnum, a sniper rifle used extensively in Iraq and Afghanistan.

Buddy's suspected mob background was vociferously referenced in follow-up news reports, but there was no evidence that could corroborate his connection to the execution. In one spirited interview, however, he provided five minutes of footage to a Seattle TV reporter and camera crew that quickly went viral. Hair disheveled, wearing a silk bathrobe, Falco was fetching his morning paper from the top of one of two sculptured topiary bushes flanking his front door. Hearing his name called out, he squinted into the sun, barely making out the long blonde hair and hourglass figure of Seattle's own, Sandy Bar. Reaching the gate, he realized two things; his robe was open and he was being filmed. "You use any of this," he warned, while closing his robe and pointing at the camera, "and I'll stuff all of you in a box."

When the cameraman continued recording, Buddy's rage grew murderous as he threw himself against the iron gate, snarling like a junkyard dog. Fearing for their safety, the camera crew stepped back, but not Sandy Bar. Unmoved by his psychotic display, she stopped Buddy cold with a question. "What would you say to Andrew Sherman if he were alive?"

Buddy released his white-knuckled grip on the gate and smoothed back his hair. His homicidal demeanor shifted quickly to contemplative. A smile formed, but his eyes remained dark pools of hatred. "I'd tell him he fucked with the wrong capo."

Up to this point, Sandy Bar wasn't sure how much of this event would be left on the cutting room floor. If she had anything to say about it, nothing would be omitted. They could digitally blur Buddy's exposed *little buddy* and bleeping-out the swearwords shouldn't be a problem. The preeminent moment, however, took place when a double shot-glass of seagull shit splashed squarely on his widows-peak. Temporarily blinded, the gangster ran screaming in circles, wiping the acrid ooze from his angry eyes. *That moment*, she vowed, *will make the six-o'clock news*. Within twenty-four hours following the broadcast, the video entitled *Sherman's Revenge* received over thirteen million hits.

Two days after the broadcast, Buddy nervously answered his cell-phone. "Hey, Uncle Sal."

"Hay is for horses you little ass-wipe. What part of laying-low didn't you understand? Shit, I got the *Feds* up my ass enough as it is. I don't need you making things worse. You looked like a fuckin' goon in that video. Calling yourself a capo. I can't even believe we're related."

Until recently, life had been tough enough on Buddy without his uncle's reprimand. Fighting the urge to scream, "*Go fuck yourself*" before bashing his cell against the bed's headboard, he managed to calm himself and instead whined, "The bitch tricked me, Uncle Sal. She said she wouldn't—"

"Oh, spare me more bullshit, Buddy. Look, I don't give a fuck about you flashing your junk all over the place. What I'm saying is that I've been working hard to give the impression we're a legitimate outfit running legitimate operations. Then you come along and within a month of being sprung from the joint, you fuck it all up. I swear to Christ, if you weren't my poor dead sister's boy, I wouldn't be wasting my time on a phone call. Capiche? . . . So no more talking to the media or saying shit about dead people like you're some fuckin' Joe Pesci in *The Good Fellow*."

Buddy's mind screamed, *That's Goodfellas you stupid old fuck!* Instead, Buddy bleated, "But Uncle Sal, he took two years of my life away from me."

"Well, boo-hoo, ain't that just too fuckin' bad. Between him saying that he's afraid someone's gonna kill him, and now him bein' dead and all . . . then you sayin' that shit on the video—" Fearing his over-elevated blood pressure, Sal took a couple breaths before continuing in a low menacing tone. "I tell you this, Franklin Buddy Falco, if you weren't my nephew, you'd be as dead as Sherman for pulling this stunt. I told you to let the lawyers deal with it for now. Maybe down the road he'd have had an accident or something, but you don't listen to me. 'What's that old fuck Sal know about things?' Well, I'll tell you this Buddy Boy, I know who and what I am in this organization, and you? You ain't shit. Now, don't make me have to pick up my phone again. You got it?"

"OK," Buddy conceded. "I tell you though, Uncle Sal, it's tough for me feeling the way I do. I really need to hurt somebody."

Sal exploded, "Have you heard a word I've said! Just let it go goddammit!" Exasperated, Sal took another deep breath, "Look, you're a free man now. Enjoy yourself. Take some ladies out on your boat for an orgy or something. Let the lawyers get what they can. Just don't embarrass me again. You're on thin ice, Buddy. Don't fuckin' blow it." The line went dead.

"The fuckin' lawyers," Buddy seethed, "won't get shit!" He stared into the gilded-frame wall mirror and contemplated going rogue. At that moment, he didn't really care about being heir-apparent to Sal as head of the syndicate. What he wanted more than anything was to *twist somebody's head off their fuckin' neck*. Smoothing back his carefully coiffed hairdo, he always found a measure of calmness while admiring his square-jawed visage. He pulled up on the corner of his eyebrows. *Maybe it's time to have these fixed?*

His cell phone's ring broke into the moment. Irritated, his fury grew as he listened to the caller's stream of excuses. He interrupted the report, "I don't give a fuck if they don't use addresses or street numbers on St. Croix. I'm telling you, Stinger, for what I'm paying you, you fuckin' better find out where he and his black bitch live."

18

Perched two hundred feet above the rocky shore, he stared sullenly over the darkened Caribbean as morning light began filling in the gray sky. Paul stood, sighed and dusted off the seat of his pants. He turned and walked the narrow foot-trail up the sloped grassy hill toward the group of cabins. He had sited the cabins on the hillside to leave as much level, open space on the property as possible. Toward the west end of the property was a twenty-five yard lap pool adjacent to the thirty-five-hundred square foot remodeled community building and covered outdoor kitchen. Further west, hidden behind an earthen berm, sat a 5-vehicle carport with an attached battery storage and water filtration shed. Just south of the shed was a ground-mounted 120-panel solar array, flanked by an 80-foot-tall 3 KW wind generator. A buried sixty-thousand-gallon bladder cistern stored collected rainwater from the compound's roofs, which was then filtered and pumped for domestic use. Completely off-the-grid, Windsol was immune to the astronomical power costs levied by WAPA, the VI Government's mismanaged and antiquated power company.

Closing the bedroom door quietly behind him, he lay beside Sienna. "You awake?"

"Now I am. How long have you been up?"

"A couple hours, I guess."

"You know, Honey, if you're worried about the meeting, maybe it would be smart to postpone it until Hank can join you."

"Hank has already done more for me than I ever had a right to ask. His plate's full enough without any more of my drama. Besides, I've gone over this a hundred times with him. Don't worry, it'll go fine."

"Me? You're the one that's not sleeping."

"It's not the meeting that's keeping me up. It's Andrew. If I hadn't said anything about meeting him, he might . . ."

"We'll never know what the outcome would have been. I just hate to see you so down over this. I understand it, but I hate to see it."

A week earlier, Roxanne had called Sienna to let them know that she, Hank and Red were headed up to Baltimore for follow-up tests at Johns Hopkins. Hank had an elevated PSA and there was some concern of prostate cancer.

Two days later, Paul had received a voicemail message from Buddy Falco's attorney. "Hello, Mr. Armstrong. My name is Craig Bell. I am an attorney representing Mr. Franklin Falco in a civil lawsuit against the estate of a former partner of yours, Andrew Sherman. I have a few questions that I'd like to ask you and will be down to St. Croix early next week. Please let me know a time and place that you would be able to meet. I'll text you my contact information."

Paul called Attorney Bell back and agreed to meet at Cafe Fresco in the Penthany Building's outside courtyard in downtown Christiansted the following Tuesday. "Cafe Fresco's chef puts out the best lunches on island," he assured the attorney in an attempt to sound unruffled.

******

Lost in thought, Paul sipped his iced hibiscus tea and watched the small streams of water spray lazily onto the bronze mermaid in the courtyard fountain. *Fifteen minutes late*, he noticed, fighting the urge to leave. An office door opened at the end of the courtyard and two men walked toward him. He recognized one of the men as a local attorney. The other, a heavy, florid faced man in his late fifties, with thinning salt and pepper hair, a dark suit jacket folded over his arm, addressed Paul as they arrived at his table. "Mr. Armstrong, I'm Craig Bell."

Standing, Paul took the offered hand. "Nice to meet you."

"Hi Paul, I'm a big fan. Charlie Johnson," the other man said, also shaking Paul's hand.

"Attorney Johnson has agreed to our use of his conference room for the next couple of hours. He assures me that the proprietor of this restaurant is capable of delivering lunches there. Shall we?" Bell asked, pointing toward a door at the other end of the courtyard.

Once inside the windowless space, Paul and Attorney Bell took seats on opposite sides of the long conference table.

"I'm curious, Mr. Armstrong. What was Attorney Johnson referring to with regards to his being a big fan?"

"I play guitar and sing, mostly at my wife's restaurant, but sometimes at other venues around the island," Paul replied, while chiding himself for being overly-verbose.

"Wow, just like Jimmy Buffett. You know, I'm sort of a parrot-head myself. Look, you seem tense. I'm just here to ask a few questions that probably won't amount to anything. Then

I hope you'll tell me what to do for fun the rest of the 24 hours I'm here. There's nothing to be nervous about. Deal?"

Paul felt himself relax. "OK, deal."

But fifteen minutes into the interview, his antennae came back up when Attorney Bell asked, "So, were you surprised when you saw Andrew Sherman alive?"

An awkward silence was interrupted by a tap on the door. Attorney Bell waited at the open door while lunch was brought into the room. Thanking the server, he closed the door, walked over to the food and began serving himself. With his back to Paul, he said, "Of course, we know that you met with Andrew eight months before he turned himself in, but that wasn't the first time, was it? You were right, Paul, this *Monte Cristo* sandwich looks wonderful."

"I'm glad," Paul replied, determined to seem unconcerned over the direction the conversation had turned. "I've never had a bad meal here," Paul added, while dressing his chef's salad. "No, I never met Andrew before running into him at The Willy T. Until then, I was under the impression he had been murdered by your client."

Attorney Bell's demeanor had changed when he returned to the table. Gone was the big, soft and smarmy parrot-head. Shrewd penetrating eyes stared into Paul's. "My client believes that you may know the location of a large sum of money that Mr. Sherman had tucked away."

"He did mention when I saw him that he had some money, but never told me where it was kept."

"Would you be willing to take a lie detector test?"

"I can't think of any reason I'd want to." Paul put down his fork and returned the attorney's hard gaze.

"Well, maybe my client was misinformed. You know how rumors can get started."

"Absolutely." He picked up his fork and tried to appear interested in the food.

The remainder of their meeting related to questions regarding the dissolution of Paul and Andrew's development company, T-Squared Development. Paul described the weeks preceding and following Andrew's disappearance and presumed death. He also referred Bell to the law firm that had handled the dissolution to confirm the lack of any remaining company assets that might be attached in the civil suit.

Following the meeting, Paul's cell buzzed in his pocket as he walked back to his truck. A relieved smile came over his face as the familiar voice boomed in his ear.

"Hey, Ace! How's those gonads of yours? Toasty, I bet. What is it, 85 and sunny?"

"Most always is, Barney. How did it go in Mexico?"

"Tapachula was depressing. I tell you, Amigo, I think if Claire had stayed in that detention center another day, she wouldn't have been able to travel. She's skinny as a fuckin' bean-pole. I'm not sure what color her hair is…kind of an electric blue, I'd say. She's sleeping now. Said she'd come home with me if I'd promise to let her stay on the farm. Said that it'd kill her to go back to the Western State Looney Bin."

It had been during their lunch together in Cartagena, Columbia's Plaza Santa Domingo, that Paulo had excused himself for a baño break and never returned. He had moved on to another mark, taking Claire's money belt with him. Scared and alone, but attractive and resourceful, she resorted to petty theft and charity to survive as she scammed her way north. Eventually, she entered Mexico posturing as the wife of an Acapulco dentist who had given her a ride from Los Pozuelos in Guatemala's Western Highlands. When they couldn't come to terms regarding his payment, he left her dazed on the side of

Route 200, with a dark welt under her right eye and a missing front tooth. She was soon picked up by the Policia and transported south to the Tapachula Detention Center. A month later, weak and disorientated, she called Barney.

"Is that a good idea . . . her staying at your house? What about her medications? Shouldn't she be under a psychiatrist's care?"

"Absofuckinglutely. Don't worry, I'm on it. Before I left to bring her back, I set up an appointment with Dr. Becker. He's agreed to see her as an out-patient in his Bremerton office tomorrow."

It wasn't the first time Paul had felt immense gratitude for the big man's generosity. Paul couldn't help carrying a nagging guilt over Claire's misfortunes. Although divorced for over two years, old patterns die hard, and Paul still had instincts to protect her and cared for her deeply.

"Well, keep me posted. Tell her that Sienna and I send our love and hope to see her down here when she's ready to travel. And Barney, thanks."

"No problem Ace. I don't see us picking up where we left off with the romance-thing, but it's good to have her back safe and sound for the time being. I'll keep you posted. Shouldn't be too long before we come down though. Now that *The Last Hurrah's* out of dry-dock, I'm anxious to take her out for a shakedown cruise. Also, I think Claire might do better with the depression in a sunnier climate. By the way, that Buddy Falco character isn't doing himself any favors. Did you see the video where the bird shit on his head?"

"Yeah. Seems like even Mother Nature is on to him. I just finished an interview with one of his attorneys. You know, he's filed a civil suit against Andrew's estate."

"And?"

127

"The attorney came down to make sure there was no meat left on T-Squared's bones when it went under. Also, he tried to trick me into saying that I'd known Andrew was alive from the beginning. I think I convinced him that I hadn't."

"Shit, that's not good. No offense, but you're fuckin' clueless when it comes to knowing what these mafia types are thinking. Was Hank with you?"

"No. He's in Baltimore having some medical tests. Look, don't worry. It went fine."

"I don't like it. That Buddy Falco is a psychotic killer. Don't even like your name bein' mentioned to him one bit. You keep your eyes open Amigo and let me know how Hank's doing."

Andy answered Paul's call on the second ring. "Hey Son, Char and I were just talking about you."

"So when are you going to make an honest woman out of my aunt? You guys must be the talk of Winthrop, sneaking around between the cabin and the girls' ranch," Paul kidded.

"Ain't no sneakin' going on round these parts, Mister," Andy bristled. "This is the twenty-first century and I'm more than satisfied to say that the woman's my lover, for now anyway."

"Yuck, gross. I'm right here for Pete's sake!" Paul heard Aunt Charlotte exclaim, followed by Andy's grunt, as her fist landed on his boney shoulder.

"So how was the interview?" Andy asked.

"I think it went well. The attorney said his client had heard that I'd known Andrew was alive the whole time, but I made it very clear that was not the case."

"Well, of course you convinced him. It's the truth. Hell, I nearly drove off the road when I heard about his turning himself in. He must have felt that Buddy and his gang were close on his tail. A lot of good it did him though. That was some shot that took him out. Heard the bullet covered close to a mile before nailing him in the forehead."

"Yeah, that's what they're saying."

"Anyway, don't worry. People like Buddy Falco are always looking for ways to mess-up people's lives. Gives them a feeling of power. But you know what? They're just yellow-bellied pussies when it comes right down to it . . . Huh? . . . Here, your Aunt wants to talk with you."

"Paul, I disagree. I don't think you should take this lightly. They sent someone all the way down to St. Croix. Let's talk about it and figure out a course of action when we're down there next week. Is Barney back yet? Will he be coming down?"

"Barney has Claire set for an appointment with a psychiatrist tomorrow. Sounds like she's pretty weak. Knowing Barney, he won't leave until she's stabilized." Paul relayed his previous conversation with Barney while Andy and Char listened, now on the speaker phone.

"I tell you, that Barney is like a knight in King Arthur's Court if you ask me. The way he goes around helping and saving people is like the stuff epic poems are written about. He's a good man to have in your corner when the chips are down," Andy pronounced.

"I just hope he doesn't get hurt if Claire runs off again," Char added. "He can say what he wants, but I'm certain he still loves her."

******

Stopping for groceries on his way home, Paul noticed two men in a gray sedan pull into the parking lot as he walked into Food Town. Catching a brief glimpse of the driver before

129

he wheeled into a spot facing away from the store, Paul thought that even with the sunglasses and a ball cap pulled low, there was something vaguely familiar about him. Not seeing the men inside the store and now finding the parking spot empty, he thought nothing more of it and headed west on Northside Road for home. It was twilight when Paul drove through the caliche stone entry columns of Windsol. As the gate swung closed behind him, he pulled into the village carport. Having heard the truck drive up, AJ greeted him on the front porch tossing a ball in the air. "Getting a little dark for that isn't it?" Paul asked.

"Ah come on, Paul. I can still see fine."

"All right, I'll be right out." He walked inside with his arms full of groceries.

On his way home, Paul had called and briefly updated Sienna about the meeting with Attorney Bell. "I think we just enjoy each day and not play the 'what-if' game," she said, as she greeted Paul with a warm kiss. "I have some great news. Roxanne called, and Hank's tests came back negative. They'll be home tomorrow afternoon. We're celebrating tomorrow night at the restaurant."

"That's a huge relief," Paul replied. "Oh, I spoke with Barney. He's back from Mexico with Claire. Sounds like she's been through hell."

"And you didn't think to tell me that when you called? I'm not one of your golfing buddies, Paul."

"Huh, what do you mean?"

"Last week, when you and Arthur played you *forgot* to ask and he *forgot* to tell you that his daughter had delivered a healthy baby girl the day before. I heard about it today from Cheryl when I ran into her at Cost-U-Less."

"Oh, man. Arthur's a grandfather. I'd forgotten Corin was pregnant."

"Exactly, that's my point. What do you guys talk about for four hours when you play?"

"I don't know, golf, poker, things like that."

Before Sienna could respond, AJ burst through the front door. "Come on Paul. It's not getting any lighter."

"Well, interesting observation, Sienna. Good discussion." Paul said sarcastically. "Better go wing a few with the little man." He turned abruptly and joined AJ outside.

Sienna shook her head, and followed him. As she stood and watched her two men play catch, her irritation quickly dissolved. Smiling, she signaled Paul over as AJ chased after a missed grounder. "Sorry about that."

"Me too. I think you made a good point."

"Well thanks, but who am I to tell you what you should talk about? It might just be that I'm a bit hormonal, what with being pregnant and all."

Paul stared, open-mouthed at Sienna, completely oblivious to AJ's play calling. "—and the runner's rounding second. They're waving him in from third. Here comes the throw to home plate." Paul dropped like a stone as the hard rubber ball drilled into *big Jim and the twins*.

"Paul, you OK?" Sienna's worried face filled his watery-eyed vision as she leaned over him.

Wincing, he slowly stood, "Kid's got quite an arm. Good thing it was a rubber ball." He placed the palm of his hand gently on her belly. "My God, Sienna."

Their lingering kiss was interrupted by AJ. "Eww, get a room."

19

Attorney Bell sat alone at the Buccaneer's terrace bar admiring the early evening view. To the west the lights of Christiansted twinkled beyond the mangrove-edged Altona Lagoon. He had asked Darrell for a strong island drink and wasn't disappointed in the painkiller, a local rum and creamed-coconut concoction that he swirled absent-mindedly in front of him. *Four or five of these and I can forget the shit I have to do to make money.*

Though he blended in with the tourists seated at the bar, he felt uncomfortable in the Big Kahuna floral print shirt. Two days ago, he had dug it out of the back of his closet up north. He hadn't worn it for nearly three years. His ex-wife had picked the shirt out on their final vacation in Hawaii. Shortly after their return, she filed for divorce, retaining a hotshot lawyer from a rival firm. He threw back the remnants of the drink and signaled for another. "A little lighter on everything but the rum, please."

The drink arrived and he gulped it down quickly. His cell vibrated in his pocket before he could order another. "Buzz killer," he said, glaring at the illuminated name. He cautioned himself before answering, *This guy's a psycho. Don't piss him off Craigy-Boy.*

"Yes, Mr. Falco. What can I do for you?"

"Look, Shithead . . . I know you think you're working for my uncle, but don't forget that I run things out here and you, being from Seattle, should remember that."

Attorney Bell's face grew even redder. His voice, however, remained skillfully calm. "Now, Mr. Falco, of course I know that we represent you. It's for that very purpose of helping you that I'm down here. Please tell me, what can I do for you?" He whirled his index finger over his head, signaling Darrell for another.

"Just tell me that son of a bitch was in on the scam from the beginning. I've got the rest covered. Got boots on the ground."

This was the part of the job Attorney Bell really hated. Working for the syndicate was lucrative, and God knows he needed the money. But fingering a seemingly nice guy like Paul Armstrong was never easy to live with. Still, his yearly retainer was in the mid-six figures and Armstrong was probably in on it anyway.

"He denied it," Bell relayed. "Rather convincingly, I might add. Maybe too convincingly. Sounded a bit rehearsed."

"Course he'd deny it," Buddy echoed. "No coincidence that he ends up down there and Sherman shows up in Tortola. You know what I say about coincidences?"

"What's that?" Attorney Bell was trying hard to sound interested.

"Ain't any."

The cold drink arrived and, fighting the urge to slam it down in one fell swoop, Attorney Bell held it to his forehead instead. It helped. He still needed some wits about him while talking to Buddy. *Make him think you find him clever,* he reminded himself. "So very true, Mr. Falco. The ancient philosophers couldn't have put it any better." He was going to say *more succinctly*, but was worried Buddy's vocabulary didn't stretch that far. The last thing he wanted to do was clue Buddy Falco in on how stupid he really was. It didn't matter. Buddy had already moved on.

"Yeah, whatever. Look, do you know where Armstrong lives? I plan on having my assets pay him a visit."

Assets? Boots on the ground? Fuck it. Attorney Bell swept the glass from the bar and drained it in one continuous motion. *How much wit do I really need here?* Burping quietly to the side, he replied, "No, we met in Chri . . . Christiansted," almost saying *Christmastime.*

"Don't matter. My guys'll find the fucker. I'm done here."

For Attorney Bell, it was just in the nick of time. "Yeah, well fucker you too," he replied to the dead line and signaled Darrell for one more.

******

He was eleven when the last person called him Vivian. In and out of foster homes, V's considerable size and strength, coupled with a constant, simmering rage left behind a trail of smashed faces, broken bones and concussions through his teen years. On his 18th birthday he joined the Marines. Trained as a sniper, he was dishonorably discharged for starting a bar fight which resulted in two Navy Seals requiring a combined 65 cranial stitches.

Once out of the military, he made money doing what he did best. It was after he nearly killed an opponent during an illegal bare knuckle boxing match, that V met Salvador Boitano. A late-model Lincoln Town Car pulled alongside V as he left

134

the Hi-Lite Fight Club. The front passenger door opened and a huge bald man unfolded himself onto the sidewalk. The man hailed V in a high-pitched, effeminate voice, "Mr. Boitano would like to speak with you."

V didn't recognize the name, but he liked the car and the whole scene seemed too intriguing to pass up. Still pumping adrenaline from the fight, he sauntered over and pinched the cheek of the behemoth. "Thanks *Nancy*."

He climbed into the back seat and was cautioned by Mr. Boitano, "You should be a little more careful, but I like your style. Hey Tiny, ease up. He was just busting your balls."

"Yes sir, Mr. Sal." The giant scowled at V in the rear view mirror.

Mob Boss Salvador Boitano had been seated in the front row of V's brief bout. He'd been blanketed by the spray of blood and tissue following V's final blow to the side of his opponent's jaw. "That was an impressive fight. I'd like you to work for me."

Initially, the job was a good fit. But after putting several slow-paying accounts in the hospital and a couple others in the East River, V's reputation alone became a sufficient deterrent. This was not to his liking. Taking V under his wing, Sal had tried to help him understand the larger picture. "If you can get the deadbeats to pay-up by just calling for an appointment, it makes us look more legit."

But V missed the face-smashing and bone-breaking. When Tiny mysteriously disappeared, Sal suspected V of running his former security chief through a wood chipper. With his loyalty to Sal now in question, V was sent to Seattle to look after things for Sal's nephew, Buddy.

V was thrilled with the assignment. He recognized in Buddy an affinity for violence that rivaled his own. Once again, he was back to using his fists, rather than his reputation. It was a perfect match, cut short by Buddy's imprisonment for the murder of Andrew Sherman. Once again, V was taking orders from Sal who provided him with little opportunity for violence. That quickly changed after Buddy's release from Leavenworth. Returning from a two week "vacation" in the British Virgin Islands, V was called to Buddy's Medina mansion to be given his next assignment.

One of the house-girls led V back to Buddy's office. "Would you like a blow-job while you wait?" the top-heavy assistant asked, smiling knowingly.

Although tolerating it from his boss, he would never take shit from Buddy's girls. "Get lost, bitch." Buddy and his entourage were well-aware that V had zero interest in either the house-girls or the extensive library of porn. Nobody, not even Buddy, dared suggest that V was gay. In fact, with his hatred for being touched, the "V" might just as well have stood for Virgin.

Resplendent in his now infamous, monogrammed blue silk robe, Buddy entered the room sporting his usual scowl. Brief nods were their sole acknowledgements as Buddy sunk low in the leather cushioned captain's chair. "Uncle Sal says we've got to lay low," Buddy began, dwarfed by the huge baroque desk between them, "at least for now."

V's disappointment was obvious, but he knew better than to interrupt Buddy before he was finished.

"In the meantime, I got something for you. I want you to go down to St. Croix in the Virgin Islands and bring me back a virgin," Buddy joked. Getting nothing from V, he complained, "Jesus, V, you got to lighten up. That was fuckin' hilarious."

Buddy, as often the case, was already wearing thin on V. But, over the years, he had learned the value of restraint. V's face moved into something close to a tortured smile, accompanied by a forced chuckle that sounded more like a cough. Satisfied, Buddy continued, "So, Stinger and you are going to mess with Sherman's business partner, a wimpy architect-prick named Paul Armstrong. For sure, the dude was involved with Sherman from the start and I want you two to find out where they stashed the money Sherman took when he blew town. Must be a million at least. Uncle Sal's fuckin' lawyer Bell won't find it. After you find the money, I want you to mess Armstrong up. Don't kill him. Uncle Sal would shit a brick, what with his reputation worries and all. Jesus, seems like he's running for president or something. Maybe I'll come down and do it myself."

******

There were several things that V didn't like about his assignment as he boarded the American Airlines 757 nonstop to Miami. The first was that he had to work with Stinger. The second was the vagueness of Buddy's instructions. *Just hurt him bad enough, but not bad enough that Uncle Sal shits a brick.* A pretty fine line he was walking. Erring on one side or the other would leave either Buddy or Sal royally pissed-off. Before falling asleep on the connecting flight to St. Croix, he had decided that as much as he'd enjoy beating the shit out of Armstrong, he would give Buddy every chance he could to come down and do the job himself.

20

Paul and Hank sat at the end of the bar, talking quietly. "Sounds like you did as good as you could," Hank replied, after hearing Paul's description of the meeting with Attorney Bell. "The problem we have now is Buddy Falco. I felt that I had a handle on things dealing with Sal, but Buddy's release from Leavenworth adds an unpredictable element to the situation."

"I'm grateful for the 'we,' Hank. Sienna and I can't thank you and Roxanne enough for your help."

"Hey, it's nothing. We're family. Look, there's no reason to become paranoid, but if anything comes up, call me immediately. I don't care if I'm having my appendix taken out. Got it?"

Grateful, Paul nodded.

The two men stood as Sienna and Roxanne joined them. "I can't believe the amount of good food you turn out in that small kitchen," Roxanne said to Sienna, following their back-of-the-house tour.

"It's a challenge, but Ambrosia has been with me since Aaron and I first opened The Green Flash. She's a big reason for our success."

"Also, I hear through the grapevine that our boy has been bringing in some pretty good sized crowds." Hank added, clinking his bottle against Paul's.

"Doesn't seem like we left these two alone for that long," Roxanne said to Sienna, looking suspiciously at the empty bottle in front of Hank.

"Well, with Sienna now eating for two, Hank and I figured we should each drink for two to demonstrate our solidarity," Paul kidded, gently placing his palm on Sienna's slightly protruding belly.

"Hey, I want in on this solidarity thing," Roxanne chirped and signaled the bartender.

Paul excused himself for the first set which, in honor of Detroit-born Roxanne, was full-blown Motown. Near the end of the set, Paul asked Roxanne to join him in *Ain't Nothing Like The Real Thing*, which she dedicated to her Hanky-Bear, before enthusiastically belting out a passable Tammy Terrell to Paul's Marvin Gaye.

Over dinner they discussed Sienna's pregnancy.

"I've been feeling good, once I get going. The early mornings have been rough, but Paul's been great getting AJ ready for school, packing lunches and fixing breakfasts."

"I still can't believe it," Paul said. "Ten years ago, I was told I'd probably never be able to have kids."

"You just needed a patient egg for your lazy swimmers," Sienna said laughing. "Seriously, we're both so happy we feel like we're floating."

"And we're so happy for you," Roxanne replied. "Do we know the sex yet?"

"Paul doesn't want to know. Says he'll be just as happy with either. I don't know if I can hold off knowing for five more months."

"What about the relatives? I bet they're excited."

"We told you that Paul's Aunt Charlotte and Andy are coming down next week. I think between my folks, sisters, nephews, and Aunt Charlotte and Andy, we may have to take a number to see the baby," Sienna joked.

"Also, Barney may be coming soon with Claire, if she's up to it," Paul added.

"Claire, as in your ex-wife Claire?" Hank asked. "Jesus you guys. How comfortable will that be? Especially, with you being pregnant and all."

"Barney's family," Sienna explained solemnly. "So is Claire. Whatever comes up, we'll just figure out a way to make it work. Look, we all have our own cabins. It'll be fine."

"AJ and Red are going to have a ball combing through ruins," Paul jumped in. "AJ's on a mission looking for small pieces of old china the islanders call Chaney. We've already paid him for several pieces that we're having made into a bracelet and pendant."

"Sounds great," Roxanne replied. "We're really excited about moving into Windsol. St. Thomas is overrun with cruise ships. We moved down here for some peace and quiet and feel like this'll be a much better fit."

From the beach below V watched yet another toast. He didn't want Armstrong to know that he was being followed. Stinger had almost blown it already in the grocery store parking lot. V wondered who the other couple was. Their chumminess, all their fuckin' toasting and laughing really bothered him. He'd see if Stinger knew who they were when he returned to the hotel. Irritated by the thought of his worthless partner, he climbed into his rented Taurus and waited.

V had tailed them from The Green Flash a few days earlier. Staying back far enough to remain inconspicuous, he'd lost them soon after reaching the rainforest's tightly curved Mahogany Road. This time, he pulled out as the four loaded into Paul's double cab truck. V's plan was to lead, rather than follow. He'd keep them in his mirror and see where they turned off. Repeating their earlier route, he climbed *The Beast*, a steep, winding section of road named by participants in the annual island-wide triathlon. Reaching the crest of the hill, he coasted down a lengthy straightaway, but soon pulled over when their headlights failed to appear behind him. Checking the road map, he saw that Scenic Drive intersected their route at the top of The Beast and continued west into the rainforest. Realizing they'd taken that route, he spun through a quick U-turn. In less than a minute he was on the bumpy, unpaved road in hot-pursuit. *I'll just come up on them flashing my lights. They'll stop and I'll say that I'm lost. I'll ask them if they live around here and maybe*—His thoughts were derailed abruptly when the air bag exploded as the Taurus plowed into a two foot deep pothole. "Shit. Oh Fuck," V croaked weakly as the air bag deflated. He clambered into the hot, humid night, stumbling though the darkness. His right arm, which had been trapped between the airbag and his sternum, felt wrenched out of its socket. His eyes burned and were blurred by the alkaline gases produced when the airbag inflated. The loud buzzing of the cicadas stopped briefly following V's screamed obscenities as he tumbled off the road and somersaulted down a thorny bank. Coming to rest on a rocky, ravine bottom, he painfully dug out his cell. Adding insult to injury, he called Stinger.

21

The breeze through the truck's open windows made the ninety degrees tolerable as Paul, Sienna and AJ sat double-parked at Henry Rohlsen Airport. Out on the tarmac, the De Havilland Twin Otter's engines were winding down after completing the sixty- mile puddle jump from Puerto Rico. Andy and Aunt Charlotte appeared through the security doorway, followed by the huge, red-bearded Barney and skinny, blonde-haired Claire.

"We're so happy you could come," Sienna said, greeting Claire and Barney.

Claire looked sallow and uncomfortable, but smiled warmly at AJ. "You've grown a foot since I saw you last. Maybe later we can play Chutes and Ladders."

Barney and Andy left to rent a Jeep Wrangler. Char and Claire climbed into the back seat of Paul's truck. Before joining them, AJ whispered to his mom, "Chutes and Ladders? Does she think I'm four?"

"She was just being friendly, Honey. Cut her some slack, I don't think she's been around many kids."

Once underway, AJ excitedly updated Char and Claire about his life on St. Croix. "There's ruins in the rainforest. There's mongoose, lizards, deer, iguana, birds, goats, sheep, horses, dogs, cows, cats and rats. No snakes though. The mongoose have eaten them all. I'm getting really good at baseball. You can play with Paul and me if you want. Paul says I have a good arm. Last week I hit him in the nuts and . . ."

A twenty minute drive brought the two-car caravan onto Windsol's quarter-mile gravel road. Wild papaya, mango and guava trees stood in dense vegetation as they passed under the mahogany treed canopy. Breaking out of the forest, they drove through the entry gate onto an expansive meadow. The metal roofs of the hillside cabins appeared on the north-slope just past the meadow. Beyond, lay the dark blue Caribbean Sea under a rose-hued sunset sky.

Sienna and Roxanne had stocked their cabins with groceries, linens, towels and toiletries. Anxious to clean up after the twelve-hour flight, they all headed to their cabins, agreeing to meet at the community house in an hour for dinner. Paul helped Andy with his luggage while Sienna accompanied Aunt Charlotte along the walking path to their cabin.

"Home again, home again." Aunt Charlotte dropped into her favorite overstuffed leather chair.

"It's good to see Claire again. She seems much more lucid than when we saw her at Western State."

"Poor dears, I mean Barney too. What they've both been through is heart-breaking. Of all the illnesses and accidents that can happen in life, losing control of your mind must be one of the worst."

"I was surprised that they decided she could travel here so soon."

"Barney told me on the flight that her new psychiatrist has a colleague on St. Croix that is well-equipped to help her with medications. Also, they're finding that diet, exercise and stress play a part in all of this. Barney thinks that Claire can work on the boat, maybe eventually run things down here for him when he has to be up at the farm. Of course, that might be kind of strange for you and Paul, having her at Windsol."

"Maybe, but we can cross that bridge when we come to it. When Paul and I married, we both inherited each other's friends and family. I know that Paul will always care for Claire and I don't feel threatened by it. I just hope she can settle into things down here for everybody's sake."

"Paul and you were lucky to find each other. I know that Claire could never come between you two, but there is wisdom to that song, *All my ex's live in Texas*, or at least somewhere other than where you live."

Sienna laughed, "That's true, but I think we're all past that now. I really hope that Barney and Claire can still make it work."

"I agree, Dear. It just isn't fair that two people who love each other have to contend with this bipolar business. It's already hard enough to keep things afloat in this day and age under normal circumstances."

******

When they reconvened for dinner, Paul and Hank offered rum drinks filled with fresh, tropical juices, garnished with banana, pineapple slices and an umbrella to the adults and a virgin version to AJ and Sienna.

Not one for lengthy speeches, Paul raised his glass. "To our wonderful friends and family, thank you for being here. We've missed you and welcome you back to your island home." Determined to keep his voice from breaking, he put his arm around Sienna, "To my intelligent, talented, and loving wife, I thought that I could never be happier than when you and AJ came into my life, but that was before you told me you were pregnant." Only Sienna heard him add, "I love you," as the group exploded into cheers and congratulations.

Andy was the most visibly affected by the news. Not even trying to hide the tears streaming down his weathered face he jumped up and wrapping his arms around Paul and Sienna said, "If it's a boy, name him Andy. If it's a girl, well, Andy works that way too."

"Andy Meyers, have you lost your mind? You stop with that right now." Aunt Charlotte scolded.

"Just kiddin', kids. Don't pay me no mind. It's just that right now, I'm about the proudest and happiest Papa in the world!"

Sienna had prepared island cuisine for their first evening's meal together. The famished travelers hunkered down on the community house's covered terrace and enjoyed the feast. Barney and Hank led the charge for seconds as they returned for callaloo soup, stewed chicken, fried plantains, rice, beans and johnny cakes.

After dinner, the men cleaned up the dishes while the women took the footpath to the new viewing platform. As she watched the surf foaming over the rocky costal shore, two hundred feet below, Claire said, "What a beautiful evening. It's so warm and clear. I could get used to this real fast."

"The breeze usually comes up about this time," Roxanne said. "It's my favorite time of the day."

"It's hard to believe that it was in the 40's when we left Winthrop," Aunt Charlotte said. "I'm so glad that you and Barney could come, Claire."

"It's been a tough year. I'm so grateful to Barney and you two. But I'm really embarrassed that I ran off the way I did. I'm just lucky to be alive." Claire broke into sobs.

145

Sienna took her hand. "We're all here for you, Claire. You have nothing to be embarrassed about."

"You're so wonderful, Sienna. After Paul and I divorced, I wanted to be the perfect ex. When Barney and I started dating, I was afraid that Paul would be uncomfortable, but he was great about the whole thing. It was all working out perfectly until—" She stopped, then shook her head. "It's such a blur."

Aunt Charlotte had been listening quietly. "Actually, I need to ask for your forgiveness, Claire."

"My forgiveness?"

"When you became manic and sent out those awful emails to Paul's friends and past clients, I was livid. All I could think about was that you were trying to hurt him. I didn't stop to think how this was being done to you as well. The *you* that I knew would never have done those things. You weren't in control of yourself and I should have known better."

Claire and Aunt Charlotte hugged, both now crying. Sienna waited until they were done. "Claire, my sense of timing may be off and maybe I'm a little hormonal, but when you sent that letter pretending you were Eric Tuckerman, you threatened AJ as well as Paul."

Claire's head dropped. "Oh God, Sienna, I'm so sorry."

"I know that, Claire. I also realize that if the mania progresses to a certain point, you are powerless to stop it. So, I need you to promise that you'll listen and follow the advice of those who love you if we say you're starting to spin out of control."

A warm wind rose from the thundering surf below as the two women looked unflinchingly into the other's eyes. Then Claire replied simply, "I give you my word, Sienna. I would give up my life before I'd hurt any of you again."

"Thank you. Enough said. I wonder how the boys are doing with clean-up?"

"If I know Andy," Aunt Charlotte answered, "he'll be reorganizing the entire kitchen."

"And if I know Hank," Roxanne added, "he'll be watching."

******

Overtired from the long trip and the evening's excitement, Andy hadn't left his seat at the table. Instead, he had appointed himself *Senior Advisor* for the clean-up, limiting his efforts to encouragement and attitude adjustment. When the boys returned the last of the serving platters to the cupboard, he called them over for "A little Single Barrel nightcap."

"To my future grandchild," Andy toasted, before the four men tossed back the smooth, golden, island distilled rum.

"To Windsol, new friends and family," Hank added.

"To living on island-time," Barney said, removing his watch and joining the others in downing their second shot.

"To Barney," Paul said. "Thanks for bringing Claire back."

"God bless us, one and all," Andy said, slamming his shot glass hard on the table. "Say g'night to the ladies for me, Boys. It's been a long day."

As they walked the old cowboy back to his cabin, Paul, Barney and Hank joined him in a hearty chorus of *Red River Valley*. Depositing him on his bed, Paul and Barney pulled off Andy's cowboy boots and socks while Andy, still singing, fell back fully-clothed onto the bed.

"G'night Boys. That was mighty nice of you pulling my footwear off, what with the stink and all. First thing tomorrow, I'm gonna go out and get me a pair of them sandals and let those doggies breathe. Yeehaw!"

Paul, Barney and Hank walked across the meadow to the old ruin on the property. Sitting on an ancient rubble wall, Barney said, "Damn I love that little guy and his Yeehaws. I hope we have half as much piss in us when we turn eighty."

"Amen," Paul agreed, reaching into his pocket and passing Barney a joint and a lighter.

"Well, well, Kemosabe. All this and herb too? This truly is fuckin' paradise."

"Well, you can thank our Rasta roofers again. Their attention to detail was amazing."

"It shows up in this as well," Barney said, pulling in a deep drag and passing it to Hank. "This is good shit and unlike that tasty single barrel, there's no acid reflux with this stuff."

"True," Paul said, looking up at the crystal-clear, night sky. "So, you and Claire?"

"Ah shit, I don't know. Truthfully, Amigo, she'll always be the one for me, but for both our sakes, we're taking it real slow. Separate beds, the whole thing. I'll tell you though; I've kept myself awake most nights fighting the urge to—'

"Have you two talked about it? I mean, does she feel the same way? Who knows, it might do you both good."

"No, I think we're both a little gun-shy after what happened. Speaking of guns, you got any around here?"

"I think Andy has a few in a cabinet we built for him. Hank probably has one or two." Hank nodded with smoke streaming out of his nostrils. "Why?"

"Why? Where the fuck in fantasy land are you living? You've got Buddy Falco on your ass. Don't you think with

148

living out here in the middle of a jungle, you'd better goddamn-well have some way to protect yourselves?"

"Actually, the new police chief seems to be doing a pretty good job of cleaning things up down here."

"Barney's right," Hank said. "We're not talking about gangbangers or dumbass hoodlums. This is the mafia. I hate to say this, Paul, but the people that killed Andrew Sherman did it right under the law's nose from over a mile away. I wouldn't count on the island police to stop them from doing anything they want."

"True, but what good would it do to have a gun? I mean, if they decide to take me out, how would that stop them?"

Barney stared into the darkness. "Yeah, well, let's hope it doesn't come to that, Amigo."

22

V had climbed back up the hill and was waiting in the car when Stinger arrived. "The Taurus is pretty fucked up," Stinger declared. "Also, you're not supposed to be on this road. It's in the rental agreement. So insurance won't cover this mess. Leaves us only one option."

"And what's that?"

"We'll torch it," Stinger replied cheerfully, as he opened the trunk and pulled out a five gallon gas container. "Happens all the time around here. Some punkass gangster boosts a car and goes for a joyride. Ends up on one of these dirt roads and has himself a bonfire. We'll just tell them the car was stolen. Insurance will cover everything."

Pulling away from the blazing sedan, Stinger talked nonstop as he drove V to the emergency room's entrance at Juan Luis Hospital. "One thing I really appreciate about being on the payroll is the health insurance. Old Sal really takes care of his crew. You might pay fifty-bucks as a copay, but that's it. Say you need physical therapy for your fucked-up shoulder, or say with those blisters all over your face, you'll need plastic surgery. I'm not saying that you will, but even if you did, it's covered. I was screwing this broad last year and all of a sudden, I get this spasm in my chest. Turned out to be something called peri-card-itis, but I think I'm having a heart attack. Of course, I'm still hard as a fuckin' rock so—'

"Stinger?" V interrupted, rubbing his temples.

"Yeah V?"

"Shut the fuck up."

"Well . . . sure, V. If that's what you want. No problem. Just thought you might want something to take your mind off your problems. You know Buddy's gonna shit when he finds out about all of this."

The back of V's left hand smacked hard against Stinger's temple.

"Jesus, V. Why'd you do that?" Stinger screamed.

"I said, shut the fuck up," V growled menacingly.

Brooding, Stinger remained silent for the rest of the ride.

There was little going on in the ER when they arrived. V was treated for burns, scratches and contusions almost immediately. When asked what happened, he explained that he had been smoking in bed, caught his mosquito net on fire and being unfamiliar with the layout of the condo, ran into a wall attempting to locate the fire extinguisher. Disoriented he stumbled outside and fell down a bank rolling through a sticker bush.

"Looks more like some kind of chemical burn," the doctor observed, as he dressed the wounds. But, with time running out on his shift, he showed little interest in pursuing the thought.

Leaving the hospital at dawn, V dropped the sling he had been given for his bruised shoulder into a trash can. The pain was manageable without the sling and he didn't want to appear injured or weak when he met with Armstrong. *The burns are ok though*, he thought as he looked in the visor mirror at his singed face.

"How about we grab some breakfast at IHOP?" V suggested, attempting to break through Stinger's pout.

"You're the boss, V. It's whatever you want to do," Stinger replied flatly, eyes on the road, hands at ten and two.

It wasn't just Stinger. V hated working with people. Normally, this *hurt feelings shit* really got under his skin. He briefly considered smacking Stinger again, but didn't want to risk another accident. As they took their seats at the restaurant, V's pain meds had kicked in. He felt almost friendly. "Hey Stinger, sorry I smacked you. I was still pissed off from the accident."

"OK, but don't ever hit me again, especially after what I've done for you tonight."

The pharmaceutical intervention pulled V back just in time from smashing Stinger's nose through the back of his head. Instead, he smiled, painfully. "Order anything you want man. I'm buying."

******

Back at the condo, V stripped down to his briefs and was about to fall into bed when his cell signaled a voicemail. "Hey, Killer," Buddy's voice greeted him. "Haven't heard much from you two and, frankly, I'm fuckin' tired of waiting for news, so I'm headed your way for some action. When I'm done pounding on that architect prick, I want you to have Stinger line me up with some tropical pussy. Coming in from Miami. Will be there a little after four. Don't fuckin' make me wait."

V set the alarm on his phone and six hours later, Buddy climbed into the passenger seat beside Stinger, with V riding in the back. Stinger pulled up in front of the darkened cashier's booth and gave their parking ticket to a seemingly disembodied hand with long, curly, green nails. With no other visual or audible contact, the gate was raised and they were off.

"You're driving on the wrong side of the road, you idiot!" Buddy screamed.

"It's OK," Stinger replied. "That's the way it's done down here. Don't sweat anything boss, I know my way around this island."

Buddy, resplendent in white silk shirt and pants, turned to look at V, whose sunglasses didn't hide the burns. "Hey V," Buddy said, chuckling, "If that's the way you tan, I'd wear a sock over your head. Your face looks like shit."

Realizing it was just a matter of time before Buddy would find out, V told Buddy about his accident. Buddy went ballistic. "What the fuck? Christ. You're supposed to be a pro, not some dumbass, sideshow clown."

Stinger jumped to V's defense, "But Boss, those roads are for shit up there in the rainforest. They don't even let you take rental cars on them. V didn't know that. Besides, I torched the car and we told the rental car dealer that some punks stole it. Everything is gonna be paid for by the insurance company."

"You torched the car?"

"She went up like a bomb," Stinger boasted proudly.

Buddy looked back at V. "And you were OK with this?"

Still pissed over the dumbass clown comment, V growled, "What would you have done?"

"What would I have done? What would I have done?" But when nothing came to him and realizing that V was approaching his flashpoint, Buddy backed off. "What kind of car?"

"A Taurus," Stinger answered.

"Why didn't you say that in the first place? A Taurus? I'd have torched that piece of shit before driving it off the lot." Buddy laughed at his own joke. Stinger also thought it was hilarious. V just stared out the window. "So Stinger, you talked to Uncle Sal lately?"

"I give him updates. You know, he likes to be kept up to speed."

"Anything I should know about? Seems like there hasn't been much to report."

"I've been working things, Boss. Investigation takes time. I need to develop sources."

"Relax, I'm just fuckin' with you. After we're done with the architect, I'll be wanting some company and I expect you to be able to fix me up."

"No problem, Boss. I've got you covered."

If he had a tail, it'd be wagging. V was growing sicker of his companions by the second.

"I appreciate that, Stinger. Oh, by the way, I don't suppose you boys have found out where Armstrong lives yet."

"It's like I was telling V on the way out here . . . I did a little investigating and found out that he built some kind of a hippy-compound in the rainforest. I think we can find it all right, but from what I hear, there's a bunch of people down from the states staying with him."

"Tell you what, Sherlock; let's just figure out a way to talk with him in private. It won't take long for him to get the message."

"I got that covered as well. I fed drinks to an old boat captain last night at Angry Nate's. He sold his boat, *The Last Hurrah*, to one of the people staying at the commune. Big guy, he says, name is Barnswollow. Anyway, tomorrow, this Barnswollow is taking the boat out. Told the captain he's bringing a friend with him, one Mr. Paul Armtrong."

"So enlighten me will you. What the fuck's your plan?"

"V came up with it," Stinger replied magnanimously. "We rent a couple WaveRunners from a place down in Christiansted Harbor and wait for *The Last Hurrah* to push out.

V moves into its path and fakes like his motor conked. He starts waving at them like he needs a tow. Once aboard, he'll take control. Then we approach and climb aboard."

"I only see two things wrong with the plan," Buddy replied skeptically. "First, we're gonna threaten Armstrong in front of a witness? And two, who is this guy anyway? He better not be anything like Armstrong's ex-police chief friend. Uncle Sal would have a shit fit. Pop all three of us. Fuckin' Uncle Sal."

"The captain said that Barnswollow used to be a crab boat captain up in Alaska. V'll make sure that he doesn't hear any of our conversation with Armstrong. When Armstrong finds out what we'll do to his wife and kid if he doesn't tell us where the money is, he'll cave like they all do."

After dropping Buddy at his hotel, Stinger and V drove into Christiansted. Reserving two WaveRunners for the next morning, they walked the boardwalk to The Brew Pub where they grabbed a hamburger and several beers.

"You know, V, you and I make a pretty good team. I'm gonna miss working with you when this is over. Maybe you can put in a good word with Buddy for me and get me transferred out to the northwest. Always thought I'd like it there."

V stared at him. They still had a job to do and V didn't want Stinger's sensitivity messing things up. Finally, he thought he had it right. "Don't take this the wrong way, Stinger, but I don't enjoy anybody's company, yours included."

23

"Release the bow," Barney ordered from the 35-foot vessel's helm.

"Bow is free," Sienna shouted, pulling in the rope and coiling it neatly on the foredeck.

"Release the stern," Barney ordered again.

"Stern is free," Claire called out. Placing the line into its hold, she joined Sienna who had already started pulling in the docking bumpers.

"Aye mates, 'tis a grand day for a voyage," Barney expounded from his perch, while taking in a deep breath of fresh sea air. They carefully passed between the channel markers leaving Christiansted Harbor.

Sienna had volunteered to take Paul's place during the shakedown when Paul was asked, last minute, to assist the coach at AJ's T-ball practice. For Claire, it was her first experience on open water. Barney moved Claire behind the wheel. "Relax, it's easier than driving a car. You're doing great."

Thirty minutes later, Sienna yelled from the foredeck, "Looks like someone's having engine trouble." Waving both arms, a man stood on a motionless WaveRunner a couple hundred yards off their port bow. Barney took over the helm and slowed to a stop alongside the small craft and cut the engines.

"She just conked out on me," the powerfully built man shouted from the personal watercraft.

"Throw us a line and you can come aboard. We'll give you a tow back to town," Barney shouted from the helm.

Expecting two men, V was startled by the two women. *Maybe Armstrong is below deck*, he hoped. "Appreciate your doing this," V said, as he took Sienna's offered hand and climbed aboard.

The loud whine of an approaching WaveRunner momentarily drew Barney's focus away from V. Removing the Glock 19 from his fanny pack, he stuck the automatic pistol squarely against the back of the big man's head and shouted, "Nobody move or I'll blow his fuckin' head off!"

Buddy carried a metal baseball bat as he and Stinger quickly boarded *The Last Hurrah*. With V keeping his gun on Barney, Stinger checked below. "Armstrong ain't onboard," he called up.

"Perfect," Buddy groaned. Recognizing Sienna from Stinger's reconnaissance photos, Buddy approached her with a plastic wrist restraint and placed a hand on her shoulder. "You let me know if this is too tight, Sweetheart." His palm traveled slowly down over her breast. Instinctively Sienna's knee slammed into Buddy's groin. "Bitch!" Buddy roared. Staggering, he kicked her hard in the abdomen, sending her gasping and moaning to the deck.

Watching the exchange, Stinger held the restraint motionless in front of Claire. She sank her teeth deep into his wrist. His howl drew V's attention. Barney spun quickly and smashed his huge fist into V's nose, sending him sprawling backwards onto the deck. Quickly closing on V, Barney was knocked off-course when Buddy slammed the baseball bat across the back of his head. The momentum of Barney's charge carried him overboard.

"Barney, No!" Claire pushed Stinger down the galley stairs and dove into the water after Barney.

Stinger slowly returned topside. "I think my tailbone's cracked."

"Your head will be next if you don't start paying better attention," Buddy threatened.

Stinger limped over to the rail. "I don't see 'em. Now what do we do?"

"V's hands were cupped over his shattered nose. Blood was pouring out between his fingers. "Let 'the fuckers drown."

Buddy crouched next to Sienna who lay in a fetal position sobbing. "Here's what you're gonna do. You're gonna tell your husband that Buddy wants the money he and Sherman stashed away. I'll be in touch with him in three days. If he disappoints me, this little incident will be the first of several mishaps. I'd put money on the next one involving AJ."

Stinger remained at the rail combing the water. "Boss, I haven't seen them come up. You want me to keep looking?"

Buddy stood. "Leave 'em for the sharks. There's no way she could make it to shore from here and he was as good as dead when he went over. Use the hose over there to douche the blood off the deck." He turned back to Sienna. "After we're gone, you take the boat back. You can do that, right?" Sienna didn't answer. Grabbing her hair, he jerked her up into a sitting position and slapped her hard across the face. "Do you fuckin' understand me?" he screamed. She nodded. Flashes of retinal light streaked across her vision.

"When you get back, the story you tell is that the skinny bitch fell overboard and the big guy went in after her. You saw

159

a big shark fin and they disappeared. You say anything about us and I promise you'll regret it." Buddy ran his index finger sideways across her throat. Laughing, he grabbed the bat and jumped on the WaveRunner behind Stinger.

As Buddy and his gang roared away, Sienna rose painfully from the deck. Holding little hope, she weakly called out, "Barney! Claire! Oh my god!"

Amazingly, from behind the boat she heard Claire shout back, "Sienna, we're here! Help me, Barney's not doing good! He's bleeding real bad!" Sienna spotted Claire holding Barney's head above water, just off the swim step. Using the power winch mounted on the rear of the boat, the two women were able to lift the unconscious giant onto the boat.

Claire wrapped Barney's head with a T-shirt, attempting to slow the bleeding. Racing back toward Christiansted, Sienna sent out a distress call on the ship to shore. "Mayday! Mayday! I have a skull fracture victim that I'm returning to Christiansted Harbor. Victim needs emergency treatment. I'm thirty minutes out and will need transport to the ER standing by."

Within minutes, their full-throttled return was stopped when a Coast Guard helicopter swooped overhead and dropped a rescue swimmer alongside the boat. After boarding *The Last Hurrah*, he strapped Barney into the lowered basket. As the three watched Barney disappear into the hovering craft, Sienna suddenly doubled over in pain. The alert Coast Guardsman signaled for the basket to be sent back down. While they waited, Claire helped Sienna to a cushion. Both women saw the gush of blood running down the inside of Sienna's leg. "Lie still," Claire said sadly.

24

Buddy's kick had caused a miscarriage and ruptured Sienna's spleen. Following a successful splenectomy, she awakened to an unshaven, bleary-eyed Paul, sitting beside the hospital bed.

"Barney?" she asked softly.

"He's still with us. I don't think Claire's left him for more than five minutes," Paul said, standing and taking her hand.

Lying comatose in another wing of the hospital, Barney was listed in critical condition after emergency surgery had stopped a cranial bleed and relieved the pressure from a subdural hematoma. According to the neurologist, it was too early to tell the extent of the damage. It wouldn't be until after the swelling abated that they would know the permanent impact, if any.

"Did she tell you how she did it? When she dove after Barney and disappeared, I thought they were both dead."

"Claire's a strong swimmer. She pulled Barney under the boat's swim step and kept his head above water until they left."

Sienna moaned and turned on her side. Paul, his face dark with fatigue and grief, gently stroked her hair.

"She's a third his size," Sienna said.

"If that."

"He killed our baby," Sienna choked.

Paul carefully lay behind her. He draped his arm over her side, gently resting his hand on her stomach.

Sienna brushed his hand away. "No, Paul."

He wished he could say or do something that would make her pain go away, but there was nothing. Pulling her knees close to her chest, Sienna repeated, "He killed our baby, our beautiful, beautiful baby . . . He killed our baby, our beautiful, beautiful baby." Helpless, he gently held her, his fury so close to the surface he could barely breathe.

A nurse appeared in the doorway and locked eyes with Paul. She dropped her head for a brief instant not wanting to interrupt the couple's intimacy. "The Doctor prescribed Demerol which should lesson Mrs. Armstrong's discomfort and help her rest."

Putting his arm behind her back and supporting her weight as she swallowed the medication, the once strong and vibrant Sienna felt small and fragile to Paul. After the nurse left, he pulled the chair beside the bed. "I've spoken to the doctors and they say you're going to make a full recovery."

"I'll never make a full recovery." Her tears flowed freely as Paul stroked her hair and gently held her hand. The medication soon took effect and her breathing slowed. Looking down at his sleeping wife, Paul left the room to call Andy.

"How is she, Son?"

"The doctors said there were no complications from the operation. I can't believe we've lost our baby." Paul worked hard to compose himself. "But she's young and strong and they expect a full recovery."

"Well there's a bunch of us down here in the lobby that love her and want to see her when she's ready."

"I'll come down now and give everyone an update, but there's no reason to stay. She's not up to seeing anyone but AJ tonight. Could you and Aunt Charlotte stay a little longer so AJ can go home with you?"

"Of course. Claire was down here for a little while. She said Barney's still in critical condition, but they think he's got a chance to make it back one-hundred percent."

"He has to. I'm coming down now. See you in a few minutes."

"Listen, I want you to promise to keep me in the loop on all this Buddy Falco stuff. I know Hank's your man, but I've dealt with my share of bad pennies too."

Returning to Sienna's room with Paul, AJ wordlessly crawled up on the bed, into Sienna's waiting arms while Paul leaned motionless against the far wall and stared out the hospital window.

******

Awakening at dawn, Sienna's bloodshot eyes held Paul's gaze. "Have you heard from Hank and Roxanne?"

"They were downstairs last night with Red, AJ, Andy, Aunt Charlotte, your parents, your sisters and most of their families. Everyone was here for hours until I told them to go home and get some rest. Knowing your family, they're probably already here, holding vigil until they can see you with their own eyes."

Reaching for Paul's hand, Sienna started to cry. "I'm so afraid Paul. Did you explain to Hank why we told the police it was an attempted boat theft?"

"He wasn't in total agreement, but he accepted the decision. He did agree that the police couldn't do much to stop them if they decided to carry out their threats."

Seeing the worry on her face, Paul added, "Look, Hank and I are working on a plan that will keep us all safe. You just need to rest and get well."

"I know you're both doing your best, but what if it's not enough? I can't stop thinking about his threats. If anything happened to AJ . . ."

******

Since hearing of the attack, Andy and Aunt Charlotte had taken care of AJ, while Paul stayed at Sienna's hospital bedside. Hank joined Paul late into the second evening to discuss potential responses to the attack. There weren't any good ones. "The best I can come up with is to contact Buddy's Uncle Sal and hope that he can rein-in the psychopath. Word's out that Sal's already pretty pissed off with Buddy, but blood runs thick with these people. Sal may have his agenda to clean up the image of the syndicate, but when push comes to shove these types usually stick together. Look Paul, they hold all the cards as long as we don't involve the police."

"They hold all the cards then. Sienna won't go for it. She's convinced Buddy will hurt AJ."

"I'll try and reach Sal. In the meantime, you need to get some sleep."

"Weren't you and Roxanne supposed to head over to St. Thomas?"

"We'll reschedule. I don't want to leave you with Buddy on island."

"Absolutely not. You're not staying here. You need to have a follow up with your doctor and Roxanne's had those appointments set up with Red's pediatrician for weeks. If anything comes up, I'll call you. They're not going to come gunning for me as long as they think I'm going to lead them to Andrew's money."

"Well, it'll be just a couple nights. You make sure to call me immediately if Buddy contacts you or anything else comes up."

On the third day, Barney regained consciousness. A relieved Claire was still unwilling to give up her permanent residence in his room. "She's fussing over me like a damn hen with her chicks," Barney complained.

Driving home to shower and change, Paul received a call on his cell. Contemplating letting it go to voicemail, he changed his mind. "This is Paul."

"Good morning, Mr. Armstrong. Do you have my money?"

"Who is this?"

"Who the fuck do you think it is? Say, that's good news about the big guy and his girl being alive. I have a friend who may want to pay him a visit concerning his smashed nose. What do the cops know?"

"It was an attempted boat theft by three masked men in a cigar boat," Paul answered, through gritted teeth.

"Good boy. That better be all they ever think. So, now, about the money—"

"I don't know a thing about it. I had nothing to do with Andrew's faked death. I thought he was dead until I saw him last summer."

"Wrong answer. I don't know, maybe all this sunshine down here has me in a good mood so I'm going to give you a little friendly advice. I say that Sherman had at least a million squirreled away and I say that you know where it is. So, here's my final offer: There's a beach called Ha'Penny on the south side of the island. You know it?"

"Yes."

"Good. Me and my boys will be waiting there at the far west end of the beach, day after tomorrow at seven in the morning. You show up alone with the money and I doubt we'll have any more problems. Believe me, Armstrong, this is your best option." The line went dead.

******

Paul found Andy on his front porch reading an old dog-eared Louis L'Amour paperback. "Sit down, Paul. You look weary, Son."

"I just got a call from Buddy Falco. He wants me to deliver one million dollars to him the day after tomorrow."

"A million, eh? I can get you three hundred thousand by then and the rest next week. That'll satisfy the crook. We've got to get this guy out of our life, and if buying him off is the way to do it, well, I'm just glad I have the where-with-all to take care of it."

They talked over the details. Andy was worried about the remoteness of the meeting location and insisted that Paul carry a pistol with him. Returning from inside, he placed a familiar .38 special on the table along with a box of bullets.

"It's the gun you used for target practice up at my range in Winthrop. It's no automatic, but you hit someone in the stomach with one of these soft tips, it'll stop 'em all right. How about I tag along?"

"Thanks Andy, but he said for me to come alone." Paul shook his head slowly. "This whole thing just isn't right."

"Yeah, sometimes you've got to plug your nose and do whatever it takes, even when it stinks."

******

Early Wednesday morning, Paul drove Andy's Yamaha ATV into the back of his truck and tied it down. The sun was still low in the sky as Paul set out for Ha'penny. The drive took less than 30 minutes. When he arrived at 6:45, a Jeep SUV was already there, its hood warm to the touch. He offloaded the ATV and put the satchel with Andy's money in the front carrier rack. Rounding a point, the end of the beach came into view. Three figures stood near the water's edge. As he drew closer, they separated and stood facing him, fifty feet from where he stopped.

Barney had done a job on the face of the largest of the three whose blackened eyes peered past a taped-on nose cast. Paul recognized Stinger from their meeting on Cooper Island. He'd never met Buddy Falco, but had seen his picture on the internet enough times to recognize him.

"Thought you'd be on foot, not barefoot," Buddy joked, noticing Paul's lack of footwear poking out from the legs of his coveralls.

"He's turned into a real island boy," Stinger added. "Married the native princess and the whole nine yards."

"That the money?" Buddy asked, as the three approached.

Something about Paul arriving on the ATV in coveralls tugged at V. Paul pulled the valise from the carrier rack and placed it on the handlebars. Unzipping a front pocket, he hesitated only an instant before pulling out the .38. From 15 feet he felt comfortable taking Buddy first with a head shot. V was desperately trying to clear his Beretta from the back of his waistband, when Paul's second shot caught him in the chest. The third bullet severed Stinger's spine as he turned to run. Paul walked over to V, who was writhing in agony, yet somehow still trying to clear his gun and shot him through the temple. He looked at the entry hole just above Buddy's right brow and added another one between his eyes. Paralyzed but alive, Stinger pleaded with him, "Please, I never hurt nobody."

"Bullshit," Paul replied coldly, then put the gun to the side of Stinger's head and pulled the trigger.

From the ATV's rear rack, Paul removed three large plastic bags that he'd brought from the battery storage room. After shoving the bodies into the bags, he sealed each with duct tape then stacked and secured the bodies onto the ATV's rear rack with large bungee cords. Confident the sea would quickly wash away any evidence on the isolated beach, Paul waded into the surf and rinsed off the blood and gore. Returning the ATV to the parking lot, he backed onto the truck bed and stacked the body bags behind the cab. After covering them with a blue tarp, he changed out of the coveralls and stashed them in a garbage bag.

Amazingly calm through the shooting, Paul now had to grip the steering wheel tightly to keep his hands from shaking. He was surprised to be alive as he drove back to Windsol. He had realized, after the attack on Barney and Sienna and the murder of their baby, that somehow he would do this. Once he knew where the meeting would take place, he was able to figure out the details. Blinded by grief and rage, he was unconcerned that he had little chance of success going up against three seasoned gangsters. Whatever happened to him would be worth the chance of freeing Sienna, AJ and his friends from Buddy Falco and Company. He had counted on the element of surprise, that no big time gangster would consider a law-abiding family man any kind of a threat.

"Guess you figured that one wrong, Buddy!" Paul shouted as he pulled the half empty fifth of rum from the glove compartment.

25

When he'd lost his business and marriage; Paul had been careful not to look for solace in a bottle. *Fuck it. I just murdered three people.* After the fourth swig his hands stopped shaking. He took one more pull as he drove through Windsol's entry gate and parked at the far end of the property, downwind from the cabins. Grabbing the valise, Paul made his way to Andy's cabin. He knew that Aunt Charlotte had already left to take AJ to school. He found Andy as expected, drinking coffee on his front porch.

Paul climbed the three steps, dropped the valise on the table and collapsed in a chair. Andy looked him over and then walked inside. He reappeared ten minutes later with a cup of coffee, scrambled eggs, bacon and toast which he set in front of Paul, who hadn't moved an inch.

"Pretty early in the morning for that, ain't it?" Andy asked, catching a whiff of Paul's breath.

Paul shrugged his shoulders, picked up the fork and started eating.

"Seems like all the money's still here," Andy said, opening the valise. "Six bullets are gone," he added, looking at Paul.

"Two for each of them," Paul replied between bites. "I need your help tonight, Andy."

Andy took a deep breath and let it out slowly. "Whatever you need, I'm here for you. Before you say anything more though, I think I need to catch up." Andy went inside and came back with a bottle of Jameson and two glasses.

******

"Char's a sound sleeper. Doubt she'll miss me, but just in case I left a note saying you needed to talk and not to worry," Andy explained, as the two met at midnight. With a new moon, the only light illuminating their work was the small battery-powered lantern that Andy carried. Paul took the upper-body end of each bag while Andy did his best to keep the leg-end from catching on sharp rocks as they dragged the bodies 200 feet down the rugged footpath to the shore below. Painfully slow, it was two hours before the first body-bag was loaded into the Zodiac that Paul kept hidden in a shallow cave at the base of the cliff. Earlier in the day, he'd brought down a half-dozen, 25 pound concrete slump-test cylinders that had been used to verify the strength of Windsol's concrete. Two cylinders and eighteen-inch lengths of nylon rope were loaded with the body. Paul started the outboard and nodding back to Andy who sat on a large rock at the water's edge holding the illuminated lantern, motored away from shore on his first of three trips. Two hundred yards offshore the ocean's depth plunged thousands of feet, but Paul took no chances and didn't cut the engine until he had been underway for ten minutes. He could still see Andy's lantern which he would use as a beacon when he returned for the second body. He rested the bag on the seat with the leg-end hanging out over the Zodiac's side. Cutting open the bag with a box knife, the odor caused him to vomit over the side until there was nothing left in his stomach. Momentarily lightheaded, he splashed water on his face and took a couple deep breaths before tying a concrete cylinder to each leg and sliding the body overboard. Between the pressure and sea-predators, there would be little left of the body by the time the concrete cylinders hit the ocean floor.

After Paul's final trip, Andy helped him wash out the Zodiac with sea-water and pull it back into the cave. They climbed the path from the beach and walked silently to Paul's cabin for a night-cap. "I killed a man once," Andy confessed, after they finished their first drink.

"When was that?"

"Back in the late forties when I was deputy sheriff in Okanogan County. There was this twelve year old girl who lived with her mom and little brother. Her dad had been killed in the war and it wasn't easy for her mom. I think the little girl's name was Ellen. She was, well, developed for her age, but not quite right up here," Andy said, pointing at his temple. "Anyways, this mean son-of-a-bitch, guy named Rupert Small, picked her up after school one day and takes her out to the reservoir and has his way with her. I get a call from the sheriff saying I should head out there. Somebody reported a woman screaming. Now, I'd been a deputy sheriff for a few years by then and had seen a lot of bad apples, but when I got out there, I found this poor scared girl naked and beat up. 'Mr. Rupert hurt me and took my clothes,' she kept repeating. I got a blanket around her and took her home. Then I drove over to Rupert's place, a piece of shit cabin with filth and garbage strewn all over the yard. When he answered the door I grabbed him by his hair and threw him hard on the ground. 'Why'd you do that?' he says. 'The little bitch's too stupid to know what I done to her.' To this day, I don't know what got into me. No witnesses, so I claimed he rushed me. Never felt good about lying though. Wanted to say, 'Hell yes, I shot him, and the world's a better place because of it.' Anyways, that pretty much finished my career in law enforcement. I guess the sheriff realized that I was too short fused and was glad to accept my resignation. Too bad though, I really looked good in that uniform."

Paul laughed darkly, "Kill anybody since then?"

"Not that I know of," Andy replied. "I guess what I'm trying to say is I know what it feels like to have killed a man. You can always talk to me about it if need be. Yes sir, that was a brave thing you did."

"I don't know how brave it was. I thought I'd feel better if I killed them." Paul drained the whisky glass and held it out for a refill. "I'm glad it's over, but I don't feel any better."

"You've been through hell, Son. Suffered a tremendous loss. It'll take some time before things seem right again, but you and Sienna will make it through all this."

"That's another thing. I've never kept anything from Sienna. This will be the first. She has enough to deal with. Can't imagine telling her that I just murdered three men and they're sleeping with the fishes."

"I don't know," Andy replied. "She's a pretty amazing woman, that one. Give her some time and maybe tell her later. You might be surprised by her reaction."

"I'm worried she'll never feel the same about me. Hell, I don't feel the same about me. Jesus, Andy, I'm a fuckin' murderer."

Andy reached over and refilled Paul's empty glass. "Then so is every war veteran who's killed an enemy. I'll tell you this, Paul Armstrong; you don't need a declaration of war to feel justified in sending those three to the great beyond."

The two men drank silently until Paul, hearing Andy's snores, took the half-filled glass out of his old friend's hand, set it on the table and gently shook him awake. Andy patted Paul on his shoulder and quietly returned to his cabin.

26

Waking late the next morning, Paul called the nurse's station on Sienna's floor saying he would be in within the hour. Hoping *a little hair of the dog* would lessen his splitting headache, he added a couple shots of Jameson before gulping down microwaved, two day-old coffee.

He walked down the path to Andy and Aunt Charlotte's cabin. "AJ's just finishing his breakfast. I woke up at seven and drove over to Lenay's to pick him up. Thought you could use the extra sleep. You boys were out late last night. Andy's still sleeping. Why don't you sit down and join me for a minute."

"Don't have much time," he replied, finding a chair across the table from her.

"AJ, Paul's here."

"Am I going to school or are we going to see Mommy?" AJ yelled from the inside the cabin.

"It's Friday, AJ. I'm taking you to school," Paul answered. "But I'll pick you up after school and then we'll go see her together."

"Are you all right, Dear?" Charlotte asked, covering Paul's hand with hers. "I know how hard this has been on you, but Andy and I are worried that you're not taking good care of yourself. You're carrying a tremendous burden and you need to make sure you stay strong and healthy for your family."

"Don't worry, I'm OK. Sienna'll be home soon and Hank and I are working on a way to keep Buddy Falco out of our lives."

"I spoke with Hank at the hospital and he's worried about you as well. He didn't seem as confident about Buddy Falco. Have you been drinking this morning?"

"I had a little whisky in my stale coffee." Paul pulled his hand back. "Look, I'm doing the best I can. What I really need is for everybody to stop worrying about me. I'm fine."

"Don't use that tone of voice with me, Mister. We're only worried because we love you."

"Why are you worried about Paul?" AJ joined them on the porch, wearing his school backpack.

Paul dropped to his haunches, "Aunt Charlotte is worried that I'm not eating enough good food because Mommy isn't home to help cook."

"P.U.", AJ gasped, waving his hand at Paul. "Your breath stinks."

Paul's face reddened as he straightened up and walked down the stairs. "Thank Aunt Charlotte, AJ. I don't want you late for school."

AJ watched Paul walk away and then looked up at Aunt Charlotte. "What's wrong with Paul? He seems mad."

"Paul," Aunt Charlotte called after him, "Why don't I take AJ to school?"

"Fine."

As he rode the elevator up to Sienna's floor, Paul reminded himself to apologize next time he saw Aunt Charlotte. Her concern was justified. Hell, he was concerned about himself too.

Paul heard a familiar voice he couldn't quite place as he approached the doorway into Sienna's room. Attorney Casey Joseph, Sienna's former boyfriend, sat beside Sienna's bed. Her reddened eyes were full of tears.

"Paul, you remember Casey," Sienna said.

Attorney Joseph stood quickly, too quickly Paul imagined. "Just checking on our girl here. Making sure she's doin' OK."

Our girl? Paul thought before replying. "Nice of you to come by. I'm sure Sienna appreciated your visit." It was the best he could come up with.

An awkward pause followed before Sienna said, "Casey's been in D.C. working on a grant for bicycle trails on St. Croix."

"My Mom told me about the attack on Sienna and her friends. I came home as soon as I heard."

"From D.C.?" Paul asked incredulously. "Isn't that what phones are for?"

"Well, I didn't know how serious it was and I wanted to see if I could help," Casey answered defensively. "Anyway, it's good to see some color in her cheeks, so I'll be leaving now."

Sienna extended her hand. "Thanks for coming by. Please excuse Paul, neither one of us is up to par right now. Say 'hi' to your Mom for me."

Casey took her offered hand and kissed the back of it. Paul handed him his briefcase and led him into the hall.

"Sorry about that, in there." Paul said. "Like she said, I'm not myself right now."

"That's not any of my concern. That's one incredible woman and I'd hate to think that she doesn't have someone protecting her from shit like this."

"She does, and it's me."

The two men glared at each other until Casey shot Paul a dismissive glance, "We'll see."

Paul's fists clenched. *Hell, I just killed three gangsters, how much more trouble could I be in if I deck this asshole.* Instead, he turned back into the room, proud of his self-control. He wasn't prepared for Sienna's reaction. "What the hell was all that about, Paul? That man was a friend long before we ever met. You embarrassed me. It sounded like you two were going to duke it out in the hall."

"Look, I'm sorry about the telephone comment, but what's with this kissing your hand business? The man isn't French."

"No, he isn't, is he?" she said, almost smiling. "Well, he probably still has a little something for me. But, I heard what my brave man told him out in the hall."

"Don't think it impressed him much."

"You don't need to impress him at all. I know what you said is true . . . but there are things that happen we just can't see coming," Sienna said sadly.

"Knock-knock," Claire announced her entry. "Well, good morning, you two. I'm headed home for a shower and some sleep. Barney's cranky as hell and kicked me out." Seeing the sadness on Sienna's face, she asked, "Is this a bad time?"

"Absolutely not," Sienna replied. "You just caught me in a moment. Actually, I may be out of here today after the doctor sees me. How are you doing?"

"I'm great. Barney wants me to start going out with Captain Marvin on *The Last Hurrah*. Says I need to learn the ropes if I'm going to run things when he's away. I think he's just tired of my asking if he's OK every time he groans."

After Claire left, Sienna told Paul, "I've really enjoyed her company. She's come by my room several times. Calls it her 'Barney break.'"

"I don't see how she could have slept much lately. In the past, one of the symptoms of her mania is that she doesn't sleep. She seems a little spun up to me."

"I know that she already contacted the psychiatrist that her doctor referred her to. His name is Pierre Brusseau."

"See, if Pierre Brusseau kissed your hand, I wouldn't have a problem."

180

"Funny boy. She said she'll start meeting with him every week. She likes him a lot. Besides medication, he believes that her bipolar disorder can be treated with meditation as well as nutrition and exercise."

"Sounds like a good match from what Barney told me. How are you feeling today?"

"I'm really sore," Sienna said, gulping back tears and touching her abdomen. "The meds help, but emotionally, not so good. I'm just so sad we lost our baby. I don't know how I'm going to ever get over this." Paul sat on the bed and took her hand. They sat quietly until Sienna asked, "Has Hank talked to this Sal-guy about stopping the attacks?"

"He was going to. I'll find out when I talk to him later today."

"I hope it was a good idea not involving the police. It seems like we're pinning all our hopes on one crook's promise to keep us safe from another crook." Paul remained silent. "And this whole thing about the money . . . what reason does he have to believe that we know anything about it?"

"Hank thinks because Andrew turned up in the BVI's and I ended up on St. Croix, Buddy's convinced that I planned the whole thing with him."

"We've got to figure out a plan. I'm really frightened he'll hurt AJ."

"Sienna, you heard what I told the hand-kisser didn't you? Buddy and his sidekicks will never get near either one of you again. I promise."

181

Sienna placed her hand on his shoulder and kissed him. "It shouldn't be all on you, Paul. I'm sorry I'm not more help. I've never felt as helpless as I do right now."

******

Paul was happy to find Barney pissed off. An angry Barney was a stronger Barney and he had a lot to be mad about.

"Goddamn bedpans and old-people food. This is a hell of a way to spend time in paradise. Tell you what though, soon as I get out, I'm going to look up Mr. Buddy Falco. Don't give a shit if he's connected to the mob. I'm gonna' tear his fuckin' arms off and stuff them up his ass."

"Has the doctor given you an idea of when you'll be out of here?"

"A punk-assed kid, just out of med school, that's who I've got telling me what to do and when to do it. Don't get me wrong, he's done a good job, but I'll leave here as soon as I think I'm ready."

"Jesus, Barney, you were bashed in the head. Don't you think it'd be smart to listen to someone who has studied this kind of trauma?"

Barney changed the subject. "I sent Claire home."

"Yeah, she came up to Sienna's room before she left."

"Well, I told her to go home, take a shower and get some sleep. Was kind of tough with her. Jesus, the woman saved my life, but I hate being fussed over. 'Let me help you eat. Now you've got food in your beard. Here, let me brush it out. Want some help in the bathroom?"'

Paul fought the urge to tell his best friend the fate of Buddy and his associates.

"Yoo-hoo . . . Paul . . . Hello? Anybody home?"

"I'm sorry, what did you say?"

"Jesus, you'd think you were the one got knocked on the head. I asked you how Sienna's doing."

"She'll recover from losing her spleen, but I don't think she'll ever get over losing the baby."

"Yeah . . . and you?"

"I'm the least of my worries. I can't help feeling that I brought all this shit down on us. Maybe if I'd—"

"Don't go there, Amigo. This isn't anything close to your fault. The fact of the matter is that there are murderous assholes in the world and sometimes you can't avoid them. Listen, I know that stringing Buddy Falco up by his balls won't bring the baby back, but I promise you the son of a bitch will feel as much pain as he can take before checking into his suite at Dante's Inferno."

"Thanks, Barney. At least that's something we can look forward to."

"Goddamn right. I'll teach that piece of shit and the whole fuckin' mafia, if need be, they fucked with the wrong family."

As Paul drove Sienna back to Windsol, he thought about his conversation with Barney. If Paul had any doubts whether killing the three gangsters was the right thing to do, his conversation with Barney had convinced him that it was. He was certain that his giant friend's promise to torture and kill Buddy, even if it meant taking on the mafia, wasn't an idle threat. Murdering the three men had also saved Barney's life.

27

It was their first dinner together since the attack. Afterward, AJ and Red cleared the dishes while Andy, Claire and Roxanne cleaned up. Sienna, still weak from the surgery, rested on a chaise while Paul and Hank walked out to the viewing platform. Hank stood at the rail looking out to St. Thomas, St. John and Tortola, all a little more than forty miles away. Paul, lost in thought, followed the visible portions of the footpath down to the beach.

"So I spoke with Uncle Sal. He says that Buddy didn't have anything to do with the attack. It figures, right? But he agreed to talk to him and see if Buddy has any ideas that might help us out."

"I appreciate your calling him, Hank. It doesn't sound like he'll do much, but at least now he's aware of what his nephew's been up to."

"Yeah, that and a ten dollar bill might get you forty quarters. You know, I've never been one for people arming themselves . . . Too many cases where a gun bought for protection ends up killing the person or a family member. That being said, I think it might be a good idea for you to accompany me over to the gun range and start the process for a concealed weapons permit. You ever shoot a pistol?"

"Yeah, some. Andy's into guns. He's got a rifle range on his land in Winthrop and brought down a few with him."

"Well I'd like to see what he has sometime. What do you think? Want to start tomorrow morning? . . . Paul?"

He remembered the six deafening booms from the pistol; how quickly and easily he had ended their lives. "Oh, sorry, what'd you say?"

"I asked if you wanted to join me at the gun range tomorrow morning? You OK there, buddy? Don't stroke out on me now. We'll get through this."

"Sorry. Just have a lot on my mind. Sure, tomorrow morning's fine."

"You know Paul, Roxanne and I talked about it and for the time being, we'd like to bunk down at the community house where I can keep an eye on the entry gate. You did a great job locating the cabins for maximum privacy, but I feel too isolated to be of any help. Also, I'd keep AJ close by. Don't let him go wandering around in the woods. At least until we have reason to believe that Buddy has lost interest."

"According to what he told Sienna, that won't be until he has this money he thinks I have. Which I don't, by the way." Paul hated stringing Hank along, wasting his time at a gun range and moving into the guest house. But there was no statute of limitations on murder and he could never put Hank

186

in the position of choosing between their friendship and his beliefs as a former officer of the law.

"Yeah, I know. What a fucked situation."

"Hey, Boys, dessert's ready." Roxanne approached the platform. "Are you two lords of the manor going to grace us with your presence or would like your ice cream and berries brought to you by us kitchen slaves?"

"How about you have a couple bedroom slaves bring the dessert down instead?" Hank winked at Paul.

"Now Hanky-Bear," Roxanne replied in a stern voice as she stopped within striking distance, "You'll get your *just desserts* immediately if you don't load up all those clever jokes and make tracks back to the terrace."

Hand in hand, Hank and Roxanne left to join the others while Paul lingered behind. He stopped suddenly, when a shiny object on the ground caught his eye. Bending down, he picked up a small piece of Chaney. Recalling how much he had enjoyed AJ's excitement when they hunted for Chaney together, he began to cry. Unable to stop, he walked back to the platform and faced the vast sea and sky. "Where did I go? What am I now?" Stinger's final plea, *Please, I never hurt nobody*, came back to him. Tightly closing his eyes, Paul tried to squeeze the words from his memory. Instead, the image of Stinger's ruined body stood before Paul and answered him, *You're a murderer.*

******

He couldn't fall asleep. Not wanting to bother Sienna, Paul grabbed his swimsuit and quietly left their bedroom. Taking a bottle of rum and an ice-filled glass onto the porch, he felt himself relax as the amber liquor calmed him. *So what now?* Taking stock of his life, it wasn't difficult to realize how fortunate he was. Making a family with Sienna and AJ brought him more joy than he had dreamed possible. He loved Windsol and all its occupants. His architectural work on the island was enjoyable, but not all-consuming-like his practice had been in the states. He enjoyed his music, golf, ocean swimming and island friends. He poured his second, then third drink. Returning inside, he found his iPhone and ear buds, brought them out to the porch and listened to old favorites by Tom Petty, Neil Young, and Stevie Ray Vaughan. He refreshed his glass with ice and downed two more drinks. "Hell, what am I so down about? I rid the planet of three scumballs. I'm a fuckin' hero."

The sky was starting to lighten when he decided to move his one-man party to the swimming pool. Normally, Paul would swim laps for an hour, but after conking his head in the shallow end attempting a drunken flip-turn, he once again shifted the venue. Putting his headphones back on, he moved into the heated whirlpool, which is where he finally fell asleep and where Sienna found her snoring husband the next morning.

"Paul. Wake up." She gently nudged him. "You can't fall asleep in the hot tub. You'll drown."

Still drunk and barely awake, he looked at her with one heavy lidded eye and muttered, "Morning, Beautiful. Wanna soak with me?"

Hank and Roxanne, returning from their morning walk heard voices by the pool and came to investigate. "Oh, it's just you two." Hank said, relieved.

"Who'd ya think it was, ol' Hanky-Bear?" Paul slurred.

"I think Paul was up drinking most of the night," Sienna explained.

"Well, I think he's probably not going to be awake much longer from the looks of things," Roxanne observed. "Come on Hank, let's help Paul back to their cabin." They started out by each taking an arm, but Paul shrugged them off, insisting he could walk unaided.

"Really, I insisssssst."

Once they were in the cabin, Paul needed to use the bathroom, "Immediately!"

Sienna went back to check on Paul a few minutes later and found him passed-out, face down on the bed, naked except for one sandal.

Roxanne was brewing coffee when Sienna reappeared after tucking Paul into bed. Hank sat at the kitchen table reading one of Paul's golf magazines. "Well, that's a first," Sienna reported. "Paul's usually the designated driver when we go out. Guess he had trouble sleeping."

"Might have trouble when he wakes up too," Hank replied. "I saw an empty fifth of rum out on the table. How much of that was last night?"

"I don't know how much was there when he started," Sienna said. "But judging from the shape he's in, I'd guess more than half."

"Well, I think you'd both benefit from a day of doing absolutely nothing together. Hank and I can fill in for you two today."

"Thanks Roxanne. Maybe you guys could take AJ and Red to the beach and I'll rest with Paul. I know how hard this has been on him. I guess he just needed to blow off some steam. I've been so down that I've barely considered what he must be going through. All I seem to do is cry."

A sleepy-eyed AJ came out from his room and started to climb into his mom's lap. "Good morning, Honey." Sienna stood and hugged him. "My stomach isn't strong enough yet for you to sit in my lap. What would you like for breakfast?"

"Waffles or pancakes please."

"Say AJ, how about you put on your clothes and head over to the community house with us and we'll fix you and Red some waffles?" Roxanne suggested.

"S'that OK, Mommy?"

"Sure, Honey. After breakfast, maybe you and Red can look for Chaney over by the ruin."

"Yippee!" AJ squealed, running back into his bedroom to dress.

"We'll keep an eye on them, don't worry," Hank said. "I'd like to find some of that Chaney stuff myself. Maybe have a bracelet or something made out of it for my woman here."

"My woman here?" Roxanne lamented. "Sometimes I think I'm married to a Neanderthal . . . or maybe Tarzan."

******

It was early afternoon when Paul awoke to find Sienna sleeping beside him. He slowly rolled out of bed. Sienna, passed him as he returned from the bathroom.

"How are you feeling?"

"Not so good. I think I was way over-served." He clamped his palm over his eyes. "Where's AJ?"

"He went with Roxanne and Hank."

Paul's cell rang. "I'd better get that."

"Good morning bright eyes!" Barney's voice boomed painfully into Paul's ear. "I spoke with Hank and he told me about your little night of shame."

Paul initially thought Barney was referring to the dumping of the bodies, but fortunately his rum-soaked brain kicked in. Fingering the bump on his forehead he replied, "Yeah, I was a one-man wrecking crew. I think I banged my head on the bottom of the pool."

"Well, Hank and I want an invitation next time you decide to party. By the way, Claire's here and it looks like I'm getting sprung today. Should be home in a couple hours."

"That's great, Barney. I'll see you when you get here. Feeling a little on the low side right now. Let's talk later. Bye."

"Wait, Ace. I haven't gotten to what I called you about. Check out this morning's paper when you get a chance. Hank called me, I guess because he figured you were sleeping. Anyway, a deserted Jeep was found at one of the beaches. The missing driver is one Clark Crabtree. Hank said that he's probably the smaller guy who came aboard *The Last Hurrah* with Falco. Says he goes by the name of Stinger. Here, I'll read it to you, *Police are investigating the disappearance of Clark Crabtree, a resident of Newark, New Jersey. The car he rented was found abandoned in the parking area of Ha'penny beach.* It goes on to say that a cop patrolling the area had noticed the car yesterday morning, but thought it belonged to somebody on the beach. By late-afternoon the beach was empty so he ran the plates. They've listed this Stinger guy as missing."

"Huh. Wonder what that means?"

"Wait, there's more. So Hank calls up the Chief of Police and has a cop-to-cop discussion with him. Turns out that the Chief's no dummy and has already found out about Stinger's priors and mob associations. Also, he goes off the record with Hank and tells him that they'd already searched the car and Stinger's condo. A neighbor tells the police that he was sharing the condo with a large man recovering from a nose job. Get this, they found several firearms with the serial numbers filed off, including a .338 Lapua Magnum which, if you remember, is the same cartridge that killed Sherman."

"Jesus, I wonder where Buddy is?"

"There was no mention of Falco in any of this and Hank didn't want to bring his name up with the Chief. Didn't want Buddy thinking one of us tipped them off. Ok, so get this, the police also found a light dusting of cocaine powder on the passenger seat of the car."

"Buddy probably sneezed," Paul speculated.

"Right, but it has the cops thinking that Crabtree and his roommate might be victims of a drug deal gone bad."

When Paul returned to the bedroom, he relayed his conversation with Barney to Sienna.

"Do you think that's what happened, a drug deal gone bad?"

"Whatever happened," Paul replied, "I think something has fouled up their plans to come after us. I think we may hear more in the next couple of days, especially if Buddy was in the car with them."

******

It didn't take a couple days. "Sal called and said he can't get a hold of Buddy," Hank reported to Paul and Sienna after bringing AJ home. "He knows that Stinger and V are missing and wanted to know if I knew anything. I told him only what I read in the paper."

"What do you make of it?" Sienna asked.

"Not sure, but if they tried to score some coke they may have run into some 'respect issues' dealing with suppliers down here. The syndicate doesn't have much muscle in this region and Buddy's used to receiving special treatment. Might have pissed off the wrong people."

"We can only hope," Sienna replied.

28

Paul held up two fingers signaling a double shot of Single Barrel as he took a barstool at *The Wall*, a local hangout just up the beach from *The Green Flash*. He had made a recent habit of stopping in for two or three shots before his first set. Sometimes, he would stop there on his way home from a jobsite and sometimes he went there for no reason at all.

Three days after the mobsters' disappearance, Barney and Claire identified all three gangsters as the perpetrators of their attack. "With Buddy apparently out of the picture, you have no reason to lie about what happened," Hank had advised. "Hell, the detectives might figure it out themselves. What if the proprietor of the WaveRunner rental company recognizes one of them from their picture in the paper? You don't want the police wondering why you lied."

******

An unsuccessful two month investigation by the St. Croix Police Department followed. With no useful evidence or leads turning up which might shed light on Buddy and his accomplices' disappearance, the initial theory of a drug deal gone bad was still believed to be the most likely cause. Even so, the investigation was still on the police chief's front burner because of the stateside publicity Buddy's disappearance was receiving.

With the two doubles already improving his outlook, Paul ordered a third which he downed quickly. Sienna had continued to struggle with her sadness over the loss of their unborn child. Paul still hadn't told her about the murders, rationalizing that it would only add to her misery. This omission had opened a chasm between them, adding to her sorrow and his feelings of guilt and isolation. Staying busy, rushing through each day from one task to another and consuming copious amounts of alcohol had become his mainstays.

Not understanding the cause, his friends and family also watched helplessly as Paul pulled further and further away. Only Andy understood the cause of his malaise. Before returning to Winthrop for the summer with Char, he encouraged Paul to tell Sienna the truth. "No man's an island, Son. You're losing your grip. As much as I enjoy being your confidant, Sienna's your soul mate. You need her to help you get through this."

Earlier in the week, Paul had driven Barney and Claire to the airport for their return to the farm in Washington State. The exotic flower business that Barney had started with his sister-in-law, Brooke, was booming and she needed help with deliveries and new orders. Also, he had promised her teenage son a horse camping trip through The Pasayten Wilderness in Eastern Washington with Kate and Andy. "We'll be back early fall and put *The Last Hurrah* through her paces," he promised Paul as they said their goodbyes.

"I'll be studying for my boat captain's license," Claire added excitedly. "We'll start booking fishing trips online before we return."

"Claire, give me a minute with Paul, will you?" Barney asked after Claire and Paul hugged good bye.

Claire kissed Paul on the cheek. "Take care of yourself," she added holding him at arm's length, a worried expression on her face. "You're the best ex-husband a woman could ever have." Hugging him a final time, she turned and walked through the *Passengers Only* door.

Paul followed Barney over to an isolated bench. "Look Amigo, I'm worried about you. I don't want to say snap out of it, but truthfully, you've got too many good things in your life to be dragged down by what those fuckin' animals, those sub-humans, did. I know a little guy that wants you to adopt him, and Sienna, well, she'll come around. You two can always try again."

Paul, fought the urge to snap, *mind your own fuckin' business Mr. Sunshine,* but instead replied, "I appreciate your concern Barney, just need a little more time, that's all. Look, you better get going. Claire is probably thinking you chickened out on the flight. Look, don't worry . . . I'll figure this thing out. Safe travels and I'll see you in the fall." Paul turned to walk away.

"They weren't human Paul," Barney called after him.

******

Now, three days later and halfway through his third double, he repeated what he had said under his breath while walking away from Barney. "If only."

"If only what?" Carley, the bartender asked.

"If only it were a half-hour earlier. I'd have another."

"Aren't you playing tonight?" she asked, clearing his empty glass and wiping the bar.

"Supposed to." Paul noticed a slight slur in his answer.

"Better have some coffee then, Hon." Carley poured a black cupful of Puerto Rico's finest.

The coffee helped and Paul would probably have made it through all three sets just fine if Attorney Casey Joseph hadn't walked into *The Green Flash*. Paul watched the big man lift Sienna off the ground with his hug, then high-fived three regulars at the bar.

Paul couldn't stop himself. "I'd like to dedicate this song to a very special Crucian." He began the acapella intro to The Beatle's *Nowhere Man*. Staring at Attorney Joseph through most of the song, the dedication's reference was not lost on the muscular attorney. Neither was his middle finger lost on Paul.

This isn't me, Paul thought, as he set his guitar on the stand. The smoldering rage he had been carrying with him for two months finally had a chance to pound on something. He motioned the big man outside. *Maybe he'll break my nose*, he thought indifferently, giving form to the self-loathing he'd been feeling for the last two months.

When they reached the parking lot, Casey shoved Paul from the side. "What d'you think is going to happen here? I'm gonna kick your ass, that's what." Joseph slapped Paul across the face.

Rushing into a right cross that landed on the side of his chin, Paul was stopped in his tracks. The left hook caught him just behind the ear and sent him sprawling. "Better stay down, Paul. Sienna wouldn't like it if I messed up her pretty boy."

Paul came off the ground with a roar. Recalling a tactic Andy had once used in a bar fight, he faked a jab which brought Joseph's guard up and planted the toe of his running shoe in the big man's groin. A gush of air and spittle flew out of his mouth followed by a low groan, but Joseph stayed on his feet. Paul smashed his fist just below his right eye, then one more on the chin. The big man went down.

Standing over him, fist cocked, Paul goaded, "Come on you piece of shit. Is that all you've got?"

"Paul!" Sienna screamed, pushing her way through the increasing number of onlookers. "Stop it! My god. I don't even know you anymore. I thought I married a man, not a fifteen-year-old hoodlum."

Paul dropped his hands to his side. He nodded at Sienna. "You're right. You're right, I—"

"Kicking a man in the balls isn't cool," Casey groaned, as he slowly stood. "Next time—"

"I'm warning both of you," Sienna said forcefully, "there better never be a next time. I'll see you at home, Paul." Shaking her head disgustedly, she turned and briskly returned to the restaurant.

Figuring he was in no shape to perform anymore that evening, Paul climbed into his truck and drove back to *The Wall*. Carley spotted his arrival and had his usual ready when he sat down at the bar. "Heard there was some excitement over in The Green Flash's parking lot," she commented, noticing his dirty clothes and the welt on the side of his chin.

When Paul didn't say anything, she continued, "You know Paul, Sienna and I go back a long ways and I can't think of a better woman for any man to be married to. That Joseph fellow never had her the way she is with you. You've got nothing to sweat there."

Paul pushed his empty glass toward her. "Thanks Carley, but how about you just pour me another drink and we'll just skip all the happy talk."

"I never figured you for such an asshole."

"Bingo. You hit the nail on the head."

"Pour your own goddamn drink then." She slammed the bottle on the counter and walked back to the kitchen.

"OK, think I will." Turning in the direction of *The Green Flash* he toasted, "To soul mates."

29

The tapping worked easily into his dream. He was a gypsy dancer; tall leather boots, billowy open-necked shirt, tight black pants and a cherry-red bandana. The stage was spongy and stuck to the bottom of his shoes, slowing him down. He struggled to keep up with the tempo. Bunches of asparagus were thrown at him from the booing crowd. He awoke with his face lying in a puddle of drool on the back seat of his truck. The tapping continued. He slowly sat up and peered in its direction. Unlocking the door, he started to climb outside when Sienna's voice stopped him. "No Paul. Give me the keys and you can sleep. I'll drive us home."

His next awareness was of Sienna wordlessly helping him into their cabin, settling him on the bed and taking his clothes off. "Where's our boy?" Paul asked.

"At my sister's."

Confused, Paul asked, "Which one?"

"Lenay's. You dropped him off earlier."

"Aunt Lenay's my favorite. You know, she's a tough one. When I first met you, she said that she'd run my ass off the island if I wasn't good to you. Sienna?"

"Yes, Paul."

"I don't feel very good."

"Get some sleep, Paul. We'll talk in the morning." She left the room, quietly closing the door behind her.

Leaning back against the door, she shook her head despondently when she heard him say to himself, "It looks like no nookie for Paul tonight." Twenty minutes later she came back in the room after Paul had fallen asleep and joined him in bed, where she would lie awake until dawn.

******

AJ dove on the bed, jolting Paul awake. "Come on Paul, you've been sleeping too long." AJ's high pitched voice pierced through Paul's hangover.

"Where's your Mom?" Paul croaked from under the pillow.

"She's at work. Auntie Lenay brought me home a long time ago. Mommy left you a note in the kitchen."

"Would you bring the note here please?"

Paul felt that he caught air with AJ's return bounce. It took some blinking and eye rubbing before he could read the letter.

Paul, I have a meeting this morning with a supplier. I thought it would be better to let you sleep and we'll talk tonight. Lenay will drop AJ off before noon. Maybe you two could do something fun together. I know he misses hanging out with you. We all do. I love you. Sienna.

"So what's it say?"

"It says that I get to have some fun with my favorite little buddy." Sitting on the edge of the bed, he waited for the room to stop spinning. "While I get ready, why don't you start making the peanut butter and banana sandwiches. We'll bring the dingy back to *Stargazer* and look for some dolphins and turtles."

Paul had run the Zodiac between *Stargazer* and the beach-cave several times since disposing the bodies. Each time, he had to shake off overpowering feelings of guilt and sadness. This time was no exception as he watched AJ scamper sure-footedly down the narrow path to the beach.

AJ helped Paul pull the Zodiac from the cave to the shore. The weather was clear with a mild breeze from the east as they motored past Annaly Bay. Still hung-over and having skipped breakfast, Paul decided to stop in Wills Bay for lunch. Climbing onto the beach, Paul and AJ scaled the rocky path into a large protected tide-pool. Careful not to step on any spiny sea urchins, Paul gave AJ a piggy-back ride through the chest-high water to a favorite flat rock terrace. After finishing their sandwiches, AJ explored the shallow end of the tide pool while Paul discreetly drained the flask he had squirreled away for his headache. Paul cannonballed into the tide pool and joined AJ in his hunt for strange sea-creatures.

An hour later, they were back underway. While the booze had helped Paul lighten his mood, the weather had darkened considerably as they bounced and rolled their way through the high swells and stiff headwind. "Maybe we should go back," AJ said, pointing at the black cloud moving toward them.

"It's just a squall. We'll be fine. If it gets worse, we'll pull into shore and wait it out."

Fifteen minutes later, with the wind intensifying, Paul turned to shore. Powerful waves crashed over the side of the Zodiac, toppling AJ onto his back.

"I'm scared. This was supposed to be a fun time and I'm not having any." AJ crawled back toward Paul.

Paul wrapped his free arm around AJ as he maneuvered through a small gap between two large boulders just off the shoreline. Pulling the boat out of the water, they took shelter and waited out the storm.

"So do we push on or go back?" Paul asked AJ, after the storm passed.

"Let's go home and play catch. I don't think today's a good day for boats."

The ride back was smoother and under sunny skies. After reaching the top of the path from the beach, AJ caught Paul off guard. "Are you and Mommy fighting?"

"Why are you asking that?"

"I heard Mommy on the phone say to Papa that you were."

Paul was surprised to hear that Sienna had talked with Andy. "Well, sometimes adults have problems and they don't agree on things so they argue. Don't worry, your Mom and I love each other and you too . . . Now go find the ball and gloves."

******

Although it was just after sunset, Sienna was happy to see Paul and AJ squeezing in as much baseball as they could before dark.

"Mommy!" AJ dropped his glove and ran toward her.

"Did you have a fun day?" She pulled AJ close to her side with one arm, while holding a grocery bag in the other.

"Most of it was really fun," AJ answered, looking at Paul, who had joined them after picking up the baseball gear.

"Oh? What did you do? Wait, let's go inside first. I need to take a shower and put on my PJ's. I bought some organic meat and thought we'd grill hamburgers."

Paul kissed Sienna and took the groceries from her. "Hi, Honey. AJ and I are in charge of dinner. You've worked hard enough already."

Paul heard Sienna singing softly in the outside shower as he heated up the barbecue. *Maybe tonight we'll make love.*

After her shower, she called from the bedroom, "AJ, come in here and tell me what you did today, while I put in a load of wash."

Paul went into the kitchen to make a salad. Sienna had picked up ripe tomatoes and arugula from the Art Farm on Southshore Road. He poured himself a rum and soda and was ready to start grilling the burgers when Sienna came outside. "I don't want AJ to hear any of this, Paul, but AJ and I are going to be staying with my parents for the time being."

Paul looked at her, speechless.

She choked back tears and continued, "You took him out in a storm and he could have drowned. I've already lost my baby girl." She saw his look of surprise. "That's right, you didn't want to know the sex, but I asked, and it was a girl."

"Sienna, he wasn't in danger."

"How would you know? You were drinking as usual and you put our son in the position of telling on you. I'm not going to risk losing AJ because you can't go one day without anesthetizing yourself from whatever the hell you're running from."

"What will we tell AJ?"

"That's your answer?" Paul looked down at the ground. "Jesus, Paul. It's really surprising to me how easily you've given up. I thought I married a man with some passion, some fight in him. Maybe Casey was right. I'm sick of this, Paul. I'm done trying."

She turned, but stopped when Paul said, "You don't need to go. Let's have dinner together. I'll move on to the boat."

"Fine."

AJ, sensing their discord, tried his best to lighten the mood during dinner. "Mom, we should go to Buck Island this weekend. Paul told me that he heard the lemon sharks are back. Right, Paul?"

"AJ, we may not be able to go this weekend, but I'm sure they'll stay around for a while."

Throughout their meal, AJ proposed activity after activity they could all do together. It was too much for Paul.

"Excuse me." He stood up from the table and walked out to his truck. She made no effort to stop him as he slowly drove away.

30

It sounded as if Andy was two inches away instead of yelling through a cell phone from Winthrop, Washington. Paul had instinctively answered his cell when it rang. He really wished now that he'd let it go to voicemail.

"Are you listening to me, Paul? You're messing up the best thing you've ever had. I can't believe you moved out over a week ago and we didn't hear about it until tonight."

"What time is it?" Paul tried to focus his blurred vision on the cell's screen. "Christ, Andy, its three o'clock in the morning."

"Yeah, so what? It's midnight here and nobody's sleepin'. Why should you?"

"I'm sorry I didn't call, but it really doesn't involve you. This is between Sienna and—"

"What kind of crazy bullshit . . . it doesn't involve me? How 'bout your aunt, who's too upset to even talk to you right now. I suppose it doesn't involve her either."

"I . . . I don't know what to say. I'm sorry for not calling."

"Well, that's a start I guess, but from where I sit, it's the least of your problems. I guess maybe Sienna had some difficulty when you told her about—"

206

"I didn't tell her. Couldn't. I don't know, Andy, maybe it's better this way. I'm not much good for myself, let alone anyone else these days."

Paul could hear Andy's exasperated sigh. "Look, Paul, I'm the last guy to give advice, but your aunt and I think you two need to see a counselor. Maybe that'd help."

"Yeah, maybe . . . Well, tell Aunt Charlotte not to worry. We'll work it out. We just need some time."

"OK, but don't take too long to work things out. Hank tells me that Attorney Joseph's been sniffing around."

"Yeah, Hank told me the same thing. Maybe it's for the best. AJ needs someone to throw the ball with him and he treats her well."

"Listen to yourself, Goddammit! She's not in love with Attorney Joseph. She's your wife, for Christ's sake. Grow a pair, will you? Go fix this thing."

After a long pause, Paul replied, "Thanks for the call, Andy. Give my love to Aunt Charlotte."

"OK, OK. I'm off my soap box. Just promise you'll keep me in the loop, will ya?"

"Will do."

"Paul?"

"Yeah?"

"We'll get through this, Son."

"Thanks, Andy."

******

Paul couldn't sleep after Andy's call. He turned on his laptop and tried working on the construction drawings for The Blossom's residence. Curtis and Deidra were arriving the following week to review the documents, but his thoughts were

207

muddled and unfocused. *Maybe one drink*. He pulled the bottle of light rum out of the cupboard. Falling asleep after his third glass, he dozed fitfully until morning when a voice outside *Stargazer* dragged him back to consciousness.

"Hey Paul, you in there?"

"Yeah, Hank." Paul pulled himself off the galley table he'd awoken slumped over. "Be right out."

While brushing his teeth, he felt Hank climb aboard. Pulling his last clean T-shirt over his head, he greeted his friend from the hatchway, "Hey, Hank."

"How's it going? Sorry I haven't been by lately. I'm doing some consulting for the police chief and that's keeping me pretty busy."

"Gonna make some coffee. Want some?" Paul turned on the stove. "Any news about Falco and his friends?"

"Nope. Not a thing. I think the chief is about ready to give up the ghost on this one. Too bad, too. Would have been quite the feather in his cap, with all the coverage it was getting. Nobody up in New Jersey seems to care anymore. Actually, I think Uncle Sal's happy Buddy's gone. My suspicion is that if it wasn't some drugged-out punks that did it, then the three of them got beamed up and are lab rats in some alien's laboratory."

Paul laughed. "I like that idea."

"Good to hear you laugh again . . . Not much to laugh about for you these days, I guess."

"Yeah, well, I'm not a victim here. I made my own bed. Can't complain if it's not comfortable."

"Look, are you going to talk to her?"

"Roxanne put you up to this?"

"Yeah, but I think you should."

208

"I'm not sure she'd want to talk to me . . . Andy called me last night at three in the morning. You know anything about that?"

"I suppose it was after he talked to me earlier. I hadn't realized he didn't know that you'd moved out. You know, this whole thing, you moving out, really sucks. I don't want to take sides, but—"

"Then don't. This isn't anyone's fault. It's just the way things worked out."

"You can't tell me you don't love her. What about AJ? The kid's heart-broken."

"Thanks for coming by, Hank," Paul said, standing up. "I've got to get some drawings done."

"Never figured you for a quitter." Hank fumed, as he stepped onto the dock.

"Say 'hi' to your buddy, Casey Joseph, for me."

"Asshole."

******

It was the call she had dreaded making. She was still so angry at him, but she had promised Andy. He picked up on the third ring.

"Hello, Sienna."

"Hi, Paul."

"AJ would like to see you and I thought you might come by tomorrow afternoon."

"Will you be there?"

This was the part she dreaded. "No, Casey and I are going out on his boat for the day. AJ will be over at Roxanne and Hank's."

"I think for now, it would be better for AJ not to see me. I'm . . . not doing so well."

She could hear his pain, but it just made her angrier. "OK, Paul, I'm sorry you're not doing so well, but I'm even sorrier for AJ that we ever met."

"It's all so black and white with you now, Sienna, isn't it? Your boyfriend helping you out with that?"

"At least he's there for me. I'd like to wish you well, but I'm so angry at you, I just can't. Goodbye, Paul."

"Goodbye, Sienna," he said to the dead line.

31

His last week on St. Croix started with an unannounced visit from the boyfriend, himself.

"Hey, Armstrong, you in there?"

Appearing topside, Paul's red-rimmed eyes stared hard at the man. "Come to gloat?"

"Nah, hell, I don't waste my time on that kind of thing. Look, I'm sure you're thinking that I'm the reason you and Sienna aren't getting back together, but—"

"I never considered you competition, Casey. Why would I now?"

The attorney glared at Paul. "Fuck it. I was just trying to be nice. Here, this is for you."

"What is it?" Paul took the manila envelope.

"It's a separation agreement. Sienna had me draw it up so you don't go trying to take something that isn't yours."

"Wouldn't imagine she'd be too worried about that," Paul replied, trying to sound casual through his clenching teeth.

"Yeah, well, it's a good idea for both parties until the divorce is completed. I'd expect we'll be drawing the petition up for that in the near future."

"That it?"

"Well, it needs your signature."

"Fine, I'll look it over and drop it off at your office."

"Chantal, in my office, can notarize it. Bring some ID."

"Great. Thanks for the help here. Glad you're so on top of things."

"Truly is my pleasure." The grinning attorney turned and walked back to his car.

Later that same day he received a call from Curtis Blossom.

"Hey Paul, how have you been? Actually, that's a bullshit question. I know you've been going through hell."

Paul didn't think Curtis knew about their breakup, but after the earlier visit by Joseph, he had no energy left to find out.

"Yeah, there have been better days. What's up?"

"Might as well tell you straight-out. The project's dead. Deidra doesn't want to live on St. Croix. We've been going around and around about it, but I've got to give in on this one. Really sorry to add to your problems, but there it is."

Paul wasn't disappointed, he was relieved. The commitment he'd made to the Blossom's was the only thing keeping him on-island. "Smart choice, Curtis. Happy wife, happy life. I understand completely. It's been a pleasure working for you," he replied as an escape plan started to unfold in his mind.

"Of course we'll pay you for your work to date. Send me the bill and let's keep in touch."

******

Paul dropped the signed, separation agreement and a sealed envelope for Sienna at Casey's office on his way to the airport. He imagined the attorney working behind his closed door, feverishly trying to speed up the divorce proceedings.

Although there were close friends he should say goodbye to, he couldn't bring himself to do it. His departure from St. Croix was as quiet as his first arrival had been almost two years earlier.

At an airport bar in Puerto Rico, he downed shots of tequila and considered his options. If he'd been drinking scotch, the idea might never have come to him.

She picked up on the third ring. "Paul! I can't believe it. Just the other day I was saying to Lew that I need to find your number and give you a call."

"It's my fault, Anita, you sent me your number and I never got back to you. I apologize."

"Don't worry about it. The last time I saw you, you looked like something the cat dragged in. I heard through some of our old associates that you're living in the Caribbean. St. Croix, isn't it?"

Anita had been the trusted office manager for twelve years with Armstrong Architects, Inc., before accompanying Paul into his business partnership with Andrew Sherman. The sudden demise of T-Squared Development, L.L.C. had pushed Anita and her husband, Lew, into an early retirement in Mexico near the southern tip of the Baja Peninsula.

"Yes, but I'm moving on now. What would you and Lew think about showing me around down there? I'm spinning the globe and my finger just landed on Cabo."

"Are you kidding? We'd love it. But you know, we're heading into summer and it can get wicked hot."

"I'm pretty used to hot weather. I think it'll be fine."

"OK, great. When are you coming? We're about 45 minutes from the airport and can pick you up. You'll stay with us, of course. We've got plenty of room."

"No, Anita, I don't want to put you out. I'll get a room."

"You're staying with us. End of discussion. You're my *former boss*. Former is the key word there. You don't call the shots anymore."

"Did I ever?"

"No, not really. Hey, Paul, you OK?"

"Yeah, just tired and a little over-served. Give me your email and I'll forward you my flight info. Can't wait to see you guys." Without further explanation he thanked her and called American Airline Flight Reservations. His indifference regarding the future was reflected in the $4,400 first-class airfare he charged on his Amex card for his next day's early morning flight through Dallas/Fort Worth to Cabo San Lucas. After securing the reservation, he returned to the airport bar until its closing. Setting the alarm on his phone, he spent the night passed out in an airport chair, his feet propped on top of his carry-on.

******

On the first leg of his journey, he pounded down free, first-class booze until the flight attendant cut him off. Heading straight for the terminal bar, once the flight landed, he resumed his effort to drown the painful memories.

"Excuse me, but I have to tell you, you look just like my younger brother. You prefer to drink alone?"

The woman, taking the seat next to him appeared to be in her mid-forties; short blonde hair, trim figure, nicely tailored navy blue jacket over a white blouse. A string of pearls and small diamond earrings were her only feminine embellishments.

"Probably best if I do."

214

"Wow, is it me or are you just—"

"Bad news," he finished for her. Paul noticed her blanch at the term.

"I'll have what he's having, tequila and—"

"Grapefruit juice, it's still early enough for breakfast."

"Well, here's to chance meetings of lost souls at airport bars in Texas." She tossed back half of her drink. "Sounds like a country-western song."

"You a lost soul?"

"Not really, I'm just scared shitless of flying. Not such a good thing when you fly as much as I do. And you?"

"A lost soul? Yeah, I suppose I am."

"I'd already guessed that. I meant what are you doing here at ten in the morning drinking tequila?"

"I'm on my way to Mexico. Thought it might put me in the mood. Where's your younger brother now?"

"That, my new drinking buddy is the question." She ordered another round for both of them. "He died, doing what he loved, six months ago."

"I'm sorry."

"Me too." Her hazel eyes clouded over. "I guess I was his lost soul project. He was always on me about not taking time to enjoy life. Oh, well, what are you gonna do?"

"At least he died doing something he loved."

She looked over at him with a sad smile. "If he could, I'm sure that's exactly what he would tell me. You know, you really do remind me of him. When does your flight leave?"

"We board in an hour." Paul nodded toward the gate across from them.

"Well, I'll see you off then. I've got two hours before I'm boarding for Albuquerque. So, look, we'll never see each other again. We don't even know each other's names. Why not fill the time and tell me a story?"

"You want a story? I could tell you a story."

"Doesn't have to be true. Just something to pass the time."

"OK, but we'll need another drink. Do you know where the bathrooms are?"

"No, but take your time. I'll order another round and watch your bag." Their drinks and the woman were waiting for him when he returned.

"OK, start talking. I'm all ears," she said.

An hour later the woman and Paul both stared silently at their drinks as the boarding for Paul's flight was announced. "It's a good story," she finally said. "This Peter-guy really must've felt like he died himself when he killed those three mobsters."

"Yeah, I guess. Wait, what do you mean?"

"Well, up until then, he'd lived a pretty squeaky-clean life. Then, bam, bam, bam, now he's a murderer. 'Where'd I go?' he probably wondered."

Paul looked over at her. "Yeah, probably so."

"A very good story. So what happened to him after he left Maine?"

"Don't know yet. What still tears Peter apart is that he couldn't bring himself to tell his wife what he'd done. Instead, he pushed her away. He left her . . . and the boy."

The woman looked at her watch and stood up. "Come on, I told you I'd see you off." At the gate, she kissed him on the cheek. "It's too good a story to leave with such a sad ending." He gave his ticket to the gate agent and turned to wave, but she was nowhere in sight.

******

As the 737 lifted off the runway, Paul was disappointed when told that the plane had apparently taken off without tequila. "No tequila? Isn't this the plane to Cabo?" He settled with multiple rum and cokes until, once again, the flight attendant notified him that he was switching to coffee.

"Been cut off a few times myself," the passenger seated next to him commented. "I remember thirty years ago, flying was the best part of the trip." A large hand came into Paul's peripheral vision. "I'm Guy."

Paul took his hand. "Nice to meet you, Guy. Paul Armstrong, I mean Armstrong, Paul Armstrong."

"Maybe coffee isn't such a bad idea. Think I'll join you."

"Yeah, probably right. It's not just the booze, haven't slept much lately."

"Yeah, been there too."

He looked out his window as the plane broke through a billowy layer of white clouds. His hand went to the spot on his cheek where she'd kissed him. "It's too good a story to leave with such a sad ending."

"Sorry. I didn't catch what you just said." Guy took Paul's coffee off the attendant's service tray and handed it to him.

"Oh, . . .nothing. Just thinking out loud."

But Guy's attention had already turned to a conversation with a couple across the aisle. Paul gazed through the window, shaking his head slowly. Even above the clouds there wasn't a happy ending in sight.

32

"Are you sure you don't want me to come with you?" Casey asked through the open passenger window of his BMW.

Sienna found the keys to Paul's truck on top of the rear wheel as he'd described in the note he'd left for her at Casey's office. "No, you've got work to do. I'll take the truck out to the marina and pick up what he left on *Stargazer*. You go back to work; I'll see you later tonight."

The cab of the truck smelled like him. Leaving the airport, Sienna scolded herself, "Stop it. Don't be sentimental. He left, skulked off without even saying where he was going." The self-talk worked until she unlocked *Stargazer's* hatchway. Most of his clothes, his guitar and golf clubs were neatly stacked in the middle of the salon.

I left the truck at the airport, near the exit booth. The key's on the back right tire. Also, I left behind some things on Stargazer. You can keep whatever you want. Feel free to sell or give away what you can't use. Always, Paul

"Always what, Paul? You left your guitar?" Suddenly she was sitting on the floor next to the pile. "What did you take

218

with you? Where did you go, Paul? Why did you leave me?" Picking up one of his shirts, her deep sobs were barely muffled as she pressed her face into its soft fabric.

******

Sienna wasn't happy to see Casey's BMW when she drove into Windsol. AJ was staying with Hank and Roxanne. She was grateful for all of Casey's help, but tonight, she just wanted to be alone.

"How'd it go?" Casey asked, as she walked up the porch steps.

"Oh fine," she replied, taking a chair next to him.

Casey stood and massaged her shoulders. "You're all tight, Hon. How 'bout we go inside and I give you a good massage. These strong fingers are magic, remember?"

"I also remember what all that massaging led to."

"Would that be so bad?"

"I told you, Casey, we need to move slowly."

"Yeah, I heard you on that. I just thought with all we're going through together, you'd be feeling—"

"Right now, what I need most is your friendship. If you can't accept that, then maybe we shouldn't be seeing so much of each other."

"You're still in love with that loser, aren't you?"

"I can't turn my feelings off like a faucet. Of course I still care for him. I'm worried about him. Why would he leave without even saying goodbye to AJ?"

"I told you, he's a loser. The sooner you realize that, the better. God knows I'm a patient man, Sienna, but there's a limit, even for me."

219

"I don't need this right now, Casey. I think you'd better go."

"I was just leaving."

As she watched his tail lights disappear through the trees, she wondered if she'd ever feel for him the way he wanted.

******

After finishing his coffee, he slept the rest of the flight and appeared passably sober as he cleared customs. Paul found a shaded bench outside the terminal and waited for Anita to pick him up. He dug out his cell and called Barney.

"Hey Champ. Been hearing there may be some troubles in paradise. You want me to come down there and give that Attorney Joseph a good reason to back off? Shit, I can just picture that prick's grin when he heard you and Sienna were having problems."

"We're past that Barney. It happened pretty fast. Sienna had him draw up a separation agreement. It's temporary until the divorce is final. They're together and I'm in Cabo San Lucas."

"What the fuck? I just talked to you a couple weeks ago. You OK?"

"Not really. But I think I'll have a better chance down here. You remember Anita from my office?"

"Yeah, sure."

"Well, she and her husband retired on the coast, somewhere north of here. They've offered to put me up until I get settled."

"Why Mexico? Why not come back here? Claire's moved back in with me so your old cabin's empty."

"That's great, Barney, you two finally together again."

"Yeah, thanks, but back to what I asked."

"I just think it's better to be somewhere that I don't know many people. I need to pull myself together. Besides, you've got your hands full up there. The last thing you need is my mopey ass dragging around."

"Hell that never stopped you before." Barney cut his laugh short. "OK, Ace, you give it a go down there, but if things don't turn around for you pretty soon, you drag that ass up here, mopey or not."

Paul wasn't looking forward to his next call. Andy was livid. "This isn't what I would consider keeping me posted. No sir, not by a longshot. Where in the hell did you say you are?"

"Cabo San Lucas, Mexico."

"Jesus, remember I'm an old man, Paul. You've got to quit with all these shocks. What the hell are you doing in Mexico?"

"I'm waiting for an old friend to pick me up. I'll let you know once I get settled. Meantime, you've got my cell number. It seems to work down here, although I'll probably need to change my cell carrier or be billed for roaming charges. I was going down pretty fast in St. Croix, Andy. Sienna's taken up with the attorney, and there're just too many memories for me there. I'm a mess. I need to put myself back together. Maybe down here, I have a chance."

"What? . . . OK, ah, Char wants to talk to you."

"Paul, I'm so worried about you. Are you all right?"

Tears filled his eyes, hearing her sweet voice. "Not really Aunt Charlotte. I'm kind of a mess."

"What can we do? Should we come down and get you?"

"No, I was telling Andy that maybe I have a chance down here, away from all my old patterns and friends, to get myself straightened out."

"Well, will you promise to call and check in?"

"I promise."

"Remember Paul, life is full of surprises, bad and good. Don't give up, Honey. You'll see. Things will turn around. I love you, Paul."

"I love you too."

"I love you too," Paul heard Andy shout in the background before they disconnected.

Paul wiped the tears away as he saw Anita jump out of a small car and run toward him. "Paul, I'm so glad you're here. Is that all you brought?" She pointed at his carry-on.

"My laptop's in there too, but yeah, that's the sum total of my worldly possessions."

"What ever happened to all those expensive suits you owned?" They walked toward the car.

"I think they're in storage at Barney's ranch. Haven't needed them since T-Squared."

"Hi Paul. It's good to see you again." Lew greeted Paul with a warm hug.

Paul set his bag in the trunk and climbed into the back seat. Anita filled Paul in on their life in Mexico as Lew drove north along the coastal highway. Arriving in the expat community of Elias Calles, named after a former Mexican president, Paul admired their casita as they pulled in the driveway. "It was Anita's idea to go with the palapa roof. Keeps things cool inside. We worked with a local architect. His brother was the builder."

"It's not an Armstrong design, but we love it. You can see the ocean from the roof terrace over the garage," Anita added.

Paul was genuinely impressed. The palm frond weave of the palapa roof covered the simple one story home, painted in desert browns, golds and reds. "It's really beautiful you guys."

They were greeted by Feliz, a ferocious-looking, but tail-wagging Rottweiler mix, who Anita warned, would probably try to sleep on his bed if he left the door open at night. Painfully reminding him of Rose, Paul forced a smile and scratched his potential bunkmate's ears as the dog's tongue slathered his wrist. They walked through the trellis-covered entry court bordered with hanging pots, overflowing with colorful flowers.

"I hope you're comfortable here." Anita opened the guest bedroom door.

"This is perfect. I can't thank you guys enough."

"Well, I made some crock-pot chili so we can eat dinner anytime you want. There's a path down to the beach, if you'd like to join Feliz and me for a walk. Lew's busy re-gripping some golf clubs. I think he's hoping you'll play with him the next day or two."

"A walk would be great, I'll change clothes. Tell Lew that I'm ready to go anytime he'd like."

"He'll be thrilled. OK, I'll meet you on the terrace when you're ready."

Anita was throwing a hard rubber ball for Feliz when Paul joined them outside. Returning the ball from the last throw, Feliz dropped it expectantly at Paul's feet. "I think he may have heard about your old quarterbacking days. Just be careful not to lose the damn ball or we'll be up all night looking

223

for it." After several lengthy throws, Paul realized that his arm would give out long before the dog ever did. Anita put the ball inside and they headed down to the beach where Felix chased after sea birds as they walked along the shoreline.

"So, pretty amazing about Andrew, isn't it? I couldn't believe it when I read he was alive," she said, throwing a stick in the surf for Feliz.

"Yeah, amazing is a good word for it."

"It seemed like I'd just come to terms with him being alive and, bam, he's dead again, this time for sure. I mean that whole turn of events was so freakin' bizarre. Poor Andrew, in spite of everything, I was actually really sorry when he was murdered the second time."

"I know what you mean."

"Paul, you want to talk about what's going on?"

"Not really. It's all pretty raw right now. I'm getting divorced again."

"I thought it might be something like that. Anytime you want to talk, let me know."

The smooth, sandy beach didn't require footwear so Paul took his running shoes off and set them on a log.

"Say Paul, would you be uncomfortable if I have some friends over tomorrow? We've had this potluck planned and I'd love to show off my former boss. We can cancel if you're not up to it."

"Sounds fun. Not sure what kind of impression I'll make, but I promise, at least, not to appear morose."

"That'd be nice. What do you like to drink?"

"Usually too much rum. Actually, I'm going to switch over to iced tea for a while so don't worry about me."

Feliz ran to greet a couple heading toward them. "That's the Siskels. You know, as in Siskel's Almonds. They own that hacienda." She pointed at a group of buildings fronting the beach, clad in glass, stone and stucco.

As the couple cut away from the ocean toward their home, Anita shouted, "Marvin, Sharon, I'd like you to meet a friend of mine."

"Is this your former employer that I've heard so many things about?" Marvin asked, shaking Paul's hand.

"He doesn't look as old as I expected." Sharon greeted Paul warmly with a hug.

"I feel a lot older than I look."

"You'll have a chance to get to know each other at the potluck tomorrow," Anita said. "You guys are coming aren't you?"

"Wouldn't miss it," Marvin replied. "So how long are you planning on staying, Paul?"

"Probably stay through the summer, at least."

"Well, if you're looking for a place, we have a guest cabin that's empty and frankly, our house sitter just fell through. We're looking for someone to look after the place for the next few months while we're up in the states visiting the kids and grandkids."

"That sounds like just what I was hoping to find."

"Great," Sharon said, "Maybe you could drop over tomorrow before the party and we'll show you around the place. Give you the lay of the land."

******

Paul volunteered to bartend for the potluck. His efforts were greatly appreciated by the cheerful gathering of expats. "I think your mojitos may be responsible for a major shift in the neighborhood, from tequila to rum," Anita observed. "How'd it go with the Siskels?"

"Great. The cottage is perfect, right on the beach. I'll move over there tomorrow morning. They're leaving tomorrow afternoon."

"I know you're looking forward to your seclusion, but just promise that you'll check in from time to time. I don't want to worry that you're lying in a ditch up in the mountains or something."

"Deal . . . I was thinking maybe you and Lew could come over this Sunday. I'll barbeque some steaks."

"I'll bring a salad. Maybe we can make Sunday afternoons a regular thing?"

"Absolutely."

"Yeah, well, you still owe me an explanation of what's going on. Don't forget."

"I won't."

"Ok, I've got to go mingle," she said, leaving him with a kiss on the cheek.

Paul watched as she disappeared into the crowd. The party had been going strong for over four hours and with the time difference and the abuse he'd been subjecting his body to over the last few months, it was all catching up to him. He was fading fast.

"I told her we should have waited longer before springing all this on you," Lew said, as he stepped in behind the bar. "You look dead on your feet, Paul. I'll take over from here. I actually make a pretty good tequila sunrise and fuck-'em if they don't like it."

"Thanks, Lew," Paul replied, relieved. "Could you explain to Anita . . ."

"Don't you worry about Anita and if anyone asks, I'll just remind them that it's almost midnight in St. Croix. Hell, they should appreciate that. Most of them are usually in bed by dark."

******

But long after Paul heard the party break up, he was still wide awake. He'd withstood the considerable temptation to drink during the party, but now with no drink orders to fill, nothing to distract him, there wasn't anything to take him away from the whole mess of his life. From his luggage, he pulled out the bottle of tequila he'd picked up at the airport before Anita arrived. Not bothering with a glass he took two big gulps. He waited for the esophageal sting to pass then pounded three more. "That's better," he slurred, and fell into bed.

33

"Jeez Paul, I didn't see you drink anything at the party."

"No, I'm just jet-lagged."

"Want some coffee?"

"Yes please."

"Lew already left for golf. Says he thought you could use the rest. You still don't take cream?"

"Still like it black."

Paul heard his cell ring from the guest bedroom. By the time he reached it, the call had gone to voicemail.

"Hey Paul, it's Hank. I'm sorry our last conversation went the way it did. Heard you left island. If you need anything, I'm still your man. Give me a call when you feel like it. Roxanne and Red send their love. OK, hope to talk to you soon."

Hank answered his cell after its first ring.

"Hello, this is Hank Johnson."

"Hank, it's Paul."

"Man, I'm so glad you called back. I've been kicking myself all over the island for being such a judgmental asshole."

"Don't worry about it. I probably would have said the same thing to you." Paul pressed his forehead hard with the tips of his fingers, but it didn't help his headache.

"But why leave St. Croix? You've got friends here to support you. Who do you have in Mexico?"

"That's one reason I'm here. If I stayed on the island, I'd just piss-off any friends I had left. Besides, after Casey stopped by with the separation agreement, I had to leave."

"Yeah, he told me about that. That prick attorney isn't wasting any time, is he? Look, Paul, I've had some experience with officers under my command who've suffered from post-traumatic stress disorder. You lost your child. Your wife and friends were brutally attacked. That kind of trauma can explain what you're going through. Maybe you should get some help. Find a counselor who's familiar with PTSD."

"I may do that, Hank. I'm not really big on counseling, but you never know."

"I can't get over that prick attorney, jumping into this before you guys even had a chance to work things out."

"Yeah, well, he's always been waiting for me to slip up. You really can't blame the guy. He's crazy about her and she's always said how well he treated her and AJ."

"I heard you kicked him in the nuts in a bar fight."

"Not my finest moment."

"No, but I wish I'd seen it." Hank chuckled.

"Look Hank, I can't put more energy into Sienna and Casey. If she's happy, then I have to let it go and focus on getting better."

"OK, I just wouldn't write off your chances with Sienna yet. I know Casey's pushing hard for divorce, but so far, she's not having any of that."

"Like I said—"

"OK, OK I get it . . . So it looks like you'll be there for a while?"

"Yeah, I think it's best."

"Well, there are a lot of us on St. Croix who don't want you staying in Mexico any longer than you have to."

"Thanks, Hank. Give my love to Roxanne and Red."

"Will do, but I have to tell you, Roxanne's pretty pissed at you."

"Yeah? Well she should probably take a number and get in line."

"Yeah, your Crucian stock has definitely taken a tumble, but I'm still there for you. Just let me know what I can do."

"I appreciate your looking after Windsol. Any problems there?"

They discussed a plugged foot valve in the cistern and returning a defective solar panel. After the call, Paul laid down, his hangover headache now accompanied by a bout of nausea.

Ten minutes later, Anita tapped quietly on his door. "You OK in there?"

"Just laying down for a minute. Stomach's a little off."

"Sorry about that. OK if I come in?"

"Sure."

"You're white as a sheet. You sure you're OK?" She leaned over and felt his forehead.

Paul considered trying to deflect her concern, but decided she'd see through it anyway. "Actually, no. I'm really not."

"Should we head into Cabo? There's an outpatient clinic there that I took Lew to when he came down with the flu."

"No, I don't think so. I'm starting to feel better."

"OK. If you're sure."

"Still taking care of me, it seems. You'd think it would get old after a while."

"Ya think? Scoot over." She sat down on the bed. "Actually, I've kinda missed all your drama. Wouldn't want to go back to it, but it kept things interesting for over twelve years. So now tell me, what brings you down here?"

Apart from attributing the disappearance of the three men to a drug deal gone bad, he didn't diverge from the truth. Anita sat quietly after he was finished. "What are you thinking?" he asked.

"I was thinking about when Andrew first walked into our office. Do you remember what I told you?"

"Lately, I've been having trouble remembering what happened two days ago."

"Probably just an early onset of your date with dementia," she kidded. "Actually, maybe your friend Hank has it right and you're suffering from PTSD. I told you that Andrew Sherman was a hustler and to watch yourself."

"If only I'd listened to you."

"No, that's not what I was getting at. He was a hustler, and hustlers tend to shake things up. Look at your life then and where you are now . . . I don't mean right now. Do you really think you could ever have been as happy without Sienna and AJ?"

"Maybe you weren't listening to that part, Anita. They're gone. I've lost them."

"Shit. Excuse my French, but you can't be that big of a fool. They're not gone, you're gone. You haven't lost them, you're lost. Seems like you've got some need to punish yourself. You're stuck in reverse, undoing your countless blessings. You know that nothing will change, until you do."

"It's not that simple, Anita. Look, can we continue this discussion when I don't feel like an ice pick is stuck in my forehead?"

"Sure. Of course we can." She turned when she reached the door. "You know I wouldn't care one way or another if Lew and I didn't think of you as family." She shut the door quietly behind her. The sound of her footsteps down the hall had disappeared before he stood up to pack.

His head felt better when he found Anita pulling weeds in her herb garden. She offered to give him a ride over to the Siskel's, but he wanted the exercise. He gave her a quick kiss. "Thanks for putting me up."

"And putting up with you."

"Yeah, that too."

"Stay in touch. Don't go getting all reclusive and weird."

Paul picked up his bag, but didn't reply.

"Come on Paul, don't be mad at me for strong-arming you back in your room. That's my job. Remember?"

Her upturned face seemed practically angelic to Paul. He frowned at her. "Bitch."

Her eyes narrowed as she stood up. "Asshole."

They were both still laughing as he set out for the Siskel's.

34

Marvin asked Paul if he would drive them to the airport. En route, Paul enjoyed talking with the couple. Marvin's dad had started their almond business on his farm in the San Joaquin Valley, just south of Fresno, California. Under Marvin's watch, Siskel's Almonds had grown into a brand name, well-known throughout the States.

Sharon had recommended an open-air restaurant in Cabo which Paul found easily after dropping them off at the airport. Realizing he still had a significant drive back to Elias Calles, he had initially decided to forgo his pre-dinner cocktails. Sitting at the bar, a martini drinking businessman from San Francisco struck up a conversation. Paul's resolve was soon displaced by two doubles, followed by two more during dinner. His coffee to go, although a step in the right direction, was definitely too little, too late.

Fortunately it was a clear night and the light from the full moon compensated for the lack of highway lighting. He cautiously drove the Siskel's mint conditioned 1972 Mercedes north along the western coast of The Baja Peninsula. "How fucking stupid are you? A DUI in Mexico. You trying to get thrown in prison for life?" He made sure his speed stayed below the limit. As slowly as he was traveling, he came up on the old pickup like it was standing still. "Really? Thirty? Go crazy old man, push her up to forty." He didn't want to pass. "Come on! Twenty-five?" Checking his rear view mirror, he gunned the engine and pulled into the passing lane. When he was even with the truck he glanced over and saw the frightened driver pointing through his windshield. The message penetrated Paul's inebriation an instant before his headlights illuminated the cow standing in his lane. *This is it,* he thought as he swerved off the road, over the divider margin and across two oncoming traffic lanes before fishtailing off the roadway through the highway's cattle fencing. Miraculously, the Mercedes stayed upright as it plunged down an embankment, mowed over cactus and finally skidded to a hard stop in a sandy bottomed arroyo. He cautiously opened the door and stepped into the night. The slow moving lights of the truck disappeared over a rise. *Maybe he'll turn around.* He dropped down in the sand with his iPhone flashlight and squeezed a look at the car's undercarriage. He couldn't spot any leaks or damage. The front bumper and grill however, were badly scratched and dented. One headlight had been smashed. The tires were buried up to the hubcaps in soft sand. The car would need to be towed. Hidden from the highway, he'd have to walk back to the road to flag someone down, but not now. He crawled into the back seat. "Maybe this'll look better in the morning."

******

The three men left their quad ATV's idling noisily behind them as they approached the Mercedes. Paul, awakened by the engines, stepped out of the car. "Hola, Amigos."

Accompanied by an animated flurry of Spanish, the men pointed to the trail strewn with knocked over cactus and skidding tire tracks. Two of the men began inspecting the car while a lanky, older man approached Paul. "I'm Chuy. Those are my nephews Memo and Alejandro. My brother was driving the truck you tried to pass last night."

They don't seem like Banditos. "I was surprised he didn't stop."

"At night he is usually very drunk. He was afraid the policia might blame him for your accident."

Paul thought it best not to volunteer his earlier evening's beverage consumption. "Can you guys help pull me out of here with your ATV's?"

"Probably, but it would be better to call Israel. He has a big tractor that he uses to pull gringos from the sand."

Three hours and $160 dollars later, ($100 for Israel and twenty each for Chuy and his friends) Paul arrived back at his cottage. He called Anita who was just leaving for a friend's house and described the accident.

"Sounds like you got off lucky. I assume you'd been drinking."

"Yeah, I'd had a few martinis in Cabo."

"Well, driving under the influence isn't really a big deal down here, unless you're in an accident. But seriously, Paul, you could have been killed."

"The booze didn't cause the accident. This cow just appeared right in front of me."

"Maybe dropped down from a spaceship?"

"Very funny. So before I email the Siskels, I'd like to find a body shop."

"Roberto does fantastic work. He's got a garage behind his house up north, just before Todos Santos." She gave directions and agreed to meet him there in an hour.

Paul stopped at a highway restaurant and gulped down a quick breakfast along with three or four shots of tequila. Arriving at Roberto's a half hour late, he drove through an open metal gate and a yard full of wrecked cars. Anita stepped out of her car as he drove in.

"Nice of you to show up, Paul."

"Yeah, sorry about that. I made a few wrong turns."

"That can happen." An older man in grease-covered overalls came out from behind the house and joined them. "Paul, I'd like you to meet Roberto." The two men shook hands. Roberto walked over to the car with a clipboard.

In spite of Paul chewing a handful of Altoids, Anita smelled the tequila on his breath. "Seems like you're really getting into the local spirit, I mean spirits. Maybe when we're done here you can help me with a list of who I should invite to your intervention."

"Enough, Anita. You're objection to my alcohol consumption has been duly noted."

"Excessive alcohol consumption, if we're being real here. Look, I'm worried about you. You spend the night in a car after being run off the road by a cow. You could have been killed. Now, you show up with booze on your breath, a half-hour late, like my time is of no value."

Paul felt himself becoming angry, but held it in check. "I'm sorry Anita, but I did make a couple wrong turns."

Roberto's proposal was seven hundred dollars which Paul told Anita, on the ride home, seemed unbelievably cheap.

"The locals treat us real well down here. Lew gets his hair cut for five dollars." She turned into the Siskel's driveway.

"So, it looks like you won't have a car for a couple weeks. You call me when you need a ride somewhere."

"I'll be OK. The Siskel's told me I could use their ATV. That should be fine for now."

"Just as long as you don't drink and drive. Promise me, Paul, you really need to pull it together."

Paul snapped. "You know, Anita, we may be like family, but you're not my fucking mother." He opened the door and stepped outside.

"Promise me, Paul. No more driving drunk, or I swear, I'll have Roberto keep the car until the Siskel's get back."

"Fine." He slammed the door and walked into the cottage, steaming. It was several minutes before he heard her drive off.

35

Paul was embarrassed by his skirmish with Anita. After leaving two unanswered voice mails that evening, he walked to her house the next morning to apologize in person. Lew's truck was gone, but a battered yellow Jeep was parked in the drive. Paul heard voices from the terrace. Not wanting to barge in on company, he turned to leave, but was given up by Feliz's bark.

Anita and Chuy appeared from the terrace. "Hey Paul, I was just going to call you back. I understand you've already met our dear friend, Chuy."

Paul smiled as the two men shook hands. "Lucky for me we did. I appreciate your help yesterday."

"No big deal, man. My cousin, Roberto, will fix the Mercedes up, good as new."

"Let's move back to the shade," Anita suggested. "I'll bring out a pitcher of iced tea and we can chat on the terrace."

Not wanting to apologize in front of Chuy, Paul followed her back to the kitchen. "Hey Anita, I'm really sorry about yesterday. You were 100% right on all counts. I promise you I won't drive drunk again. I was a complete idiot."

"Thanks for that, Paul. You're forgiven." She kissed him on the cheek and handed him the pitcher. "Take this out and I'll bring the glasses."

Paul complemented Chuy on his English. "Have you always lived on the Baja?"

Chuy laughed. "Oh, no. I grew up in Oakland, California. My parents moved there in the late 50's and opened up a Mexican restaurant."

"Chuy was the oldest of four brothers and two sisters. Growing up, they all worked at the family restaurant."

"Vietnam was in full swing and I was about to be drafted, so I joined up with the Marines. Couldn't have picked a worse time to enlist. Ended up in the battle to retake Hue from the Viet Cong and North Vietnamese, during the Tet Offensive."

"Chuy was one of the few in his platoon to make it back alive. Tell Paul about your battles with the VA."

"I was sent home and got the Purple Heart for being shot in the thigh, but there were other injuries." Chuy sipped his tea. Paul, uncomfortable with his own dark past, wondered if he'd continue.

"You've probably heard about Agent Orange. Our war strategists decided that it was better to hold our positions and be doused by the stuff than to move troops out of a target area. Monsanto had mixed up the concoction to defoliate trees and falsely claimed it wasn't harmful to humans. I got off pretty easy with a mild form of peripheral neuropathy. My hands and feet itched, mostly at night. Not serious enough to qualify for disability, as it turned out. That came later with the PTSD."

Anita stood, as if on cue. "I'll leave you boys to talk. I have some paperwork I need to get out this morning. Yell if you need more tea." Paul now suspected that Chuy hadn't just dropped by, but was summoned by Anita.

"Actually, I have somewhere to go, myself." Chuy stood up and pushed in his chair. "Tell you what, Amigo, Anita says that you like to run. I do a little of that myself. How about I come by your place just before sunset and we'll head down to the beach? We can talk more then."

After Chuy left, Paul followed Anita inside. "So, nice move, General . . . calling in reinforcements."

"What are you talking about?"

Not buying her feigned look of innocence, Paul just smiled.

"OK, maybe I did ask him to drop by."

"To work out a strategy for pulling my head out of my ass, if I know you."

"If only it were that simple. Look, Chuy's been through a lot. He's an exceptional human being. You would enjoy getting to know him. If this helps with the extraction of your head, then all the better."

******

Paul didn't think he'd have a problem keeping up with Chuy, who had to be pushing seventy. Careful not to tire out the old man, Paul set out at a slow pace. Chuy immediately pulled alongside. "PTSD has been around forever, but it wasn't really acknowledged as a disorder until about 1980. When I returned from 'Nam, I'd never heard of it. I was just constantly angry and scared. Booze and dope, that's how I dealt with it. My family tried to help. They organized an intervention and I spent six months in a northern California sanitarium that specialized in substance abuse. Two months after being discharged, I was back on the booze, heavier than ever. I ran a red light, narrowly missed hitting a school bus and crashed through the front of a car dealership. I broke some ribs and smashed my face, lost my driver's license and developed an addiction to the drugs I was taking for pain." Chuy had ramped up the pace while talking. Paul was working hard to keep up.

"After the accident, I moved into my parent's basement apartment. I was supposed to look after the place while they visited relatives in Mexico. Instead, I got loaded one night, started a grease fire, burned down the house and killed their dog."

"Jesus."

"Yeah. I was one fucked up hombré." The pace had again quickened.

Chuy glanced over at Paul. "You OK?"

"Fine, just haven't exercised much lately."

"Wanna slow down?"

Paul perceived or imagined a subtle challenge behind Chuy's offer. Either way, his self-esteem was already at rock bottom. He didn't need his ass handed to him by the old man. "No, feel fine."

With the exception of Paul's panting, they ran in silence across the wet sand until Paul gasped, "K," to Chuy's suggestion they turn around.

"Look at that sunset, Pablo. This is my favorite time of day. You know, running's been the key to my salvation. I replaced booze with it. Eventually I was able to make amends for all the trouble I'd caused, forgave myself and wrapped my arms around the whole PTSD thing."

"What do you mean?" Paul gasped, sweat streaming across his face, insides shaken and stirred, dangerously close to hurling.

"That's for another run, Amigo. We're back." Paul resisted the strong desire to collapse in the sand as they slowed to a walk. He trailed Chuy back to the cottage. "Tomorrow, same time then?" Chuy asked, climbing into his Jeep.

241

"OK. You want anything to drink before you head out?"

"Already taken care of, Bro." Chuy lifted a water bottle from an ice chest on the passenger seat. "Mañana, Amigo."

What was that all about? You almost killed yourself trying to keep up. He went inside, showered, laid down and fell asleep in seconds. His mouth was cotton dry when he woke just after midnight. He drank a tall glass of water, crawled under the blankets, but couldn't fall back to sleep. Like a dark, evil mist, he could feel it coming on. Guilt, regret, sorrow, anger all gripped him in a familiar wave of pain. He got up and filled a tumbler with ice and pulled the cork out of a tequila bottle with his teeth, but was stopped suddenly by Anita's words *You know that nothing will change until you do.* He set the bottle down, spit out the cork and opened his wallet. The only picture he hadn't removed was of AJ in his T-ball uniform. The wave of pain was now all-consuming, a regular fucking Tsunami. He held the wallet in front of him and kept his eyes on the photo, his hands trembled with the effort. When it finally passed, he poured the tequila in the sink. "I'm fucked-up, but I won't drink it away anymore." Five minutes later Paul was walking barefoot on the beach. He started to jog. Picking up his pace, he accelerated into an all-out sprint before collapsing to the sand. He rolled onto his back and stared at the clear, night sky. He couldn't remember ever feeling more alone. He missed Sienna, AJ and the life he'd left behind. Feeling himself sinking again, he shook his head, stood up quickly and walked back to the cottage. One last thought gripped him as he fell exhausted into bed, *I may have lost Sienna, but I don't have to lose AJ.*

36

After a sound sleep, Paul awoke late in the morning and signed into Gmail.

Dear Sienna,
Maybe you heard already from Andy, but I'm in Cabo San Lucas, and am doing better. I know there are important things we need to talk about and I hope, one day soon, to have the opportunity.
I am attaching a letter that I've written to AJ. I hope you agree that it's important for me to stay in touch with him and that the letter seems appropriate given the circumstances. I wish you happiness Sienna. I'm sorry to have let you down.
Love always,
Paul

******

Dear AJ,

I'm living in Mexico near the city of Cabo San Lucas. I live in a neighborhood called Elias Calles. Although I'm a long ways away from you, I think about you all the time and can't wait to return to St. Croix and see you. But, before I come back, I have some problems to work out. In the meantime, let's stay in touch through email and maybe we can video chat too.

How are you doing? Have you and Red been hunting for Chaney? Have you seen any iguanas lately? I bet Rose is getting big.

I hope to hear from you soon.

I love you buddy,

Paul

He warmed a leftover chicken enchilada and made coffee. His iPhone announced an incoming email as he sat down to eat.

Paul,

Of course you can write to AJ. I'm at the restaurant, but I'll print your letter and give it to him when I get home. I know he'll be very happy to hear from you. He misses you, Paul. This has really been tough on him.

Send me your address so I can forward your mail. There's something from Curtis Blossom.

I'm glad you're doing better.

Sienna

Paul reread the message several times. She didn't seem as mad as the last time they spoke. Maybe he'd call her at the restaurant some time, although when he imagined their conversation, he couldn't think of anything he'd want to know about her life now that she was with Casey. Besides, stopping the binge drinking and dealing with his anger and guilt were challenging enough without the flood of emotions he felt every time he thought of Sienna.

Anita's call broke his train of thought. "So how was the run?"

"Still alive, but barely. I'm in much worse shape than I thought. Call me a glutton for punishment, but we're going again this afternoon."

"Maybe I should have mentioned that Chuy runs in the Mexico City marathon each year. He says it's for fun, but it's in the August heat and sounds nuts to me."

"Thanks Anita. You know a little warning might have been nice. I almost killed myself trying to keep up with him."

"Well it's good to hear your competitive juices haven't dried up. Other than that, how are you doing?"

"Are you wondering if I got drunk and drove the Siskel's ATV into the Pacific?"

"Well, did you?"

"Actually, for the first time in a long while, I went to bed sober. Don't know what possessed me," he added, joking. "Actually, that's not true. I know what possessed me. I can't keep running from myself . . . I've got a little boy who needs me."

"One day at a time, Boss. One day at a time."

******

Paul sent the Siskels an email notifying them of the accident and that he was taking care of the costs for the repairs with Roberto. He poured himself more coffee and began a google-search on PTSD. While the symptoms of the disorder matched his own, he was put off by the lengthy sessions of psycho-analysis prescribed as an effective method for healing. Discouraged, he was about to close his laptop when Sharon Siskel's email arrived.

Dear Paul,
We're so sorry to hear of your accident and thankful that you weren't injured. You are not to pay one dime for its repair. That kind of accident can happen to anyone down there. It used to be more of a problem before Highway 19 was turned into a four-lane and the cattle fencing was installed to keep the livestock of the road. I feel bad that I didn't warn you when you dropped us off at the airport.
We'll get in touch with Roberto to settle the bill.
Warmly, Sharon

Paul appreciated her insistence on covering the cost of repairs, but there was no way he'd let them do it. If necessary, he'd confess that he'd been lit up like a Christmas tree when the cow dropped out of the space ship in front of him. He hoped it didn't come to that.

Hearing the Jeep drive up, he switched off his computer, and steeled his resolve for the impending overexertion. This time when they reached the beach, Chuy suggested a walk instead of a run. "You don't want to come back too fast, Pablo. Yesterday, I found out that you have the will to come back. Today we'll talk about a way."

Paul feigned ignorance. "What do you mean by 'come back'?"

246

Chuy smiled. "Actually, 'come back' isn't the term Anita used."

"More like, pull my head out of my ass?"

"Sounds closer."

"Did she offer you anything for your efforts? You've got to have things you'd rather be doing."

"Actually, Lew and Anita have already overpaid me with their friendship. She really cares for you, and whenever I get the chance, this is what I do since I returned to Mexico."

"What? Running out of shape sad-sacks into the ground?"

"Seems to help reduce the sad sack's desire for a drink. How was last night?"

"Listen, Chuy, before you suggest that I join you at AA, I just don't think I'm interested in that route."

"No problem there, Amigo. In spite of what most people who call themselves alcoholics say, quitting excessive drinking isn't all that hard. You just stop doing it. The hard part is working through the reason for the excessive drinking."

"Which is?"

"Trapped energy." Chuy stopped and turned toward the ocean waves rolling into shore. "When I was in Vietnam, there was a local boy we called Elvis. He was around fourteen and lived with his mother in a small village that we used as an outpost. A bright kid; always smiling, laughing, and singing Elvis Presley songs. I'd give him rations, and sometimes he'd bring me a warm meal his mother had fixed. One evening, three Marines were smoking weed around a small fire. I watched Elvis toss a grenade into the fire. The three soldiers were obliterated. I was concussed and wounded, but managed to shoulder my M16 and framed him in its sights as he ran away. I saw and did terrible things in Vietnam, but the image of

Elvis's head exploding from my bullet will haunt me for the rest of my life. Later, after returning home, I realized what a huge fucking mistake the entire war had been and that the real enemy was the military establishment that sent us over there. I was outwardly furious at the politicians and generals for their lies and corruption, spewing my hatred to anyone who'd listen. Inside, I felt isolated, frightened and guilty for what I'd done to Elvis and the others I'd killed. Drugs and booze were my only escape from a deeply rooted desire to punish and ultimately, destroy myself."

Chuy can't know of my killings. Anita probably did relay the story of the attack on the boat, the loss of our daughter and my drinking. Yet, Chuy's story strongly resonated with Paul.

They resumed walking. "I appreciate you telling me this Chuy. What about the trapped energy?"

"Energy gets trapped when something happens that we can't accept or forgive. What finally saved me was forgiving myself."

"But how do you forgive something that's unforgivable?"

"Make amends the best you can, then let it go. The past is the past, Pablo. Nothing's gained by dwelling on past mistakes."

"Easier said than done."

"Exactly, Amigo. The how is different for everyone. I had to get off booze and quiet my mind. I started running and learned to meditate. I try to let difficult emotions and thoughts pass through me instead of getting crazy over the things I can't change. The big thing for me, though, was forgiveness. Forgiving others, sure, but mostly forgiving myself."

His eyes pierced into Paul's. *He knows there's more to the story than Anita told him.*

"You got to love yourself, Amigo, or you ain't shit, as my uncle likes to say."

When they finally turned around, the sun was dipping into the ocean. Even though he was still stiff and sore from yesterday's run, it was Paul who suggested they run back.

37

She was born an over-achiever. At Princeton she ranked nationally in the javelin and graduated summa cum laude with a degree in psychology. She went on to obtain her JD from Harvard Law School, graduating first in her class. In spite of several lucrative offers from well-established East Coast firms, Constance Hunter decided instead to join the FBI. Combining a strong-willed self-discipline with uncanny intuition in complex investigations, she soon reached the upper echelon of the bureau's agents. Fifteen years into her career, she was now special agent in charge of the FBI's Seattle division. Constance was responsible for the cohesion and effectiveness of over 300 FBI personnel. However, her passion remained in solving complex crimes. To this end, she was often consulted by field agents working on difficult investigations.

Her meteoric rise through the ranks of the FBI had come at the expense of a personal life, a subject her younger brother, Adam, had often chided her about. In their last phone conversation, he brought up the subject again, "Look Connie, you need to lighten the fuck up and live a little. Do something for no other reason than it feels right. In two weeks I'll be hiking in the Patagonia. Remember when we were kids, and we talked about seeing faraway places together? Come on Sis, you've got a cache of personal time off, use some of it and join me."

"We have several investigations going on that would suffer if I were out of pocket," she had replied stiffly, sorting through her email while they spoke.

Frustrated by her continued unavailability and a growing belief that his sister had been swallowed up in the nation's terrorist paranoia, Adam had pushed it. "I think the investigations would be fine. I'm not sure how you'd make out though, with nothing to do but relax. You know, Connie, there are more important things in life than locking people up. I worry about you. You're so *by-the-book* now. Everything's so fuckin' black and white."

Connie was irritated enough to stop her multi-tasking. Punching out of the speakerphone setting, she picked up the handset and barked, "That's easy for you to say. Your liberal friends have quite the pity party going over all the poor detainees- 99% of whom are guilty as hell."

"But what about that one percent? Don't you ever feel remorse for the innocent lives you guys are ruining? Why not go against your rules and order and make an exception if you believe a person's innocent?"

"Because, Dear Brother, without rules and order all that's left is chaos. Besides, I'm not the one who decides. We find them and examine them. Somebody else decides what happens next."

Polar opposites, Constance had been both older sister and surrogate mother to Adam, five years her junior. Most of their mother's attention had been directed toward scoring prescription drugs. Dropping out of his third as a philosophy major at Seattle University, Adam worked as a masseur. Happily bouncing from one northwestern resort to

251

another, he was able to save enough money for his real passion-travel. Since Constance took over command of the agency's Seattle office, their relationship had been stretched thin by her job obsession as well as their divergent perspectives on the nation's *War on Terror*. Still, Adam was the only family Constance had and, all differences and distractions aside, she loved him deeply. "Someday I'll retire and we'll have lots of time for backpacking," she assured him, as they ended their final call.

Three weeks later, Constance received word that Adam and three members of his hiking party were missing and presumed dead. Witnesses described the massive mudslide as catastrophic with no chance of survival. Still, she brought her considerable agency resources to bear and joined local Chilean authorities in an all-out search for the missing hikers. Although the walking poles he was using at the time of the landslide were discovered, after three days of dangerous excavations, the bodies remained unreachable, entombed in fifty feet of mud and ruin.

Constance flew back from Chile buried in sorrow. Recalling the number of times she had declined Adam's invitations to join him on one of his adventures; she was devastated by his death and riddled with guilt. Before leaving for Patagonia, he had left her a voicemail when she had been too busy to take the call. Crying softly, she listened to the last words she would ever hear him speak, "Hey Sis, it's your bad news brother calling. I'm boarding for Santiago in ten minutes and really bummed you're not joining me. Next year it's Iceland, so you'd better start planning for three weeks off. OK, that's it. I love you. Oh wait, by the way, here's a thought for you to chew on while I'm gone . . . Rules and order may be keeping us from chaos, but they should never be a substitute for conscience. Just something to think about. I love you, Sis."

Forced by the Bureau to take a month-long leave of absence, she kept herself afloat by feeding her active mind and imagination with investigations that intrigued her, making notes for her field agents and offering suggestions during informal meetings held at a downtown Seattle coffeeshop.

It was during this time that Andrew Sherman had been gunned-down in Tortola. Although agents investigating the killing were certain it was Buddy Falco who ordered the hit, there was no evidence that could be used to identify the shooter, let alone link Buddy to the killing.

When Buddy disappeared, Constance, now back at work, was immediately skeptical of the theory that Buddy and his two mobster associates had been taken out by a gang of drug pushers. Her doubt was strengthened with the discovery of the 338 Lapua Magnum, which not only provided a link with Buddy to Sherman's assassination, but also the murderous skill level of at least one of Buddy's companions. From home, Constance pulled up Buddy's file. It's a given that mob murders are usually related to money and/or revenge. It was obvious that Buddy had taken his revenge on Sherman for framing him, but what about the money? In Buddy's trial for Sherman's alleged murder, FBI investigators had uncovered a multi-million dollar gambling debt that Sherman had owed Buddy. It was also disclosed that Sherman had skimmed over a million dollars from his development company just prior to disappearing. Buddy, she was certain, would try to recover any leftovers.

She found it in a report buried deep in the digital file; a violent assault perpetrated by Buddy and his two cohorts just days prior to the mobsters' disappearance. Quickly scanning through the report, she stopped when she recognized the last name of one of the victims, Sienna Armstrong. She returned to the report's beginning and carefully read every word. There it was, "Sienna Armstrong suffered a ruptured spleen and a miscarriage as a result of Buddy Falco's kick to her stomach."

She had it. Her mind leapt ahead as she pulled up the fall announcement of Sienna's marriage to Paul Armstrong. She recognized Paul's name as the former partner of Andrew Sherman, who coincidentally had reported running into Andrew Sherman months earlier at a bar in the British Virgin Islands. She could easily imagine Buddy's reaction to Sherman and Armstrong showing up in the same restaurant, 4,000 miles away from where they had last seen each other. *That's no fuckin' coincidence. Armstrong was in on it from the start.* The pieces fell together, and she felt confident Buddy was in St. Croix to put the squeeze on Armstrong for the money. But he miscalculated. Every man has a flash point. When Buddy kicked Sienna in the stomach, killing their unborn child, he had pushed the architect too far. Buddy Falco had created the worst kind of enemy; the kind he wouldn't see coming.

She was looking up the number of the special agent in charge of the Bureau's field office in St. Croix when the Armstrong's wedding announcement and photo came up on her laptop screen. Stunned, she studied the black and white newspaper photo. Paul Armstrong, stared back at her. Only it wasn't Paul Armstrong's face that she was seeing, it was Adam's.

38

An hour before the Johnson's were picking him up for a day on their boat, AJ crawled into bed with Sienna. "Mommy, are you going to marry Casey?"

"I don't know Honey. Paul and I still need to figure things out."

"Are you still mad at him for drinking alcohol when he took me out in the Zodiac?"

"No, Honey."

"Do you still love him?"

"Yes, I do." The words tumbled out of her mouth before she had a chance to think.

"Then why can't Paul come back, Mommy?"

"Paul's trying to get well so he can come back and see you."

"I really miss him."

"I do too Honey," Sienna said, hugging him. "I do too."

******

When Roxanne and Red arrived, Red took AJ out to the car to show him his new remote controlled helicopter.

After the boys left, Roxanne asked, "So give, sister. What's up?"

"What do you mean?"

"What I mean is there has been a certain someone's BMW parked in the carport the last week and it's still there when Hank and I take our morning walk."

"Very clever of you Sherlock, but Casey has been sleeping in the guest bedroom."

"Terrific. The man looks like he could be a model on the FDNY's beefcake calendar and you have him sleeping in your guest bedroom."

"He's a great guy, Roxanne. I know that I'm lucky to have him in my life, but I just don't feel the chemistry."

Their conversation was interrupted by the sound of a vehicle driving through Windsol's gate, followed by two toots from its horn. Roxanne and Sienna walked out on the porch. The boys had already reached the white van and pointed up to the porch as the driver stepped out carrying a bouquet of long stemmed white roses.

"Sienna Meyers?" The man approached the two women.

"Shoot, I thought they might be from Hank," Roxanne kidded, pointing at Sienna. "You found her."

"It wasn't easy, but the fellow gave good directions over the phone. I own the flower shop in Frederiksted. My name's Eldon and these are for you."

Sienna read the note accompanying the flowers as Eldon drove away.

Nowhere near as beautiful as you . . . C

"All chemistry aside, it looks like you're being courted, and in fine style, I might add. Come on boys, Hank will be wondering what's taking us so long."

She kissed Sienna on the cheek, "Enjoy this, Sweetie. We girls deserve all the fussin' over we can get. In fact, I think I'm gonna mention Eldon's shop to my Hanky-bear."

She watched Roxanne's car pull away. *Would she ever feel chemistry for another man?* Her cell's ring broke into her thoughts.

"Hi Honey." It was Andy. "How's life on the island? How's our boy?"

"Hey Andy, things are alright. AJ's doing better now that he and Paul are communicating regularly."

"Well, I'm glad to hear that. I know how much he loves him." When Sienna didn't answer, Andy cleared his throat and continued, "I know how much he loves you too, Sienna."

"He has a funny way of showing it."

"You can't judge him, Sienna. You don't understand what he's been through."

"Andy, I went through everything he went through . . . and don't forget, it happened to my body. I didn't drink like a drunken sailor, get into fights, and leave the island. I didn't—"

"Sienna, please, stop! I didn't call to upset you. You've been through hell and you don't need some old coot giving you a hard time about anything."

Sienna took a deep breath. "No, I'm sorry Andy. I know how much you love Paul. I'm just . . . I don't know. Do you know why he hasn't contacted me? It's been over two months since I've talked to him. What's he expect from me?"

Andy carefully considered his response before answering. "I think he feels that you're with that attorney fella now and he doesn't want to cause problems."

"Well, how noble of him, Andy. Maybe he should have been a monk instead of my husband and AJ's daddy." Andy didn't reply. "Look . . . maybe we should agree to disagree and change the subject. When are you coming down? Your grandson really misses you and Aunt Charlotte."

"Well, that's what I'm calling about. Char and I were talking and, well, we think you should come up here. I've reserved Kate's last Pasayten ride in September for the entire extended family."

"September, huh . . . Well, AJ and I are up for it. I'd have to ask Casey if he wants to come. He's part of our lives now."

"Yeah, I suppose."

"Would you be nice to him, make him feel welcome?"

"Yeah...for you I would. Sure, bring him along. I'm paying for the trail ride and your and AJ's tickets, but the attorney can pay for his own airplane ticket. Seems like he can afford it, driving around the island in that hotshot sports car of his."

"His name is Casey, Andy. Please stop calling him 'the attorney.'"

"OK, got it. So you'll let me know after you talk with him? I need to make a passel of reservations. Char, Barney, Claire, Brooke, Joey, Tex and Sally, they're all coming. It'll be like old times."

"Almost," Sienna said, thinking of the one person not coming. "I will Andy. I'll let you know tomorrow."

******

AJ had already eaten dinner and was in his bedroom with Rose when Casey came in and found the dinner table set for two.

"Get out of that suit and wash up. I roasted a chicken and if I wait much longer to serve it, you'll think it's leather." Casey reappeared a few minutes later and joined her at the dinner table. "Still plenty moist to my palate. Thanks for waiting on dinner for me."

"Well, you did send me these beautiful flowers." She pointed with her fork to the crystal vase filled with the white roses. "It's the least I could do."

"Beautiful flowers for my beautiful lady."

"Andy called today." She passed Casey the wine bottle.

"What'd he want?"

"He invited us on a horse camping trail ride in Washington, early next month."

"I bet he's real excited about my coming along."

"He promised that he'd make you feel welcome. Come on Casey, the other Windsol people from Washington will be there. It'll give you all a chance to get to know each other."

"Windsol." Casey made a face. "Armstrong came up with that name, didn't he? Did you ever think he might be gay?"

"Not funny, Casey. Anyway, what should I tell Andy?"

"Why do you want to go up there? Those are Armstrong's people. We've got our own families down here."

"Andy is AJ's grandpa and the other people are friends of mine. They're my people too."

"Well, if you two are going then I guess I'll come along. Find out the dates and I'll make sure Chantal signs me out on my calendar. I gotta say though, I've never cared much for horses."

259

39

Significantly exceeding Paul's final billing, Carl Blossom posted in the memo section of his generous check.

Includes a ten thousand dollar expense for wear and tear on the architect. CB

Except for food, Paul had very few living expenses. He had decided to take the summer off from any money-generating efforts and focus on his recovery. So far the strategy was working.

His sunset beach runs with Chuy were now over six miles and he still hadn't touched a drop of liquor. His diet was mostly organic and vegetarian. In the evening, he devoured books on recovering from PTSD that he had downloaded to his Kindle. At Chuy's assistance, he made sure he didn't become too isolated. Sunday afternoons he joined Anita and Lew for a barbecue and attended at least one neighborhood function every other week. Most of his days were spent hiking alone through the nearby foothills of the Sierra De Laguna mountain range. Twice a week he spent his afternoons at an eight room eldercare center. Anita had mentioned that her friend Remy had started the center after her husband died, leaving her with a house way too big for one person. When her aging aunt moved in, Remy, a former registered nurse, realized that caring for elderly residents would provide her with an income as well as a family of friends for her aunt to enjoy. Anita described how appreciative the residents were when visitors showed up. Paul decided to give it a try.

It turned out that Paul wasn't the first of Anita's referrals to visit Remy's eldercare home. "Do you know a handsome fellow, a little older than you, named Lew?" Paul was asked by Smokey, an ascoted, pencil-thin, 93 year old Brit, as Paul wheeled him outside onto the shaded veranda.

"I know a Lew who's married to Anita."

"That's the fellow. That's right, he is married, isn't he? Say, be a sport and reach inside that pack on the back of my chair and pull out a fag for me, will you?"

Paul wasn't sure what he'd find inside the small fanny pack, but did as he was told. There were several single-shot bottles of Gordon's gin, a couple vials of prescription medication, some Kleenex, a Zippo lighter and a half-empty pack of filtered Marlboros.

Paul, now understanding the origin of his nickname, lit Smokey's shaking cigarette. After a deep draw, the shaking stopped. "This Lew fellow, I bet he's a hit with the ladies. Kind of reminds me of Frank Gifford in his prime. You know . . . the American footballer. I always thought he was quite dishy."

Paul had to work hard at not laughing. "I'll tell Lew you think so. I'm sure he'll be pleased."

"No, don't you dare. I wouldn't want to scare the poor fellow off."

"He's a retired prison guard. I don't imagine he scares easily."

"You're probably right, but still you never know how people are. Say, Paul is it? If you look inside my pack you'll see a few small bottles of gin. If you'd be so kind as to go into the kitchen and grab us a couple glasses and a bit of ice, we could have ourselves a nice time of it out here."

Paul took one of the small bottles out of the bag and headed to the kitchen.

"Say, Handsome, where'd you come from?" Paul was filling Smokey's glass with ice from the freezer and hadn't heard the five foot nothing, eighty-something redhead come up behind him. Thoroughly giving him the once over through her thick glasses, she said, "Well, I'll be. The view in this place is improving daily. I'm guessing that you're Paul, Anita's friend. Remy said that you'll be dropping by once in a while. A word to the wise . . . Next time you come, don't let Smokey corral you. That old prune thinks he still has the moves. Had that other poor fellow—"

"Lew?"

"Yep, that's the one. Had Lew massaging his shoulders. He might be 93 but he still fancies himself a playboy. Enough about Smokey though. Where's your glass? Didn't that cheap old goat offer you a drink?"

"Yes, but I'm off booze for a while."

"Good idea. Better to keep your wits about you with Smokey sniffin' around. By the way, I'm Remy's Aunt Ruby. She and I started this place ten years ago. OK, I gotta go and make the rounds." She turned to leave. "Don't be a stranger."

Paul returned to the veranda. "It's about time. I thought you might have taken off with my gin." Smokey took the offered glass.

"I thought about it, but ran into Ruby."

He signaled Paul to lean down. "She's a bitter woman, that one. Still can't get over my preferences, if you follow my drift. Thinks every man over eighty should find her irresistible. Don't get me wrong, she's bright as a light bulb. Good company, that one, but she shouldn't expect an old dog to change his spots." Taking a long pull on his gin, he continued. "You know, Remy and Ruby are the reason I'm still on this planet. By the way, where's your drink?"

"I'm off booze for now."

"Is that right? Well, better you than me." Smokey toasted Paul with his glass.

"What did you mean that you wouldn't be on this planet if it weren't for Remy and Ruby?"

"After my Alfred died, I had no one. No children or grandchildren to visit me. I was totally alone. When we first got together, it wasn't like it is now where gay couples can adopt. He would have made a great mum, he just loved children. I was always too busy trying for the almighty pound, or dollar, but not Alfred. He'd see me chasing my tail, all worked up about something, and before you could say vacation, he'd have us flying off to somewhere exotic. That's how we ended up retiring down here on the Baja. We bought a condo near Todos Santos. We had 41 wonderful years together and shared the last ten down here. Then one day, right after breakfast, he just stood up and dropped to the floor. A massive coronary and he was gone, just like that."

"I'm sorry."

"The heart attack that killed my poor Alfred broke my heart as well. I wasn't doing a very good job of taking care of myself. I wouldn't cook and I only ate out a few times a week . . . I guess I wanted to join him. Remy had heard about me through mutual friends. Showed up one day and told me that I needed to sell my condo and move into her place. She said that I needed someone to look after me. I came over a couple times, I was still driving then, and decided to give it a try and, well, here I still am."

The story reminded Paul of other familiar stories, including his own, where someone helped bring a person through a rough time. He felt compassion and without being asked, stood up and gently massaged the old gent's shoulders.

"Well, that's very nice of you. I get so bound up in this chair, that really helps," Smokey reached up and patted Paul's hand.

Paul didn't even mind Ruby's disgusted head shake as she mouthed, *I warned you*, through the window.

40

Dear Paul,
Casey, Mom, and me are going to ride horses in the
Pasayten Wilderness with Papa. We get to fly in the big airplane. It will
be loads of fun.
Hope you are feeling better.
Love,
AJ

Paul was conflicted over AJ's cheerful message. He had already spoken to Andy and Barney about the ride and decided that it would be too uncomfortable with Sienna and Casey there. But reading AJ's message had him rethinking his decision. *If I'm going to have a relationship with AJ, and live on St. Croix, then I'm going to have to get over the fact that they're a couple.*

The ride was in ten days, which coincided with the Siskel's return. Whether he joined the ride or not, he might as well purchase his airplane tickets and spend some time in Washington before heading back to St. Croix. Either way, he'd be seeing AJ in less than three weeks. He'd decided that he would rent a condo on St. Croix instead of moving back into one of the vacant Windsol cottages.

"Damn it, Paul," Andy's voice blazed from his cell. "The whole idea of building the place was so we could all live there together. Now that damn attorney's gone and screwed the whole thing up."

"I hate to stick up for Casey, but it's not his fault, Andy. I can live nearby. I like the idea of AJ growing up surrounded by our friends. He and Red are like brothers and now that Hank is there to look after things, Windsol will do fine. Maybe one day, I'll live there again, but not right now."

"Yeah, well, I still don't like it very much. How are you doing by the way? You sound good. About ready to re-emerge?"

"I still get down and feel anxious, but it doesn't usually last very long. Anita introduced me to my running partner, Chuy. He saw a lot of action in Vietnam as a Marine and recovered from PTSD. He's been a big help to me."

"Sounds like a good man. Our family just keeps growing doesn't it? I'd like to shake his hand one day."

"You will, soon I hope. You'd really love Anita and Lew too. So, I'm still on the wagon, and I feel strong enough to step back into my life on St. Croix."

"Yeehaw! Finally. When will we see you?"

"In less than a month, I'll come to Winthrop for a few days to see you guys after you get back from the ride."

"Well, I'd better tell Kate and Carmen. They're so anxious to see you. They're gonna be beside themselves when I tell 'em you're coming."

"Let's keep it between the two of us for now. I don't want Sienna to get wind of this yet. It could throw a damper on their plans to come up for the ride."

"You're always so concerned about everyone else. Maybe you should be a little more concerned about me. I ain't getting any younger, you know."

"What can I do for you, Andy?" Paul braced himself for the answer.

"You can get off that damn high horse and quit worrying so much about messing up Sienna's relationship with Casey. Christ, mess things up for God's sake; make a fool of yourself if you have to. Goddammit, win her back, Son."

"Well, how do you really feel about it, Andy?" Paul laughed. "Look, you may have a point. Believe me, if I find out that she's done with Casey, I'll look into it."

"I'll look into it? That's the best you can do?" Andy groaned. "My God, I'm already an old man. At this rate, I'll be worm food before you make your move."

Paul was due at Anita's in a half-hour, and still needed to shower off the dust and grime from his hike in the hills. After calming Andy down by assuring him that he wouldn't hesitate if there was ever an opportunity, they disconnected. His cell rang just before he stepped into the shower.

"Hola and Que Pasa, Amigo."

"Hey, Barney."

"How are you doing, Slugger? Miss me?"

"Of course, life just isn't the same without you. I'm doing well Barney."

"Well, it's about fucking time. So, now that you're back in the pink, when are you going to haul your ass up this way? I'm not asking for me, you understand. It's Claire, Brooke and Sally that keep pestering me to find out."

Paul told Barney his plans before cutting the call short and stepping into the shower. Fifteen minutes later, Kate heard the news from Sally. Ten minutes after that, Andy got a call from Carmen.

"Andy, we just heard that Paul's going to meet us up here after the ride."

"Well, that's great Kiddo, but you sure as hell didn't hear that from me. I just talked to our boy, and he filled me in on his travel plans which he told me he wanted to keep on the QT. I told him that I thought he was being ridiculous, in so many words."

"Well, the cell lines are abuzz now, so maybe you convinced him to go public. I was going to give Sienna a call tonight to coordinate their arrival next week. Do you think I should tell her she might see Paul after the ride?"

Andy moaned, "Where is Char when I need her?"

"She told me she's visiting friends in Port Townsend."

"It was a rhetorical question, Carmen."

"Rhetorical? Well done. You are becoming a force to be reckoned with on the holy battle field of Scrabble. So what do you think? Should I tell Sienna?"

Rubbing his temples, Andy finally answered, "No, don't tell her. Let's just let it play out on its own."

******

She could fly anywhere, on a moment's notice. The FBI had a fleet of jets gassed up and ready to go. In spite of this, she was drinking scotch on an American Airlines 757, crossing over the Cascade Mountain Range, en route to the Dallas/Fort Worth International Airport.

Usually not one to drink on duty, Constance was perplexed as she swirled the amber-colored Glenlivet in front of her. *Maybe I didn't take enough time off after Adam died. Maybe there's something wrong with me. Maybe I'm fucking crazy.* She chuckled derisively and sipped her drink. Whatever the cause, she was definitely operating *out of bounds* or, *off the reservation* as she had heard it labeled. She had always been a rules girl, the right way or the highway, a by-the-book agent. But something now was amiss. She hadn't shared her theory regarding Buddy and his accomplices' murders. She hadn't called the St. Croix bureau. The one thing she had done was to order an alert that would notify her if Paul Armstrong booked a reservation on a commercial airline flight leaving St. Croix.

She thought little of it when she received a notice that he had purchased a one way flight from St. Croix to Puerto Rico. However, when she was notified that he had dropped $4,400 on a one-way ticket to Cabo San Lucas, with a three hour layover at Dallas/Fort Worth, she decided it was time they should meet. But now, sipping on her second drink, she couldn't think of one single reason, for the life of her, why.

41

"Casey, will you help AJ finish packing?" Sienna asked as she transferred a load of wash into the dryer.

"Yeah, OK," Casey sighed, slowly rising from the sofa and turning off the TV. His apathy for the horse camping trip had become more and more apparent as their next morning's departure drew close.

Barely stopping herself in time from suggesting that he take his lazy ass and grumpy attitude home with him, she drew in a deep breath and began humming *Amazing Grace*.

From AJ's room, Casey's loud and angry voice abruptly ended her Zen moment. "Christ, AJ, we don't want Paul on this trip. What the hell are you doing?"

Casey towered over AJ who sat at his computer desk. In spite of the size difference, AJ shot back at Casey, "I can ask him to come if I want."

"Casey," she said with a forced calmness, "can I speak to you outside, please?"

"Before you start," Casey said as they walked out onto the porch, "I realize I didn't handle the situation well in there. I'll apologize to AJ, but Jesus, Sienna, I look over his shoulder and he's practically begging that loser to—"

"Casey, please listen carefully," Sienna interrupted. "In this house, in front of me or AJ, it's not acceptable to refer to Paul as a loser."

"OK, I won't say it anymore, but you know how I feel."

"Everybody knows how you feel, Casey . . . and just so you know, I do understand your reaction. Frankly, I was hoping to enjoy this trip and I don't want Paul on it either."

After he apologized to AJ for his outburst, Casey left to button up a few final matters at his office. Sienna called AJ into the kitchen for a PB and J sandwich. "AJ, do you understand why Casey got mad?"

"Because he doesn't want Paul to come on the trip."

"That's right, Honey. I know this is hard for you to understand, but I don't think it would be a good idea for Paul to come either."

"Because you want to marry Casey."

"No, AJ . . ." Startled by his assumption, she attempted to explain, "because I want to enjoy this vacation and it would be uncomfortable for me if Paul was there with us."

"But I want to enjoy this vacation too and it would be uncomfortable for me if Paul *wasn't* there."

Impressed by his spirit, Sienna once again found herself stumped by his logic. She had to pull out the adult card. "Look, Honey, Casey and I work hard and this trip is something we need. We need to relax and since we're the adults here, you'll just have to wait a little bit longer to see Paul."

"OK, but it's not fair."

"You're right." She hugged him. "But let's try and have a good time anyway, OK?"

"OK, Mommy."

******

All packed and ready to go, Sienna went over a mental list of the things she would need to do in the morning before leaving for the airport at nine. The light tap on her bedroom door preceded Casey's entry. Wearing only his boxers, Sienna felt a stirring as she admired his muscular body. Sensing her eyes on him, he moved quickly over to her bed and lay next to her.

"I thought we might talk about the sleeping arrangements on the trip," he said, moving his hand across her thigh.

She covered his hand with hers. "I'm listening. What would you suggest?"

"I'd suggest that we do this every night."

He kissed her, tentatively at first, until Sienna moaned and kissed him back, her lips parting. He caressed her breasts, and though she lay back and parted her legs, he felt her grow rigid when his hand moved down across her stomach.

"What is it, Baby?" he asked, sitting up.

"It's just . . . I don't know, Casey. You're a wonderful, beautiful man, but I just don't think I'm ready for this."

"OK, let me ask you this. Do you see yourself ever being ready?"

"I don't know, Casey. I'm sorry."

After a moment, he got up and walked toward the door. Turning, he said, "You know what I think?"

"What?"

"I think you're never going to be ready *for me*." When she didn't reply he added, "They're your friends up there in Washington. I'm not going. Besides, if the loser shows up, I'd probably wind up in jail for beating the shit out of him. I have needs too Sienna. Fuck this."

To his credit, he didn't slam the door when he left, although she wouldn't have blamed him.

******

On the day of his departure, Paul and Chuy set out, in the early morning, for their final run together. With Paul's physical conditioning now greatly improved, the pace was fast with very little conversation. Afterward, Chuy opened the glove box of his Jeep and handed Paul a tarnished silver dog tag. Paul read the inscription,

ALVEREZ
J. A.
2271550
USMC
CATHOLIC

"Was this someone in your platoon?"

"No amigo, Jesus Alejandro Alvarez is me. Keep it as a reminder of our runs on the beach and the power of forgiveness."

On the ride to the airport, Paul repeated Chuy's parting words, as he handed the dog tag to Anita. Lew, who was driving, looked over as his wife kissed the dog tag. "I can't think of a better symbol of forgiveness than this," she said, wiping her eyes with a tissue, she added, "I just wish we all didn't live so far apart."

Paul carefully slid the dog tag back in his wallet. "We'll be seeing each other again soon, and often. I promise."

Anita and Lew parked their car and walked beside Paul into the airport. After picking up his boarding pass, they found three empty chairs at an airport coffee shop.

"Hey Lew, sorry we didn't get a chance to play golf."

"No problem, as long as you don't wait too long to come back. You know, Tiger's building a course down here. El Cardonal, I think it's called."

"How many strokes will you give me?"

"No way, you used to be a five at Sahalee. I want two a side." Lew walked up to the counter to give their order.

"Have you heard from Sienna?" Anita asked.

"No, but I didn't expect I would. AJ and I, on the other hand, are in constant communication. Poor little guy. He really wanted me to join the ride in the Pasayten, but that would be too awkward with Casey and Sienna."

"You had all summer to pull yourself back together and get healthy. Isn't it about time you put all that good work to use? Come on Paul, get over yourself. It seems pretty clear to me, in spite of all the 'don't want to interfere' bullshit you've spouted, that it's not just about AJ. It sounds to me like you and Sienna are the real deal. You haven't received anything from her lawyer. My guess is she's not ready yet to throw in the towel. Get on that plane, Paul. Stop being so damn polite and go win her back."

"Win who back?" Lew asked, as he delivered their coffees.

"Paul's been telling me that he shouldn't join the Pasayten ride, because Casey will be there with Sienna."

"Well, what's the worst that could happen? You might get punched, right?"

"A very likely scenario," Paul replied, smiling.

"Well, stay close to Barney then, he'll take care of you."

"I think Paul's more worried about the awkwardness with Sienna, than being punched. But even so, I'd listen to Lew's advice just the same."

"OK, don't worry. It'll all work out regardless of what happens. You guys have been terrific. I owe you both, big time. I'll be back, but you have to come visit me in St. Croix before then."

He stood when it was time to leave. Lew gave him a burly hug and stayed at the table, while Anita walked him to the security check point. "Anita, you've always told me straight-up what you think and I can never thank you enough."

"We love you, Paul. Now, maybe it's about time you start listening to my straight-up advice." She punched him on the shoulder. "Go get her, Boss."

******

The first leg of his flight ended in Los Angeles, where he cleared customs. By then he had reached his decision. He found a seat at the gate of his connecting flight, pulled out his iPhone and went online. He booked a flight, departing Seattle 90 minutes after his arrival.

At Sea-Tac, he picked up his bags and headed back up the escalator to the Horizon Airlines counter. Sixty minutes later, he was on Horizon Air's commuter plane to the tiny, single-gated Pangborn airport, located four miles east of the eastern Washington town of Wenatchee.

Since the trail ride had started that morning, he knew that unless he could arrange a ride with Carmen, he'd have to take a bus from Wenatchee up to Winthrop. But she hadn't answered when he had called from Los Angeles nor when he had landed at Sea-Tac; so he'd left a message on her cell. "Hey Carmen, it's Paul. I'm landing in Wenatchee at four-thirty this afternoon and was wondering if you'd be able to come down and pick me up. No problem if it doesn't work for you. I'll grab a bus. Either way, I'll see you soon."

But Carmen had gotten the message. She greeted him at a full run, practically knocking him over from the force of her hug. "Paul, we've been so worried about you. We love you so much. Don't ever scare us like that again."

"It's great to see you too. I'm fine now. Let me get my bags and we'll catch up on the drive home."

When they came out of the small terminal building, Paul was elated by the sight of his red turbo '86 Saab, top down, ready to roll.

"I was hoping you'd come in this. Mind if I drive?"

"Figured you might want to." She dropped the keys into his open palm.

Even in September, Eastern Washington's dry heat reminded Paul of Cabo as he drove north through the golden hills and apple orchards on Highway 97.

"So, lots of surprises going on," Carmen said.

"Yeah?"

"First, Sienna and AJ show up without Casey. Then, I get this call from my long lost friend, Paul Armstrong, saying he's arriving in Wenatchee in less than two hours."

"I did try you earlier from Los Angeles . . . Wait! . . . Casey didn't come?"

"Nope, and from what she told us last night, that ship not only has sailed, but apparently never made port . . . if you get my drift. Uh, Paul? . . . Look, Honey, you can't do anything about it today. Slow down for God's sake!"

42

The first day is usually the toughest. After 16 miles and a three-thousand foot climb, the riders were exhausted when they finally arrived at base camp. Barney slid off his horse, Bamboo, and rubbed his tailbone. "So when does the fun start?"

"Need any help with that rubbing, Cowboy?" Claire needled him.

"Just because you barely have any weight bearing down on that beautiful ass of yours."

"Hey Uncle Barney, isn't this the coolest thing ever?" AJ rode up on Willy, a small brown and black spotted pinto. "When do we get to ride again?"

"Watching Barney take his first uncertain steps, his 16-year-old nephew, Joey, teased, "We might have to pull Uncle Barney in a wagon."

"Don't you worry about your Uncle Barney. I've got reserves and stamina, the likes of which you youngsters have never seen."

"What's stamina?" AJ asked Joey, as they brought their horses over to the picket line.

"Means he doesn't get tired."

Andy and Tex had already set up the tents and had started the cooking fire. Barney went in to rest while the women found a nearby stream to clean up. Even with Andy ringing the dinner triangle, Claire had to send AJ and Joey to wake *Mr. Stamina*.

After dinner, Andy walked over to Sienna who was watching Joey and AJ brush down their horses. "It's great to see those two together again," Sienna said. "Joey has always been so good with AJ."

"Yeah, they're both good kids. Say, I'm sorry Casey wasn't able to make it. Everything OK there?"

"Congratulations, Andy, you waited almost 24 hours before asking if we had broken up. That must have been difficult for you."

"You can't imagine how difficult. So, I saw you chatting with the girls last night. Do I have to get all the details from them?"

"No, I'm just frustrated with myself for letting it go on so long. He's always been a good friend, but I never felt—"

"Like you do with Paul?"

"Andy, will you please give it a rest. I have no idea where Paul's head is at this point. Also, I'm still angry and hurt over how easily he bailed out on us. I don't know if I could ever really trust him again."

"I hate to hear that," Aunt Charlotte said, joining them. "I'm not saying that you don't have good reason for your feelings, Sienna, but you must wait until you talk with him. Find out what happened. I've never seen him behave the way he did. Maybe it was the attack on you, but I think something more was going on."

"I agree with Aunt Charlotte," Kate said. "I know how much he loved you and AJ. He must have felt totally powerless after the attack."

"Actually, I remember telling him in the hospital how powerless I had felt and he said that he would never let those three get close to any of us again. It was after those thugs disappeared that he started drinking. Maybe it was a delayed reaction, but I think it was the binge drinking that was the major problem. Hank said he'd seen similar behavior with officers on the force suffering from PTSD."

Andy was about to explode, listening to their theories and analysis of Paul. He knew what they didn't, but he also felt that it wasn't up to him to tell Sienna, or anyone else for that matter. "Well, you'll probably have a chance to ask him all of your questions when we get back from the ride."

"What? What are you talking about?"

"Paul mentioned that he's planning on being in Winthrop when the ride's over."

"Oh, I see." Sienna grew furious. "And you thought, what? That I might swoon or have a seizure if you told me?"

"Of course not, we—"

"We? What do you mean, we? Does everybody know about Paul coming to Winthrop?"

"Well, maybe not everyone. I didn't talk to Tex and Sally."

Sienna gave them all a withering look, the final glare directed at Andy, before disappearing into her tent for the evening.

"Good job, Andy," Barney shouted. "Compared to you, our boy's looking better and better."

******

The next morning, Andy asked Sienna to join him for a short walk.

"I'm sorry Sienna. It was my idea not to tell you about Paul coming to Winthrop. I guess I was worried that you'd try and avoid seeing him, or something."

"Andy, I'm not the one who left the island. I want to have a conversation with him. I need to have a conversation with him. Look, I realize our problems have been tough on the people who love us." She took a deep breath before continuing. "I love you, Andy, I'm not mad. It's a beautiful day and AJ and I are so thankful to you for this trip."

"Well, OK, then. Thank you, Honey. I just wish—"

"I know Andy." She took his hand. "I miss him too."

An hour after breakfast, everyone but Barney and Sienna rode out for a day ride led by Kate. Sienna opted to catch up on some well-deserved rest while Barney's excuse of a tender tailbone, provided Andy and Tex with good material for future ribbing.

"But don't you worry, 'Little Ace', I'll be back in the saddle tomorrow," he promised a disappointed AJ. "Besides, somebody has to look after your Mom. Wouldn't want the Indians to get her, would we?"

"Uncle Barney, you're joking," AJ replied, "and you should call them Native Americans."

"Schooled by a six-year-old," Claire said, after AJ ran over to help Andy saddle up his pony.

"He's really something, isn't he?" Barney said. "I know how much Paul misses him."

"Paul always wanted kids. I'm sure he's broken up over their separation."

"Saddle up," Kate shouted. "Day's a-wastin'. Let's get a move on."

"I'll see you soon," Claire said excitedly, as she stood on her tip toes to receive Barney's kiss.

Andy, last in the line of cow-pokes, shouted back, "If we're not back by three, send out the Cavalry. Yeehaw!"

******

Barney moved the camp chairs into the sun. Sienna joined him with two mugs of cowboy coffee.

"I wonder what cowboys have against coffee filters?" Sienna asked, handing him a mug of Andy's steaming, dark brew.

"I think it's an image thing," Barney spit out a few coffee grounds. "You know, like the Marlboro Man, strikes a match on the side of his face and lights his unfiltered cigarette."

"You know, maybe it's the mountain air, but this stuff actually tastes good. So, how's it going with you and Claire?"

"Claire and me? It's going great. Life is good. We're excited about coming back to St. Croix in November. *The Last Hurrah* will be a sturdy little vessel for our charter business."

"I'm really happy for you, Barney."

"Yeah. I just wish Claire would relax a little more. She's so determined not to have another episode; she's always looking over her shoulder. I keep telling her that between her doctor and me, we'll warn her if we ever see her spinning up."

"God, what a terrible ordeal."

"She's strong. We'll make it through this. I'm a lucky guy."

"You both are, to have found each other again after what you've gone through."

"A good lesson," Barney replied. "Never give up on love."

"Why Barney, I didn't know you watched soap operas."

"Very funny. Actually, I think it's something Paul said to me once."

"If only he hadn't."

Before Barney could answer, she got up and splashed the rest of her coffee on the ground. "Well, assuming I'm not too buzzed after drinking this stuff, I think I'll try and take a nap. I'm a bit jet-lagged and haven't gotten much sleep the last few nights."

"Speaking of getting buzzed." Barney pulled out a joint.

"Enjoy your Rocky Mountain High and I'll see you in a few hours." Sienna smiled and disappeared into her tent.

43

Barney looked at his watch. It was close to two-thirty and Sienna still hadn't come out of her tent. *Guess she really needed the rest.* He walked over to the picket line and gave the nickering Bamboo a handful of grain. Next to Bamboo, Sienna's horse, Belle, raised her head, her ears perked. She neighed loudly, which brought the pack horses' heads and ears up as well. Barney heard an answering neigh. As the rider drew close, Barney smiled in recognition. "Well, if it isn't the long-lost *Senór* Armstrong."

"Hola Amigo," Paul replied as he dismounted and braced himself.

"So damn glad to see you." Barney's hug lifted Paul off the ground. Setting him down, a worried expression came over his face. "Jesus, you're just skin and bones. Didn't anybody feed you down there on the Baja?"

"Mostly fed myself, but don't worry, I can still kick your ass."

"Been eating that Mexican Peyote it seems, from the way you're hallucinating." Barney took a phantom swing over Paul's head. "Man, it's good to see you. Been worried about you. A lot of people've been worried about you."

"Yeah, I know. I've been a lot of fuckin' work lately."

"Ain't that the truth?"

"I owe a lot of apologies." Paul looked around the campsite. "Are you it? Everybody else on the day ride?"

"Aren't I enough for you? Actually, Sienna's in her tent over there. She said she needed to rest, but I think she just needed a break from my jabbering."

Barney sensed Paul's hesitation. "If I were you, I wouldn't wait, even if she's asleep."

"I'm not sure how this will go. Do you mind taking a walk to give us some privacy?"

"No problem, Amigo. I was just thinking of taking a little stroll with a shovel and toilet paper."

Paul stopped outside Sienna's tent and called quietly, "Sienna? It's Paul."

"I know who it is. I've been listening to you two since you appeared." She came out through the tent flap. "Or should I say, reappeared?"

Paul knew that many things needed to be discussed, but he couldn't hide his pleasure. "God, it's good to see you."

Standing close to him was difficult. His eyes looked crystal clear. She fought the desire to kiss him. "Let's sit by the fire. There's some of Andy's cowboy coffee still on."

"Sure, that'd be great. Give me a minute. I gotta pull the saddle off JJ and give him some feed."

By the time he joined her, Sienna's anger had returned. She handed Paul a mug of coffee. He winced as it splashed onto his hand. "Sorry about that," she said glibly.

"That's OK. So, how have you been?"

"How have I been? Really? You come riding in, unannounced, after I haven't heard anything from you in over three months and that's how you start? No . . . I'm sorry for breaking your heart. I'm sorry AJ worried that I left so I wouldn't have to adopt him. I'm sorry for—"

"Jesus, he said that?"

"You think I'd make that up? Of course he did. You can't just pick up and disappear without hurting the people who love you." Sienna stood, tears streaming down her face. "Losing our daughter was bad enough, but at least we had each other."

"Daughter?"

"You didn't want to know the sex of the baby. I did. The nurse told me, Paul, and it was a girl . . . We lost our daughter and you weren't there for me. You ran. Mexico? Really, Paul? I don't even know who you are."

"Sienna, I can never expect you to forgive me, but I want you to know that I've never stopped loving you."

"Olly, olly, oxen free," Barney's voice boomed. "OK if I come out?"

"No, Barney, we're not done yet," Sienna shouted, but Paul held his hand up.

"I'd like Barney to hear something I need to tell you both." He yelled back to Barney, "Sure, come on out and grab a chair."

"Everything OK?" Barney noticed that Sienna had been crying. "You working some things out?" he asked hopefully.

Sienna stood up. "No, Paul. This isn't one of your performances, and you sure as hell aren't calling the shots."

"Sure, sure. You guys take all the time you need," Barney replied, shuffling back off toward the bushes.

"Sienna, I think that if—"

"Paul!" None of them had heard the day riders returning, until AJ and Joey rode into camp. "You came!" AJ jumped down from his pony and ran into Paul's outstretched arms.

"I missed you AJ. I can't believe how much you've grown."

"Are you still mad at Paul, Mommy?"

"Hey there, Cowboy!" Andy shouted as he and Kate led the other riders into camp. Sienna's anger diminished slightly as she stepped back and watched Paul's warm reception from the rest of the family. Only Aunt Charlotte picked up on the discord between Sienna and Paul.

"Bad timing, our arriving when we did?" she asked.

"I suppose it could have been better. Actually, I was throwing a fit . . . so maybe it was a good thing."

"I'd say you have every right, Dear. After dinner, maybe you two should take a walk together."

During dinner, her mind was a jumble. It was difficult for Sienna to follow the conversation. She watched Paul mingle. He looked good. Maybe a bit on the skinny side, but he was animated when he spoke and laughed often. She had to admit that his time in Mexico seemed well spent. She was certain he had noticed that she wasn't wearing her wedding ring. If he asked, she wouldn't tell him that she wore it on a gold chain around her neck. Barney approached her nervously. "Are you and I OK?"

"Of course, Barney. I'm just so angry. At Paul mostly. But, it kinda sucks being the only one who isn't overflowing with joy, now that he's back."

"Yeah, I get that. Actually, I'm pretty pissed off at him, too. Never will understand how he pulled away from everybody the way he did. Just doesn't seem like something the Paul Armstrong I grew up with would ever do."

Seeing Barney and Sienna talking, Paul walked over and joined them. "Since you guys are judging me, wouldn't it be fair to let me say a few last words before sentencing."

"I'd say it's only fair," Barney replied, looking toward Sienna, who shrugged her shoulders and gave a weak nod of agreement.

Lowering his voice, Paul said, "We can't do it here."

"OK, then, lead on sir," Barney said, theatrically bending with a full arm flourish, in a feeble attempt to lighten the mood.

In the dim light of a quarter moon, they walked away from the campfire through the sparse pine scrub. Paul stopped when he found two large logs, about three feet apart. He sat down, motioning Sienna and Barney to sit across from him. "Before I start, I want you both to know that I trust each of you completely, and I fully acknowledge that I should have told you about this sooner."

"Told us about what?" Barney was growing suspicious of the dramatic build-up. "Did you find Jesus, or have you come back a gay *caballero*?"

"Oh God," Sienna moaned. "I hadn't considered either one of those options."

Paul smiled, "You guys done?" Both of them nodded yes. He took a long, deep breath. "When you both were in the hospital after the attack, I got a call from Buddy Falco demanding a million dollars. Andy offered to provide the funds and gave me $300,000. for a down payment. Buddy told me to meet them at Ha'Penny Beach with the money or there would be another attack. I assumed he was threatening AJ. I met them early in the morning at the west end of the beach. I brought the ATV . . . and a gun."

Paul stopped his narrative and looked off as he gathered his thoughts. His voice dropped, barely audible. "They never saw it coming. I killed all three."

Sienna gasped, looking at Paul in disbelief.

"They're not the only ones who didn't see it coming," Barney said, equally stunned.

"Later that night, Andy and I dragged the bodies down to the beach below Windsol. I dumped them off the Zodiac in 10,000 feet."

"Why'd you wait so long to tell us?" Barney asked.

"I felt like a monster."

Kneeling in front of him, Sienna took his hands with tears streaming down her face. "You didn't do anything wrong. You weren't the monster. You saved us from the monsters. They killed our baby. They could have killed AJ. I just wish that you'd told me."

"Andy and I talked about it that night. We knew you two would be questioned by the police after their disappearance. We didn't want you to have to lie."

"Nobody's talked to me about it for over six months. Sienna's right, Paul. Why'd you wait so long? I could have helped. Maybe kept you from sinking so damn low and scaring the hell out of everybody."

"I didn't really understand the reason, until Mexico. The truth is that I didn't kill them just to protect us. Andy's million dollars may have gotten them out of our lives. The truth is that I wanted them dead for what they did to my family. I couldn't tell my wife or my best friend, when I couldn't even admit it to myself."

"I planned on killing those fuckers as soon as I got out of the hospital," Barney said. "I told you, before I found out they'd disappeared, that I wasn't going to be satisfied just dreaming about it. I meant it."

"I remember, and that helped me, because I knew that they'd have seen you coming."

"You're probably right . . . Jesus, it's hard for me to even imagine what you've been going through. I should have been the one to do it. Wouldn't have bothered me a bit."

"So who else knows?" Sienna asked, moving beside him.

"Just you two and, of course, Andy."

"I can't believe, with all the bitching I did about you, he didn't tell me. God knows, I bet he wanted to," Sienna said, taking Paul's hand.

"I was adamant with him. I didn't want you to know. I'm sure this has been rough on him."

"Yeah, I know that for a fact. But, I also know what's going to make him feel better." Sienna said smiling.

"What's that?" Paul asked.

"Telling him that we're back together."

"We're back together?"

"I'm never letting you go." She opened the collar of her jacket and pulled the ring out from under her shirt. He undid the clasp, pulled the ring off the chain and slid it onto her finger.

After their long and passionate kiss, they looked expectantly at Barney. Smiling, he stood. "Looks like my work here is done. I'm already gone."

44

Even before Adam's death, Constance was prone to insomnia. Her high-energy metabolism and a job that required constant attention usually left her with a maximum of four hours sleep on a good night. Since returning from Patagonia, however, it had gotten worse. Haunted by regrets and sorrow, she'd often take late night walks before bed. Returning home this afternoon from the Dallas/Fort Worth Airport, tonight was no exception. Leaving her downtown Seattle condo, just north of The Pike Place Market, she followed her usual route south on Western Avenue. Dropping down to sea level she crossed the Elliott Bay Trail and headed north along the waterfront sidewalk of Alaskan Way. Under the anonymity of her hooded sweatshirt she enjoyed deep breaths of the saltwater-laced air as she passed by long commercial piers stretching far into the bay. Music and laughter spilled out from waterfront bars and restaurants as she continued her brisk walk. Although nobody seeing this hooded walker would have guessed it, she was a key figure in an organization dedicated to preserving the freedom most people took for granted. However, since Adam's death, the pride she used to feel was replaced by a growing sense of isolation.

"You want a story? I could tell you a story . . ." Paul's words from the tape recording came to her. She stopped and gazed into the foaming tidal water below. While there was always a question as to the admissibility in court of hidden recordings, it certainly would be a starting point for an aggressive investigation. She was confident Paul Armstrong would be unable to withstand the pressure and would confess to the killings for a reduced sentence.

Before boarding her return flight, she had emailed three senior agents scheduling a meeting in her office for the following morning. She imagined their reactions when she broke the news. *How did you ever put that together? She's done it again! That's one for the books.* This would be just one more feather in her cap.

But lifting her gaze, tears filled her eyes as she watched a brightly lit cargo ship slowly passing a half-mile offshore toward the Straights of Juan De Fuca. This crying thing was relatively new for her. She'd done very little of it over the years. Now, it seemed that she was crying constantly. The counselor she had been seeing encouraged it. *But why cry at a passing ship?* She knew the answer. She would rather be on that ship, headed anywhere, than at tomorrow morning's meeting. She wiped her eyes, shaking her head. *What's wrong with me?*

"Everything OK there?" She recognized the authority behind the question even before she was framed by the spotlight.

Turning toward the black and white police cruiser, she shielded her eyes from the light's glare. "Everything's fine officers. Just taking a walk."

Surprised that the hooded figure was a woman, the two SPD officers stepped out of their car. "You know Ma'am," the larger of the two began, "this isn't the safest place to be out walking by yourself."

"I need to see your ID," the other officer demanded.

"We have to stop anyone we spot loitering along the waterfront," the first officer explained. "Just for security . . . you understand."

Constance regretted that she had stopped. If word got back to the bureau that she was taking unaccompanied late-night strolls, an escort would be assigned to accompany her. "I'm FBI special agent Constance Hunter." She took her badge wallet out and showed it to the surprised officers. "As you know, I'm required to carry a concealed firearm and I would appreciate it very much if my name didn't show up on your evening's log. You see . . ." she stumbled, now unsure of what to say. Her eyes were drawn to the kind face of the larger officer. "It's hard to get away by myself."

The two officers recognized her name and knew of her position with the bureau. They agreed to overlook the encounter. While his partner returned to the cruiser, the first officer remained at the guardrail with Constance and watched the receding lights of the cargo ship. "I grew up on Queen Anne Hill," he said. "I used to ride my bike down here just to smell the salt water and watch the big ships come and go." Sensing his partner waiting, the officer pushed back from the rail and pulled out a card, "I hope you don't consider this inappropriate or forward, but if you ever feel like company on one of your walks, give me a call." As the patrol car pulled away, Constance looked down at his card and smiled. *I just might do that Officer Wyatt Howard. I just might.*

Spending time with a stranger that she met by happenstance made little sense logically. But stepping into her sparsely decorated condo, his card was still in her hand. She looked at it one more time before setting it on a table next to her favorite photo of Adam hang gliding over Black's Beach in San Diego. She picked up the photo. "D'you know this Wyatt Howard guy? Yeah? Must be OK then." She set the photo back on the table.

Walking into her bedroom, she stripped off her clothes, showered, brushed her teeth and was asleep as soon as her head hit the pillow.

******

Constance had called the meeting for nine a.m. At eight she left her condo's garage and turned the windshield wipers on high-speed against the blanket of rain pounding her car. She deviated from her usual route to the downtown FBI building and pulled her car into Waterfront Park, at the foot of Queen Anne Hill. Leaving her jacket in the car, she walked quickly toward the rock bulkhead that marked the boundary between the park lawn and the frigid Puget Sound waters of Elliott Bay. As she drew close to the shoreline, she kicked off her shoes and began to run. The rain streamed down her face. She built up speed, like she used to when she threw the javelin in college. Raising her throwing arm, she prepared to launch the small tape recorder as far as she could into the turbulent gray water. She planted her foot just short of the rocks. Her hand swept forward.

Looking to the heavens, the rain mixed with her tears. Her conscience told her that Paul Armstrong had acted in self-defense. Yet the laws, the rules, and order required that he be held accountable. How could she balance her position in the force with this newly discovered voice of her conscience? She knew that Adam had a hand in all of this. She looked down at the tape recorder still in her hand. She couldn't let go. Not yet anyway. "I'm trying Little Brother . . . I'm trying."

Reaching her car, she placed the tape recorder in the glove box and took out her cell. Dialing the office, her assistant picked up on the first ring. "Hi Rhonda, it's me. I need you to cancel the meeting I've got scheduled this morning. Clear everything else that I've got on the books. Something important's come up and I'm taking a personal day. I'll see you tomorrow." She dialed another number.

"Good morning. Officer Howard."

"Hello Wyatt. I don't know if you remember me . . . This is Connie Hunter."

"Of course I remember you."

"I'm ready for our walk."

THE END

The authors live with their two rescue dogs, writing novels and creating timeless, energy efficient designs from their architectural practice in the Virgin Islands.